# THE LEGACY OF BOONE WILSON

## LEE ANN SONTHEIMER MURPHY

**World Castle Publishing, LLC**
Pensacola, Florida
Copyright © 2024 Lee Ann Sontheimer Murphy
Paperback ISBN: 9798891261549
eBook ISBN: 9798891261556
First Edition World Castle Publishing, LLC, March 11, 2024
http://www.worldcastlepublishing.com

# Dedication:

To my Kentucky ancestors who continued to roam and to my grandfather who headed off to Texas as a young man to bring back an authentic chili recipe the family's been tinkering with ever since.

# CHAPTER ONE

Boone Wilson knew he'd die before the month was out, and although he would rather live, he accepted his sad fate. After all, with a bullet lodged in his chest, he couldn't expect anything else. Two weeks after he'd been shot, playing faro at the Out of Luck Saloon in Laredo, he remained both alive and sore. The sharp, burning pain he'd experienced when the bullet slammed into his chest had faded, but he still hurt. There hadn't been any more bleeding, not since that first night when not only had the wound bled like hog killing time, but he'd tasted the iron bitterness of blood in his mouth. He'd wondered if there might be pus inside the wound, but the sawbones who told Boone that he was as good as dead hadn't offered any further treatment. Doc Smitty – likely not the man's actual name – spent more time drunk than anyone Boone had ever known, and that was a remarkable record. The fever that still made Boone's bones ache and his skin burn were the reasons he thought it might be infected, but since no one figured he'd live, no one bothered to do anything.

He'd trailed cattle all summer long, as he had for the past five years, driving herds from southern Texas to Dodge City or Colorado. If he'd made a mistake, it'd been taking that last drive, one in the fall after the summer grasses were about gone on the trails, then coming back to Laredo to spend the winter. Boone bunked on a ranch that lay between San Antonio and Laredo, but he liked to gamble, so he'd come into Laredo to play.

Boone regretted that now. If he'd stayed on the ranch, he wouldn't be about to die. After spending a week or more tucked into a bed upstairs at the saloon, he had begged to go outside, and so, each morning, his buddy Deacon Lee carried him downstairs, then tucked him into a chair on the saloon's front porch. His feet were propped onto part of a busted table, so he was lying down more than sitting up.

Miss Mary, who owned the place, objected and said it was bad for business, then relented. She'd decided Boone could be propped out on the porch each day, at least till it turned cold, and spend his nights in the smallest room upstairs. After all, she'd figured they would bury him before long, but he hadn't died.

Since it was too hot for a blanket, they'd kept Boone wrapped in white linen sheets. He hated them – they were too much like a damn shroud, and each day, they became filthy from the dust that blew through the streets of Laredo. Because just about everyone believed in the adage feed a cold and starve a fever, he figured if the bullet didn't kill him first, he'd starve to death. He drank all the coffee anyone would bring him, but he was lucky if he got a biscuit or bite to eat. Most everybody who patronized the Out of Luck knew who Boone was and what had happened to him, so they didn't waste much time passing pleasantries or sitting down for a conversation. More than once, he heard them whisper that he had one foot in the grave.

Boone was mortally wounded, grave bound, hungry, usually thirsty, and lonely, none of which made him happy. He had no legacy to leave to anyone, not his compadres here, his friends, or his family in faraway Kentucky. That changed, though, the day Miss Rachel Rose Shaw stepped onto the porch and took a seat near Boone.

He knew who she was – the school marm who'd arrived for the new school term, a pretty woman with her waist-length hair pulled up into a tight bun at the back of her head. Miss Rachel didn't look any older than Boone, who was twenty-six.

"Good afternoon," she said. Her voice was soft and melodious, not the sharp teacher tone he'd expected. "Is there anything I could get for you? You look so uncomfortable. I'd be happy to get you some water or food or fix that sheet so it's not so tight."

Boone cleared his throat. "I'd be most obliged, ma'am, if you could bring me something to eat. I'm near starved."

She reached out and messed with the sheet bound around him until it was looser. "I can do that. I've seen you out here for a week or more. Have you been sick?"

"I'm dying," he told her. "Got shot in the chest near two weeks ago, and the doc said there wasn't naught he could do about it. Guess that's why no one wants to bring me much to eat."

"I'll get you some food," she told him. "I'm Rachel Rose Shaw. I teach school."

"Boone Wilson, cowboy, from the Double B Ranch," he replied. "I'm pleased to meet you, Miss Rachel."

She nodded. "I'll be back."

He watched as she picked up her skirts and marched into the saloon. Boone waited for an outcry, figuring they would toss her out. Mary didn't like respectable women in her establishment. He heard Mary's strident voice, then Rachel's gentler tone. When Rachel returned, she had a tin plate heaped with frijoles, refried beans topped with a bit of salsa, and a spoon, along with some water.

"There weren't a lot of options," she told him as she settled onto a chair. "I hope these beans will do."

"Ma'am, they're like manna from heaven. I haven't had much but coffee and a biscuit on occasion."

Boone reached for the spoon, but she shook her head, filled it, and extended it toward his lips. He opened his mouth just in time and sighed with pleasure as the rich taste of beans filled his mouth. The warm food slid down to his stomach and he managed to eat about half of what she brought.

"Thank you," he said. "Bless you."

"I brought you some water, too."

He sipped the tepid water and then closed his eyes. Rachel laid one hand across his forehead, and he opened them again.

"You're feverish," she said. She pulled a handkerchief from a dress pocket, wet it, and laid it across his forehead.

"That's nice."

She gave him a smile. Then, she tried to reposition him into a more comfortable position.

"I'll be here again tomorrow," she told him.

"Don't you have school?"

"Today's Saturday, so no, not on Sunday tomorrow."

Boone liked her company, and he enjoyed the way she fussed over him. He might be dying, but he wasn't dead yet. "Can you stay awhile?"

Rachel scooted her chair closer, and when she did, he caught a sweet whiff of the sachet she wore. "I certainly can, Mr. Wilson."

"Call me Boone, please." He hated the way his voice sounded so weak and the fact fatigue made him want to sleep. He'd rather savor every moment the lady spent at his side.

"Boone, then," she said. "You may call me Rachel, no need to stand on formalities. How do you feel?"

"Hot and tired," he said. "And I hurt."

She removed her bonnet and fanned him with it. Boone welcomed the rush of air.

"Sleep if you can," Rachel told him. "I won't leave until you're asleep. I promise."

"I'll hold you to that," he said, as if he could. He didn't have the strength to shoo away a fly.

The last he recalled before he drifted asleep was that she had refreshed that handkerchief across his head and the rhythmic sway of her bonnet as she waved it back and forth. Boone thought she might have been singing to him, not the songs they sang to the cattle on the trail but old, familiar songs, maybe hymns.

When he woke, he realized he was holding her hand tight. For a moment, he had trouble remembering where he was and what had happened. He started to stretch, then winced when it hurt.

"Rachel?"

"I'm still here," she said. "It's getting close to evening. Some of your friends wanted to carry you upstairs, but I asked them to wait till you were awake."

"Who was it?"

She touched his forehead and cheeks again, then frowned. "One said he was named Deacon, the other one Mac."

"They're two of my pards," he said.

"I gathered that," she said, stroking his hair back away from his face. "They were fierce until they decided I was helping, not hurting you. They'll be back soon – I should go home."

"Wait."

Rachel remained until the cowboys came back. Boone saw her flinch when they lifted him up, and he jerked his head to indicate he'd like her to come upstairs, too.

"I think he'd like you to go with him," Deacon said. He'd noticed, and Boone was glad of that.

She hesitated, but not for long. "I will," she said. "But will one of you please tell that Mary to leave me alone? She tried to throw me out earlier."

Boone tried to laugh. "She don't usually let nice gals in the saloon, Rachel. I'll square it with her."

"Save yer strength," Mac said in a gruff Scots accent. "I'll tell Mary for ye."

Whatever he said, Boone couldn't hear, but Mary didn't protest when his pals trailed him up the stairs at the back of the saloon. He kept his jaw clenched tight, and his lips pressed in a hard line to avoid groaning, but by the time they laid him on the narrow bed in the smallest room, he wanted to moan aloud. He did cry out as he tried to settle into a position he could stand. The exertion of being brought up, then settling in, took a toll, and Boone shut his eyes, willing himself to catch his breath. Then, maybe, the pain would return to a level he could stand.

Before he could, however, Rachel leaned down. "I'm going to move you," she told him. "It's probably going to hurt, but when I'm done, I think it will be better. Will you let me?"

He'd rather fight a wild steer, but he nodded. Deacon tried to intervene. "It's gonna hurt him," he said. "We been keeping him shaved 'cause he wants to be, but every time, it puts him in mortal agony."

Boone gave a faint nod in agreement. Rachel took it as permission to put him in a different position.

For a woman who couldn't stand any taller than five feet and appeared slight, he thought she had a lot of strength. With a few moves, Rachel had him rolled onto his right side, his head propped against the pillow. He wore a pair of long-handled underwear pants and a worn shirt. When she tugged at the shirt, he raised a feeble hand to stop her.

"Hurts," he said.

"I imagine so, but you should have clean garments. Do you have more?"

Boone shook his head. "At the bunkhouse in my pack, but I'll need 'em to be buried in."

The sentence took more effort than he had to give.

"I gotta rest," he muttered.

From the swish of her skirt, he could tell that Rachel had stepped away from the bed.

"Ye do ken he's dying?" Mac asked, making no effort to soften his voice. Boone heard it, but it wasn't anything he didn't know.

Her reply, however, surprised him. "I don't know anything of the sort. He may well live if he's not starved to death and allowed to get some strength back."

*I might not die? She's the only one who seems to think so,* Boone thought with something like wonder and a faint stirring of hope. He struggled against sleep to eavesdrop.

"Bullet's still in," Deacon told Rachel. "Digging it out now would be more than he could take. The doc said so."

"Would that be the one who stays drunk?" she replied, her tone sharp as vinegar. "I don't know as I'd trust his opinion."

Deacon's voice lowered. "Do you know any healing? Cause unless you do, you can't give Boone or us any hope."

"I know a bit," Rachel said. "I was raised by my granny, and she was a mountain healer. The shape Boone's in, nothing I try will hurt him, and it might help. If nothing else, he might die – if he does – with some comfort."

"The thing I'm wondering is why ye took up with Boone." Mac sounded suspicious.

Boone inhaled her lavender scent and sighed when Rachel put her hand across his forehead, light and gentle.

"He looked like he needed someone," she said.

God knows he did, Boone thought, and then he let his body relax into sleep with one precious thing he'd lacked until now – hope.

# CHAPTER TWO

Rachel hated to leave Boone, but she figured if she tried to stay, the proprietor of the saloon would throw her out. If she had a home of her own, she would have asked the cowboy's friends to carry him there, where she could tend to him proper, but as the schoolteacher, she boarded with first one family, then another. She had been in the West Texas town of Laredo for less than a month, and the winter school session had just begun. So far, she had been boarding with the Kurtz family, a unit of six with both parents and four children, all under five. Mr. Kurtz ran the blacksmith's shop, and in their modest three-room house, Rachel had a bed in the children's room. The man of the house paid her far too much attention, in her opinion, and often had an eye on her. Privacy didn't exist, and already, although it was Saturday, her absence had probably been noticed.

Although born in southwest Virginia, her family eventually headed west, settling first in Mississippi, then in Texas. She'd finished what schooling she had in the Piney Woods of East Texas, and she'd been teaching school in one place or another since the age of sixteen. She'd taught in Rusk, then left there for San Antonio, then, after hearing of a vacancy in Laredo, she'd written to the school superintendent who hired her sight unseen. Until her arrival, Rachel had no idea that there hadn't been a schoolteacher for more than two years.

It was true enough her granny had been a healer and had taught her. Teaching school was the only trade Rachel had, but it was a lonely life. In her daily trek through the streets of Laredo, from the Kurtz home to the one-room schoolhouse, she had noticed Boone on the porch. Despite his pallor and obvious weakness, he was a nice-looking man, and he stirred something in her lonely heart. At twenty-six, she hadn't married, although she came close, discovering on the eve of her wedding that her groom had a wife and children in Tennessee. Since then, she hadn't courted or looked twice at any man. But Boone, long before she knew his name, tugged at her heartstrings.

When she stepped onto the saloon porch, it had been out of a desire to help. When he told her he was dying, it hit her hard, and she resolved to prevent it if possible. The hours spent with him convinced her of three things – she thought he didn't have to die, she liked the brave, quiet young man, and he seemed as lonely as she.

As soon as she entered the Kurtz home, Rachel became the center of attention. In the largest room, the family had gathered around the table for supper, but all of them paused and stared.

"There you are," Martha Kurtz said. "I wondered what became of you. You left this morning, and I feared you might have fallen into the river or got attacked by thugs."

"Oh, no, nothing like that."

"Where were you then?" Harold Kurtz asked. "Mart could have used some help with the children."

Rachel bit her lip and avoided any comment. She'd been hired to teach school for a meagre amount that included her board. So far, no one else had offered other lodgings, but additional chores hadn't been part of the deal. It wasn't that she minded offering a helping hand, but she did object to being treated like a servant.

"I was visiting," she said, almost adding visiting the sick as

Christ urges us to do but didn't. Religion was a sore point between her and her hosts. The sole church in town was the San Agustin Church in a small structure in the shadow of the new church being built. Rachel, a lifelong Catholic, sometimes attended. Mr. Kurtz wasn't too happy about that. The Episcopalians had begun having sporadic services. There were other occasional prayer meetings for Methodists and Baptists. The Kurtz family sometimes attended one of those.

"Well, come sit down and eat," Martha told her. "We're having some fried 'taters and a bit of beef if you're hungry."

Rachel wasn't, but she took her place at the table and managed to eat a small portion. If she were to help Boone, she had to keep her own strength up. Afterward, she helped Martha clear the table and wash the dishes. Although it was November, this close to the border in south Texas, the days remained warm, even hot, but at night, temperatures dropped. The small house remained over warm.

"We're going to try our hand at fishing in the river tomorrow," Martha told her as they put away the dishes. "Harold fancies some fried fish if we can catch any, and there's no church, not this week."

"I reckon Miss Rachel will be going to church again with the heathens and Mexicans," Kurtz said as he walked into the kitchen. "But she's welcome to come along if she wants,"

Even if she hadn't planned to tend to Boone again, Rachel wouldn't go. She spent more time than she'd like with the Kurtz family now, and although she enjoyed an occasional walk down to the Rio Grande, she hated the snakes, and there were many.

"Thank you, but I have lessons to prepare for the week," she replied. "But I might walk down now for a breath of fresh air."

Lessons for an entire school term were tucked into her trunk, but since it was early, Rachel decided she might stroll down there now to find a willow tree. The bark could be brewed into a bitter tea that would help Boone's pain and fever. The two oldest children, Maisie and Mark, accompanied her, but she didn't mind. With the bark she would need, Rachel walked them home, teaching them a new song along the way.

In the morning, despite little sleep, she rose as early as the Kurtzes and attended the early Mass. By the time she returned home, they had gathered fishing poles and a basket lunch and headed down to the water.

Rachel rolled up her sleeves and set the willow bark to steep. Then she minced the piece of beef she'd bought on the way back from church and added some salt and water to a saucepan to boil it to make some nourishing beef tea. As soon as both teas had steeped, she packed them into a basket and set forth to the saloon.

To her surprise, Boone wasn't on the porch. She frowned and walked through the open saloon doors. Miss Mary, who had to be at least fifty with a worn face and hair going gray, met her and blocked the way.

"Where do you think you're going this fine morning, missy?"

Her rough tone failed to intimidate Rachel, who asked, "Where's Boone?"

"Upstairs in bed where a dying man ought to be. I don't want you in my place, not a respectable woman. It's bad for business."

"No, it's bad for Boone," Rachel replied.

"You could lose your reputation, schoolteacher."

"If Boone can get better, it's worth it."

Mary stared at her, eyes round and dark with anger. "You ain't like most of the women. I'll give you that. Most wouldn't dare be seen in this place, but the young man's dying, and for the life of me, I don't know why you'd care."

"I do, though," Rachel said. "Do you want me to pay you? Is that the problem? I have a $20 gold piece I'll give you if you'll leave me alone."

Mary laughed, a dry wheezing sound that became a cough. "You've got some spunk. I don't want your damn money – go on, then go up to him for all the good it'll do."

The barroom smells of cheap whiskey, tobacco smoke, and strong perfume choked Rachel's nose as she climbed the stairs. The door to Boone's room was shut, but without knocking, she entered. He lay in the same position as when she'd left. His eyes were shut, but she didn't think he was asleep. It was hot and stuffy in the room, so once she put the basket down, Rachel worked the window until it opened with a screech.

"They said you wouldn't come back," Boone said, his voice little more than a whisper.

"Who said it?"

"Deke and Mac," he replied. "But you're here."

"I told you I would," she told him. "I keep my word. Did you sleep?'

He shook his head and winced with the effort. "Not much. Hurting too bad and thirsty."

She put her hand on his forehead and found it too hot. "Didn't anyone give you any water?"

"Not since you did."

There was a pitcher on the table beside his bed, so she poured some into a tin cup and then held it to his lips. She supported his head with one hand as he drank. Then she dampened a cloth and put it across his blazing forehead.

"I've got willow bark tea to help," she told him. "And beef tea if you think you can drink it."

"I likely can, Rachel. Thank you."

First, she repositioned him, rolling him to his back, then propping him up on pillows high enough he could drink without danger of choking. It caused pain, she could tell, but Rachel was as gentle as possible. She also unbuttoned his shirt, seeing the bullet wound for the first time. The uneven hole was ringed with red, a sure sign of infection. When she finished, he'd gone pale and grasped her hand tight.

"I know I'm dying, but let's don't hasten it," he told her, voice rough and low.

"If I have my way, you'll live," she told him. "Let's try the beef tea first. You need the strength."

He managed to sip a tin cup's worth with her help. Then he downed some of the willow bark tea, pungent and bitter despite the sugar she'd added. The effort seemed to leave him spent, so Rachel let him rest.

She bathed his face, neck, and wrists with water, hoping to bring down the fever. If he were to live, though, she thought the bullet had to come out and the wound be treated. Boone either slept or fainted for a bit. She wasn't sure which. But, after a while, he rested easier, and she remained beside him.

Around noon, someone knocked on the door, and a young woman stuck her head into the room.

"Mary sent me up to see if you needed anything."

Rachel stood up and stretched. "More water, laudanum if there's any to be had."

"How's Boone?"

"He's fevered and weak. Is he your fellow?"

The girl shook her head. "No, he ain't mine – he don't have a gal that I know about either. We all like him, but he's one to keep to himself, mostly, quiet and such."

Boone's eyelids fluttered.

"Rachel?"

"I'm here."

"Who else?"

"It's Peggy," the girl said. "Boone, how you feelin'?

"Bad to worse," he told her.

"I'll go fetch the water and all."

She dashed away like a rabbit running from hounds, Rachel noted. Most folks didn't like to be around sickness. It made them skittish and fearful they might be next. When she looked over at Boone, however, Rachel frowned. He did appear worse, or else she hadn't noticed before how ill he looked. He remained ghost pale, but his hair was in disarray, sticking out in multiple directions. His eyes, a deep grey color, glistened with fever. The lines of his mouth were set hard as if he hurt – which she realized he did.

"Do you mean what you told her, about bad to worse?"

"I don't feel good, and that's a fact, but if you got more of that beef tea, I'd do my best to get it down."

Sick as he looked, he spoke with more volume than earlier.

"All right."

This time, he finished it and managed to eat some of the soft beef scraps she'd strained from the tea and brought. After, he wanted some of the water Peggy brought up but refused the patent medicine laced with laudanum.

"I'd rather have my wits about me for now," he said. "Closer to the end, I may want it, though."

"What if you're not going to die?" Rachel asked.

Boone stared at her and shook his head. "I won't make old bones, that's for sure, not with a bullet in my chest and a raging fever. 'Sides, that's what that drunken sawbones said, and I guess he'd know."

Rachel settled her skirts onto the bed and sat facing Boone, cautious not to jar him. Her fingers stroked back his unruly hair from his face. "I think he may be wrong. They had you near starved, but I'm here to feed you. If the wound can be healed, you won't die."

His expression changed. "Do tell."

"I am – I think you have a chance to pull through."

"Woman, you do beat all," he said. "Ain't never known one like you."

Boone caught her hand in his and held it.

"Is that good or bad?"

"Oh, it's good, all the more so if I don't die. I reckon I will, but it's pleasant to think maybe I won't."

The more she got to know Boone, the more Rachel liked him. She thought him handsome and figured he had to be close to her age. More than his looks, though, she admired his resolute courage, his pleasant speech flavored with more than a little wit and humor. His accent reminded her of home, back in the Appalachian hills where she'd been raised, and she guessed he might be from Virginia or Kentucky.

Rachel noted, too, how the shortest conversation sapped his strength. The beef tea had helped, but he needed more. Fever burnt the back of her hand when she laid it across his forehead, and she frowned, worried.

Footsteps pounded up the stairs, and three cowboys, hats in their hands, burst into the room. She recognized Deacon and Mac but not the third one, who appeared younger than the others.

"How's he faring, Miss Rachel?" Deacon asked. "I see he's still on this side of the grass."

"He's a very sick man," she said. "But he's had some willow bark tea and some beef tea. He still has a fever, though, and I think the gunshot wound is festering."

"Aye, I ken that fine, 'tis pus-filled as anyone with an eye can see," Mac told her. "But we'll take him down to the porch if he wants. Boone?"

The ill man shook his head. "I'd rather stay here for now, as long as Rachel will stay with me."

"We brought you another visitor, Boone," Deacon said. "He nagged at us until we did."

Boone tried to raise his head to see but failed. Rachel reached beneath him and pulled up the two pillows. If she had more, she could better prop him up. He groaned with the movement.

"Who'd you drag in here?"

The younger man came toward the bed, twisting his hat between his hands. "It's me, Boone. I reckoned I ought to come see how you were, at least say farewell in case you died."

Whoever he was, Boone reacted to his voice with a wild attempt to scrabble higher on the pillows. Rachel rose and put her arm behind him for support.

"Don't hurt yourself," she said, and turned to the newcomer. "Come over here if you want to talk to Boone. Sit on the edge of the bed if you'll be easy, and don't jostle him."

"Ezekiel," Boone said. "Kid, you ought not have to come."

Zeke did what she suggested and sat on the bed.

"I had to, Boone. Ma'd have my head on a plate if I didn't. You know she would."

Rachel glanced from the boy to Boone and back. They looked something alike, and she said aloud, "You're brothers."

"Yes, ma'am," Zeke said. "I'm the least one. He's the oldest. I ain't been here only since the spring. There's five of us brothers altogether, Boone, Jacob, Garrett, Moses, and me."

"And this one should've stayed in Kentucky," Boone said. "He's not but fifteen. I'd lick you, Zeke, if I could get up from this bed."

The tough sounding words were delivered with gentleness, however, and the boy put down his head, but not before Rachel saw the tears tracking down his cheeks.

"I'd hug you if I weren't scared that I'd hurt you more," he told his brother.

Rachel reached over to pat Zeke's arm in comfort. He began to sob, which upset Boone. Already on emotional overload, with the room packed to capacity, Rachel's head whirled. The powerful scents of men, horses, leather, tobacco, and sweat permeated her senses, and despite the open window, she struggled to draw a deep breath.

If she found it so hot and close, it must be doubly so for Boone.

"Gents, you either need to take Boone outside or clear out. This room's not big enough for all of you."

Deacon Lee nodded. "We'll clear out for a spell, but we'll be downstairs. The place ain't open, but I don't reckon Mary'll toss us out. Want us to fetch anything?"

"Beans, if there's any cooked, the *frijoles refritos*," Rachel replied. Boone needed to eat, and she was more than a little hungry. "Or something."

"You stay," Boone said. "And Ezekiel."

"Count on it," she told him. "We'll both be right here."

Rachel meant it. For now, she had no thoughts about lesson plans or school tomorrow or the Kurtz family, nothing but healing Boone. Whatever happened after that, she'd face it when it came, but for now, this was the center of her small universe.

# CHAPTER THREE

The last person on God's green earth that Boone had expected to see was his youngest brother, but Ezekiel was here, and although he wouldn't admit it, he was glad to see the kid. If he was going to die – and despite Rachel's hopes, he still figured he would – it was a comfort to have someone of his blood at his side. He'd been half mad at the boy since he showed up at the ranch in late April, figuring he was too young to trail cattle and sure that he ought to be at home to help Ma. Boone had tried to send him back, but Zeke proved to be as stubborn as he was, so he'd stayed, even gone on the drives with them. Despite the fact they'd made him ride drag, the worst position with dust in his face, Zeke didn't complain. He'd begged to come to town with Boone two weeks ago, but Boone stood firm. Zeke may have proved he could be a cowboy, but he was too young to visit a saloon. Even though Boone went for the camaraderie and the occasional game of cards rather than women and strong drink, it wasn't a place for a boy barely fifteen years old. The only reason Boone had even gone into Laredo that day had been to play cards, hoping to win a big enough stake to return to Kentucky. His plan had been to take Zeke home, and somehow, he'd decided he might want to go home too. His return after the war hadn't been what he expected, though. His family welcomed him right enough, but he felt out of place and disconnected. Their lives had moved on while he had been gone, and he'd changed. War had a way of doing that to a man. If he brought Ezekiel home, he'd find out if he felt the same or wanted to stay.

Although Boone hadn't been much older, just eighteen, when he went to war, he wanted to protect Zeke from the worst that life that could deal. And, since he got shot, he thought it was for the best that the kid hadn't been present. Boone still had no clue why Mad Mike had walked into the Out of Luck and shot him with his .44 at close range. He barely knew the man, and he hadn't been up to any hijinks with anyone. He didn't cheat at cards, and he had no favorite gal among the sporting ladies at the saloon. He'd never done more than dance with one or two of them, and he drank very little liquor. That Boone would go to the grave without knowing why he'd been shot bothered him, but he couldn't ask Mike – he'd been strung up within the hour because everyone thought Boone was a dead man.

"Zeke, hush that noise," he told the kid, who still snuffled and wept.

"I cain't help it," Zeke answered. "They told me you were shot and that you'd die, but I never thought to see you abed, looking so sick."

Boone wanted to reassure him, tell him he'd be fine, but it would be a lie. Besides, he felt rotten. The fever that cooked his bones now made him shiver with a chill. Rachel noticed his shaking and pulled up the sheet. Then she touched his face again, cheeks and forehead.

"Your fever's up," she told him as if he wasn't aware. "Can you finish the rest of the willow bark tea? I think it helped a bit."

"It might, but I gotta piss," he told her. He would have been squirming with the need if it didn't hurt to move. Her quick reply surprised him – he figured she'd balk at helping with that.

"There's a chamber pot," she said. "Zeke, can you grab it for me?"

In less than five minutes, Rachel had taken care of that pressing need, then helped him drink more of the willow bark concoction. Even with the sugar she'd added, it was bitter. The effort drained his strength, though, and he closed his eyes, ready to sleep. The wet cloth Rachel put across his forehead was soothing, and he drifted to sleep, secure in the knowledge she was at his right side, his kid brother at his left.

Boone didn't think he slept long, but he woke to the aroma of refried beans, and his stomach rumbled with interest. He thought Rachel had it right not to starve him because eating, even though it'd been little, did make him feel a tiny bit stronger. As he awakened, he listened to his brother and Rachel talk in quiet tones.

"If you would, could you go to the house where I board and get a few things for me?" Rachel asked his brother. "There shouldn't be anyone home yet – they went down to the river to fish. It's three rooms, and my trunk's in the only bedroom, at the foot of the cot where I sleep. I could use the comb, the quilt, two towels, two bars of castile soap, and some lavender. And my reticule, too."

"I'd be right happy to, ma'am. Just tell me where to go."

"It's the house next to the smithy. If the Kurtzes do come home, just tell them I sent you, and I'll sort it out later. But eat first if you want. They sent up plenty of food."

"I ate this morning," Zeke said. "I'll go so I can get back. Are you my brother's sweetheart?"

Boone cocked an ear to hear the answer. He'd known her a few days, and he surely hadn't been able to court her, but he felt a connection to Rachel he couldn't explain.

"I'm the schoolteacher," Rachel said and dodged the question. "Anything else has to wait until he's recovered."

"So, you don't reckon Boone's gonna die after all?" The hope in his brother's voice hurt to hear because he didn't want to disappoint him.

"I'm going to do my level best to see he doesn't," Rachel said. "I can't promise he won't, but I think he can pull through this. It won't be easy – I think the bullet needs to come out, and that wound is festering. If I can take care of that, get his fever down, and keep him fed, he's got a chance."

*From her mouth to heaven's door*, Boone thought. She sounded certain and competent like maybe she'd nursed sick folks before now. He found her both smart and pretty, and he wouldn't say no if she wanted to be his sweetheart if he lived. If he died, Boone figured she'd mourn him, and that offered an odd sort of comfort.

Her notion that the bullet should come out scared holy hell out of him, though. It would hurt and might finish him off. The doc had said no, but then he did tend to stay drunk, so maybe Rachel knew something the sawbones had forgotten.

"Boone?"

His brother's voice interrupted his thoughts, so he opened his eyes.

"I'm awake, kid."

"Miss Rachel has beans if you're hungry. I'm going to fetch back some things for her – I ain't leaving."

"Didn't figure you was," Boone said. "I could eat a bit, I think, but I need some water first."

Rachel had a cup at his lips, and when he'd drank, she spoon-fed him all the beans he could eat. The refried frijoles were still warm, and he savored the flavor. Boone hated eating from a spoon like a baby, but he could barely raise his right hand, and when he did, it trembled. As delicious as the food tasted, it didn't rest easy in his belly. He shook his head to refuse the next spoonful, so she put it back in the dish with a worried frown.

"I need to take a good look at the wound," she told him. "I'm afraid it's going to hurt, though."

"Go ahead." At least if she did it now, if he screamed, Zeke wouldn't be present to hear.

Boone tried not to flinch as Rachel's hands undid his shirt and peeled it back. Although she kept her touch light as a flittering butterfly, her fingers hurt where they touched. She pressed on the edge, and he let loose a wild cry, almost a Rebel Yell.

"I'm sorry," she said, pulling back her hands. "I know it's painful. No wonder you're fevered, though. It's inflamed, and there's pus."

"So, it's bad?" Boone asked through clenched teeth. His faint hope that he might survive faded.

"If it was your arm or leg, they'd want to amputate," Rachel said. "But that's not an option."

"Then I am a dead man." Yesterday morning, he had been resigned to his fate. Now he realized he wanted to live, very much.

"No," Rachel told him, voice firm. When he looked up at her, though, he saw tears in her eyes. "We just have to get that bullet out and treat the infection right away."

"I might die anyway."

"And you might not," she told him. "I don't even know how you got wounded or why."

Boone attempted a laugh, but it sounded more like choking. "Neither do I," he said. "I was minding my business, playing faro, and Mad Mike walked up and shot me."

The more he spoke, the worse he felt, but Boone ached to converse with Rachel. He wanted to share his thoughts and past with her and then hear about hers. If he managed not to die, which most of the time he doubted, it would happen.

"That scalawag!" Rachel exclaimed.

He couldn't help but try to laugh. "That's not a word most ladies use," he said, but he wasn't offended. Her answer surprised him.

"I never said I was a lady," she told him. "I'm just plain hill folks. A proper lady wouldn't be sitting upstairs in a saloon, in a room probably used by the soiled doves for business, especially not without a chaperone."

It required him to draw on what little strength he could muster, but Boone managed a smile.

"I'd rather a woman than a lady any day."

Boone reached for her hand and grasped it. She smiled back. "Rest awhile, Boone. You look tired."

"I'm wore out," he agreed and shut his eyes. Heavy fatigue claimed him, and he slept, deep and hard, but not for long. The door slammed open from the hallway, the sound echoing through his head and firing a headache. Then he heard Zeke's raised voice and a loud thump as something heavy dropped into a corner.

"You'll wake Boone with this racket," Rachel cried. "You didn't need to bring the trunk, just the things I wanted."

"I had to, Miss Rachel," Zeke said. "I'm awful sorry, but that Mr. Kurtz came home, and he didn't like me being in his house. I told him you sent me, but he called you some terrible names, ones I don't want to repeat, and told me to take the trunk to you. Said you won't be coming back under his roof."

Boone forced his eyes open and saw Rachel positioned in front of the window, mouth open wide.

"Oh, my."

"What is it?" Boone asked. A headache on top of his other ills was the last thing he needed.

"Nothing to worry about," Rachel said, but he heard the dismay beneath the cheerful tone she attempted.

Before Boone could disagree, they heard Miss Mary shouting downstairs. Mac's low rumble rang out, and a shot was fired before someone dashed up the stairs, feet pounding. Kurtz appeared in the open doorway, red-faced and perspiring.

"You!" He yelled and pointed at Rachel. "You're no better than one of these fallen women. No respectable lady would be in a saloon and on the Sabbath, too. I heard you were here yesterday, too, out on the porch with that, that gunslinger. You're not fit to be the schoolteacher. I thought you were an upstanding woman when I hired you, but I was wrong. You're not welcome in my house, and don't you even think about coming back to the schoolhouse. Your kind ain't wanted here in Laredo. You're a wicked bitch without any morals at all."

Rachel didn't flinch as the blacksmith spat his ugly words at her, but Boone saw her mouth turn down, upset, and the hurt in her eyes. He tried to pull himself up in bed and failed.

"Shut your dirty mouth," he growled, speaking louder than he'd managed in days. "Don't talk about Rachel that way. And get out of here."

Boone would have shot him if he had his guns, but they were tucked into a drawer in the room's single chest. The effort cost him, though, and his head whirled. He figured he'd faint in a moment, which would make his words meaningless.

"I'm not leaving until she pays me back for the months she taught school," Kurtz said. "I wonder now what she's been teaching our young ones. If I'd known she was so free with her favors, I'd have had her myself."

The unmistakable sound of a pistol being cocked caught Kurtz short, and he fell silent.

"Leave now, or I'll put you down on the floor like the dog you are," Zeke said, weapon in hand. The menace in his voice surprised Boone, but it made him proud, too. The kid had some sand, he thought. "And apologize to Miss Rachel before you go."

Whether or not Kurtz would have done so would remain unknown. Mac appeared behind him in the doorway, with Miss Mary peeking around him. When Kurtz opened his mouth, Mac hit him on the top of the head with a single fist. Kurtz toppled to the floor, landing with a clunk.

"Get him out of my place," Mary said, shrill.

"Is he dead?" Rachel asked, twisting her hands together.

"Knocked out," Deacon Lee said. "He'll come round in a bit."

"Take him home," Mary cried. "I want him gone now."

Dizziness made Boone's head spin worse than a pinwheel. His effort to sit up overtaxed his already weak body and his vision wavered as bright flashes of light all but blinded him. Although not aware of it, he must have made some grunt or groan because Rachel returned to his side.

"Boone?"

He heard the concern in her tone but couldn't answer as he slipped into darkness.

His sight returned, dim but clear enough he recognized Rachel hovering over him, a worried frown dividing her forehead. His brother loomed over her shoulder with an expression just as anxious. The pungent stink of smelling salts rankled in his nose, strong and stenchy enough to make his stomach roll over. Boone thought he might be sick, but the moment passed, and he realized he'd been repositioned in a way that offered as much comfort as possible.

"Rachel?"

"You fainted."

"Shouldn't have tried to sit up," he muttered. "That skunk gone?"

"Yeah," Zeke said. "Don't reckon he'll show his face here again."

What happened was all jumbled in Boone's head, but if he recollected right, Rachel no longer had a place to stay, and it was his fault. He tried to ask her about it, but she hushed him.

"Don't fret about it, Boone," she told him, her tone softer than the first colors of daybreak. "You need to lie still and be quiet till we get that bullet out and do something about the festering. All the commotion didn't help any – you're burning up with fever. Can you drink a little water?"

With her hand supporting his head, he could, but not much. Boone sank into the pillow, grateful when she bathed his face with cool water. He shut his eyes as he enjoyed the small respite. Rachel cupped her hand against his cheek, her skin cool against the heat.

"You're going to pull through this," she told him.

He doubted it, but he didn't bother to say it again. Rachel wanted to hope, and he wouldn't take that from her until the end.

"Rest awhile, if you can."

Then, to his amazement, she kissed his forehead, her lips a silk brush over his skin, and then she kissed him again on the mouth, a light, fleeting caress that both shocked and pleased him.

If he'd felt better, he would have smiled, but Boone realized he wouldn't give up on living without a fight, not when he had a woman like Rachel at his side.

# CHAPTER FOUR

Unemployed and homeless in a tiny Texas border town, Rachel's concern should have been centered on her future, but it wasn't. Boone remained her focus. He was worse, she knew, and getting weaker as the fever and infection sapped his strength. By the shadows on the wall, she guessed it had to be evening, likely five o'clock, and would soon be dark. After the long day and the unanticipated turn of events, weariness lay over her like a heavy shawl. But Rachel had no desire to leave Boone's side, and if she hadn't been thrown out of the Kurtz home, they would have expected her back well before now. Small blessings, she thought and tried to think through her fatigue on how to go about saving Boone's life. She knew that the bullet had to be dug out, despite the risk, and she had to get rid of the infection, but choosing the best way, the method that would do the least damage, fell to her, and it was a quandary.

Although outside, temperatures were mild enough, Rachel had sweated through her dress. She brushed back stray hairs that escaped from the figure-eight bun she'd pinned up and wiped her face. Boone quieted, and she thought he slept, but his stillness worried her. She wasn't the only one with concerns.

"You still think he'll make it?" Ezekiel asked her, turning around the room's other chair to sit backward in the seat. "He looks awfully bad to me."

"I believe so," she replied, praying it was true. "He's getting worse, that's true. That bullet has to come out, and then I have to get the wound to heal."

She'd repeated the same so often Rachel thought she could chant it in her sleep. It wasn't just a theory anymore, though, but reality, and it had to happen soon.

"Should I fetch up that doctor? He's downstairs even though the place ain't open."

Although she knew the man by reputation alone – and it wasn't a good one – Rachel nodded. "It's worth a try. He wouldn't before, but maybe he'll change his mind."

Zeke nodded and headed downstairs in a rush. When he returned, he brought not only Doc Smitty but Deacon and Mac as well.

The powerful fumes of rotgut whiskey rolled in waves from the doctor as he approached the bed.

"This young man says you wanted to consult me about this patient," he said. From his speech, Rachel could tell he must be from back East, some civilized big town and wondered what brought him to this frontier place. "I fear I've nothing good to tell you, miss. I examined him two weeks ago when he got shot, and to be honest, I'm surprised he's lasted as long as he has."

He'd been drinking, she thought, but he wasn't completely inebriated — yet.

"The bullet needs to be removed," she said.

The doctor peered down at Boone with an expression that reminded her of an owl, and then he shook his head. "It's too risky. He looks extremely ill to me with a fever, and that wound is tainted. My advice is to give him plenty of laudanum, and if that doesn't work, pour some whiskey down his throat. I'd hazard a guess he's in a great deal of pain, so make him as comfortable as possible."

Ezekiel turned pale and steadied himself against the wall,

but Rachel shook her head.

"I'm not giving him up to die just yet," she told the doctor. "If you won't remove it, I'll find someone who will, or I'll do it myself. Boone deserves a chance to live."

Dr. Smitty turned to face her. "My dear, are you one of the girls here? A dance hall girl, perhaps? You look a bit too fresh to be a...."

"She's the schoolteacher," Mac growled.

"Is that true?"

Rachel gave the doctor back the stare. "It was."

"Do you know anything of medicine?"

She nodded. "My granny was a healer, and she taught me."

He bent with a formal bow. "Then I concede to your knowledge. Mr. Wilson is now your patient and your case. I wish you well, my dear, I do, but I fear you'll be disappointed."

The man's disdain fired her anger.

"He'll live to dance on your grave," Rachel said in a ragged voice. "If you won't help, then go back downstairs to your bottle."

Smitty shrugged his shoulders and headed through the door. No one spoke until his footsteps ended at the foot of the stairs.

"Miss Rachel, I'll help you," Deacon said. "I'm no sawbones, but in the war, I helped some of the wounded men. We all did, Boone too, and I'll do what I can."

Rachel realized she should have figured out that Boone and his comrades would have served in the war, and she didn't need to ask which army they had been with. With Boone's Kentucky accent, she figured he'd worn gray, one of those many young men who fought not for slavery or states' rights but for their homes and farms and families.

Tears knotted up in her throat, but she did her best not to cry. "Thank you," she told him. "We'd best do it soon if Boone's to have a chance."

"It's aye late today," Mac said. "If ye think the lad can hold on till morning, 'twould be best to do it then."

It made sense, and Rachel admitted it. Still, there were things she could do now that might help, and she planned to do them. Drawing on the folk cures learned at her granny's knee, she decided to do what she could. *Maybe I should have thought of some of this before now but although it seems like I've known Boone a long time, it was just yesterday that I came up on the porch where he was sitting.*

Ezekiel stood, gazing down at his brother with the saddest expression she'd ever seen.

"Do you still think Boone might live?"

Rachel put her arm around him, the way a sister would, then wondered if they had any sisters. "I do, Zeke. Will you stay with him while I go gather some things I need? If he wakes, see if he can take some water and tell him I won't be long."

"Yes, ma'am, I can," the kid replied. "It's gettin' dark, so I'll light this lamp, too."

She untied her apron and tried to straighten her hair. Then she picked up her reticule, picked out the gold piece, and marched downstairs to conduct a little business with Mary.

The saloon keeper sat at a table, smoking a thin cheroot. Rachel advanced from the foot of the stairs to stand.

"What do you want now?" Mary said. "I should have booted you out this morning. From what I heard, your reputation's ruined like I warned you, and Boone's still dying."

"I still intend to heal him," Rachel said. "I need some supplies, though, and I wondered if you might know where I could get them."

Eyes narrowed with suspicion; Mary blew out a stream of smoke from the little cigar.

"What kind of things?"

Rachel took a deep breath. "I need a clove of garlic or at least several heads and some dried comfrey root. I could use a small, sharp knife and a good set of tweezers or small forceps if they can be had, and some clean linen or cotton cloth, stuff I can tear up to make bandages. I brewed what willow bark I had into tea for Boone, so if there's any to be had, it would be convenient, too, so I can make more. I'm not asking for charity either – I'll pay for it all."

Mary ground out her cigar but saved the stub. "You do beat all, Rachel. Hand over the gold piece. I can lift the forceps from the good doctor's bag – as you can see, he's over in the corner, drunk again. There's garlic in the kitchen, and if Graciela, my cook, can't come up with the rest, I'll eat my best bonnet. I can see you haven't given up on Boone Wilson, and I admire a stubborn woman. I'll see what can be gathered and send it up. I'll send some more food, too, not so much for Boone, but you and that kid need to eat too."

The gold piece weighed heavy in her fingers as Rachel laid it down on the scarred table.

"Thank you," she said. Then she lifted her skirt and headed back upstairs. Zeke sat at Boone's bedside but the other cowboys had sat down on the floor, backs against the wall.

"Did you get what you wanted?" Deacon asked.

Rachel nodded. "Someone will bring it up. Are you both staying the night?"

Both nodded.

"Aye," Mac said. "It's twenty miles back to the ranch, but we'll not sleep here and trouble you, missus. Mary will let us sleep on the floor downstairs."

"We'll have our bedrolls from our horses, too," Deke added. "Zeke probably would rather sleep in here if you don't mind."

"I don't."

"You ought to sleep too." The soft, weak voice came from the bed, and Rachel turned to find Boone awake.

"I will," she said. "There's a few things I want to do first, then I'll get some rest."

He nodded, but the slight gesture appeared feeble, and he closed his eyes as if the effort had been too taxing.

Graciela brought the items upstairs in less than an hour. Rachel had first met the cook when she begged beans from her for Boone on the day she first knew him.

"I brought the things you wanted," she told Rachel. "And a few others, some honey and some oregano. Miss Mary told me why you needed these and those help with a bad wound, too."

"Thank you," Rachel told her.

"I've made some enchiladas with chili gravy if you want to send the niño to the kitchen," she said. "By then, the willow bark tea will have steeped enough, too."

Rachel craved sleep more than food, but she nodded and thanked Graciela again. She might not want to eat, but her body needed fuel, so she would. She doubted Boone could eat, not tonight.

She peeled two garlic heads, then used the paring knife provided to slice it thin. As carefully as possible, Rachel pulled away the bandages on the wound and dropped them to the floor. They were nasty, with old blood stains and fresh pus. She layered the garlic slices over the open laceration and then wrapped a fresh bandage over it, tying it to stay in place. She reserved the comfrey, oregano, and honey for morning, for after the bullet came out. With any luck, the garlic would draw out some of the inflammation.

Boone stirred, his nose wrinkling at the strong aroma of the herb.

"What do I smell?" he muttered.

Rachel perched on the edge of the bed and cupped his hot

cheek with her hand. His whiskers had grown enough he needed a shave, but she didn't want to risk it, not when there were more important things ahead.

"Garlic. It helps heal, Boone. I'll have more willow bark tea soon. Are you thirsty?

"Dry as riding drag," he said.

He drank most of a cupful of water with her help, then lay back, his face paler than the pillows. Rachel bathed his face and wrists, then laid a wet compress across his forehead. As she tended him, the coal oil lamp cast tall shadows on the wall and flickered as the cooler night air wafted in through the window.

Boone shivered, and before she could ask, Deke shut the window.

"Mac and I are heading downstairs," he told Rachel. "If you need anything or Boone does, send the kid or just holler for us."

"I'll fetch my bedroll," Zeke said.

Ezekiel returned with two plates of the promised enchiladas with gravy, his bedroll, and saddle bags. Behind him, Peggy delivered a pot of steaming willow bark tea. Zeke devoured his plate, then rolled out his bedding and settled down.

"If you'll wake me, I'll sit with Boone later," Zeke told her. "Then you can sleep."

Rachel nodded. She coaxed some of the tea down Boone, and then he managed a few spoons of the hearty Mexican dish. After that, she ate most of what remained and wondered just how she would manage to sleep upright in a straight chair.

Although she was weary enough to sleep on the floor, she doubted it would happen. Boone watched her and said, "You gotta rest, too. Lay down with me. It ain't like I'm able to do anything."

"I don't want to hurt you," she protested.

"Zeke!"

His brother popped up from the floor with such speed she knew he hadn't been asleep.

"What is it?"

"Help her move me over so Rachel can lay down too," Boone said.

The young man's eyes widened. "In bed with you?"

"Ain't like I'm gonna ravish her," Boone said. "Unless you want to bunk with me."

Zeke swallowed hard. "I'd be afraid I'd kick you or something."

Together, Rachel and Ezekiel moved Boone to the left side of the bed, leaving a narrow space where she would lay down. She took down her hair and put it in a single braid, then removed her petticoat but not her dress. Rachel joined Boone, doing her best not to jostle him, and lay facing his uninjured side.

He turned his head toward her, his fever-bright eyes staring into hers.

"Someday, God willing, and if I live, we'll do this the right way," he told her. "Ain't never had a woman in my bed and always figured when I did, it'd be a wife."

His words moved her to tears, but Rachel closed her eyes so he wouldn't see them. He might take it wrong, she thought, but his near proposal brought home the realization that she'd like to be in this man's bed – for good.

With that revelation between them, she slept until the early hours of the morning, then roused Zeke to prepare for the effort that would either save or end Boone's life.

# CHAPTER FIVE

Boone doubted a dying man could ask for much more than to die easy, but a pretty lady tucked in beside him in bed was far beyond any expectations he'd had to make that transition pleasant. Tomorrow, he figured he would most likely die despite the combined efforts to save his life by removing the bullet. No one had to tell him that the wound festered. The pain radiating from it was too deep and bad not to be. Besides, he could smell a faint foul odor, something more than old blood. A man didn't serve for four years in a difficult war as a foot soldier without recognizing a wound gone bad. Boone had seen too many of his friends and fellow soldiers give up the ghost not to know now.

It had to be worse, not better, he reckoned, because it hurt more, and his fever burned hotter. His strength was fading, and he was aware of it. Boone appreciated the efforts that Rachel, dear, sweet, kind Rachel, would make and his friends too but he doubted he could be saved. There had been low times in his life when he maybe wouldn't have cared much, but he didn't want his youngest brother to watch him die or bury him. And Boone would rather stay alive to court Rachel. He'd been more than a little particular about women, never meeting one he had any desire to keep until now. That he would meet the kind of woman he'd dreamed about on his deathbed represented a huge irony.

Tonight, though, he wanted to savor what he could despite

his pain and fever. Even though she'd tended him for long hours, Boone could still catch a whiff of the lavender sachet she wore, and he liked it. Turning his head to face her required effort, but he made it so he could look on her face, her dark blue eyes closed now with near black lashes resting on her cheeks. He thought her small, upturned nose was cute, and he liked the way her lips were both full and naturally pink. He recalled how that sweet mouth had kissed his forehead, then his lips, and he longed for more.

He conjured up enough strength to touch her with his right hand, a talisman, while he yielded to sleep, and for the first time since he'd been shot, Boone dreamed.

*He climbed the hill to the house where he'd been raised, the split rail fences around the dooryard intact. It had to be autumn because Ma's prized maple tree flamed orange, and the oak trees had shifted from green to a yellow gold. The walnut trees were already bare of leaf, but some nuts still hung on the branches while others were scattered across the ground.*

*There was a pleasant chill in the air, not cold but cool enough he could see his breath. Boone approached the house, aware he had no pain, and moved without difficulty. Either he was dead, or it was a dream – he wasn't sure which. It seemed real because he could smell the tang of woodsmoke wafting from the chimney and feel the rush of a breeze as it rippled through the nearby trees. Behind the house, he saw the harvested corn field and the garden, picked clean. By now, he reckoned Ma would have everything put away for the coming winter, leather britches beans strung up to dry, pumpkins and apples for pies, cabbages, and potatoes in the cellar to keep, and more.*

*It was silent, he noticed, which was odd. He didn't hear the chickens clucking or fussing. There should be at least one cow, a milk cow, to moo, a mule, and a corral of horses and pigs rooting in a pen. Although the children raised here were grown, too, save for Ezekiel. They would help his mother, long widowed. His brothers, save for Zeke,* lived nearby and still did, as far as he knew.

By the way the sunlight slanted through the trees, Boone knew it was morning and still early. Ma was one to sing while she baked biscuits for breakfast and cooked some meat to serve with it. But no songs echoed in the air, and he wondered why not and was curious why he'd seen no one.

It's as if I'm the only person here, he thought, but he knew that shouldn't be. Puzzled, Boone halted where he stood to think. He sat down on a stump that had been there as long as he could remember, gazing at the familiar surroundings. Everything sparkled, he thought, and seemed new. The colors of the fall leaves, the whitewashed house, the faded green shifting to brown of the grass was vivid.

Boone had been happy to be home, but now an uneasiness crept over him. He thought of a Bible verse he recollected from church, one that said now we see through a glass darkly but then face to face. The preacher had said it meant that in heaven, things would be clear and bright.

He wondered if this was heaven, then, and if he'd come to stay. Or, idly, he considered the fact it could be hell and what seemed so perfect could change to torment. An odd sense that he had a choice to make hit him, and his anxiety increased.

When he glanced over at the porch again, this time, it wasn't empty. His father, dead since he was Ezekiel's age, sat there in one of the chairs. Although he didn't speak or wave, Boone thought he was aware of his presence. Part of him yearned to step up onto the porch, take a seat, and join his daddy, but Boone didn't.

Somehow, he thought that if he did, he wouldn't wake up from this dream if that's what it was, that he'd be dead for sure. He wanted to go home, to come back here and raise a family of his own. He'd wanted to bring Zeke back where he belonged, but if Boone stayed now, the kid would be left in Laredo. So would Rachel.

There was a pull toward his pa and another to go back, to wake up fevered and dying.

*Before Boone could decide, he heard a sound for the first time in the dream, a woman's voice, but it wasn't his mother's.*

*"Boone," she said with urgency and more than a little fear. "Boone!"*

*"Is he gone?" Ezekiel asked, his voice rough with grief.*

*"He can't go," Rachel said with a sob. "He'll wake up."*

*Their voices gave him the direction he needed. Boone rose from the stump, and without a backward glance, he turned away from the house and started down the hill.*

Pain and reality slammed into him with enough force that he gasped and then opened his eyes. Rachel, no longer lying beside him, stood beside the bed, a worried frown on her face with Zeke beside her. The kid looked like he was about to bawl.

"Hey," he said, surprised at how hard it was to form the single word.

Rachel cried out, then dropped to her knees beside the bed. Zeke put a fist to his mouth.

"Boone, oh, Boone," she said. "You wouldn't wake up and…"

"We were scared spitless," his brother interrupted.

Boone attempted to grin but doubted he did. "I ain't dead, not yet," he told them. "I reckon I could have been, though."

Rachel clasped his hand in hers. "You're on fire with the fever. Can you drink some more willow bark tea?"

He nodded and managed a few sips. "Is it morning?"

"Almost," Rachel replied.

"I gotta tell you what I want," he told them. "If I die."

"You won't," Rachel said.

Boone shook his head a little and stopped. The slight movement made his head whirl.

"Just in case," he said. Speaking took a lot of effort and strength he didn't have. "You get six cowboys to carry me to bury. I want you both to walk behind, you're all the family I got here. Then, the gals from the saloon can follow if they will. And I want a dead march. I reckon they should be in there somewhere with a drum to beat slow and a fife. Mac'll know what I mean if you don't. And get a preacher or someone to read that bit from Corinthians about seeing through a glass, and faith and charity."

"Boone, you're going to live," Rachel said. She'd released his hand and was bathing his fevered forehead with cool water. "Don't fret about all that now."

He shut his eyes and tried not to worry. She sent his brother to fetch his friends, and when they returned, he listened.

"Get him to drink the laudanum," Deacon said. "Mac, go down and see if you can't get some hot water, maybe a cot or table. If one of us digs out that bullet where he lays, it's gonna bleed all over the bed."

Rachel lifted his head up so he could drink the opiate, and once he did, it wasn't long until he could feel the numbing effects of it. Her capable fingers also undid the bandage and took away the garlic. Then, she washed the wound. The lye from the soap burned, and although she used a light hand, it hurt where she touched.

A cot was brought, and his friends lifted him onto it. Boone moaned, couldn't help it because the movement sent pain radiating out from his chest through his body. The cot was lower than the bed, but as he began to slide into darkness, he was aware that Rachel held him on the right side, his brother on the left.

They were speaking to him, but it didn't make much sense by that point. Boone liked the sound of their voices, especially Rachel's, but his thoughts drifted toward Kentucky and home. His mind rolled back the years, and before he slipped into drug-induced oblivion, Boone relived scenes from his past, from his boyhood to the war to on the trail. He remembered when Ezekiel was born on a cold March day and the night his father died, sick with an ague. Boone saw his mother's face when he rode away to war and remembered dancing with Ma at Jacob's wedding.

Then, it all faded, and he knew nothing at all. His last thought was wondering if he'd wake again or if he would be dead.

# CHAPTER SIX

Somewhere not too distant, a cock crowed to greet the morning, and Rachel prayed it wasn't a black one because that could herald death. If not, then all was well – it was normal and a good omen rather than a bad one. Although she'd slept a little, she hadn't rested easy beside Boone, too afraid she'd jostle him. Then, when she and Zeke were going to change places, he couldn't be roused, which terrified them. Rachel had feared the worst, but young Ezekiel had been certain his brother had died. He hadn't, but the possibility remained.

Faced with the necessary task, now she was also more than a little afraid. Once the laudanum had worked, Boone lay very still, his face paler than anyone she could recall. Worse, despite all their talk that they had worked with the wounded, Rachel was designated to remove the slug. She accepted the responsibility and prayed her hands would not tremble.

In the two weeks since he'd been shot, the round wound had become increasingly inflamed, but a scab had formed. She would not only have to dig for the bullet but cut first to gain access. Deacon and Mac held down Boone's shoulders to prevent him from moving. It shouldn't happen, not with the laudanum, but no one wanted to take the risk. Zeke sat on the floor at his brother's feet with the same purpose. It also gave him less of a view of the wound, which Rachel thought best since he was the youngest present.

With the same knife she'd used to slice the garlic in hand, Rachel put the forceps borrowed from the doctor's bag nearby, along with some old towels for blotting away blood and pus. This was the first time she'd ever dug for a bullet, but under her Granny's training, she had staunched a few wounds, helped bring a few babies, some in a rush of blood, and tended a snakebite. There had been no personal connection, though, not like the one she felt for Boone, which made it hard.

For a moment, Rachel thought she couldn't do it after all, that she would have to hand the knife over to one of the men. She cast a glance at Boone's face, though, and resolved she would manage for his sake. If she didn't, he would die, that seemed certain now, and although she knew little more than either cowboy, she hoped that she would use the most care.

She drew a long breath, held it, then released it. "I'm doing it," she announced. "Hold him still."

Her hand didn't shake as she used the blade to cut across the wound, wincing as blood welled up where it sliced. She patted the wound to staunch enough of the flow to see, then put two fingers into the wound. If she could locate the slug that way, it would be easier than probing. The warm slickness within the gash sickened her stomach, but Rachel held her gorge. When she touched something hard that wasn't bone, she tugged at it, and despite the opiate, Boone moaned.

Rachel picked up the small set of forceps and prayed she could find the bullet again. She latched onto it with the tool and, with slow, measured motions, drew it from the wound with a gasp. It was larger than she expected, probably a couple of inches long, with a serrated bottom.

"Is it all there?" Deacon asked. "It ain't broke in pieces?"

She held it up and studied it. "No, it's all there."

"Thank God," the cowboy said. "Sometimes they break,

and if there's still pieces, they'd fester."

Mac took it from her fingers. "Aye, I'd say it's a .44 slug from a Colt Dragoon pistol and 'tis all there."

"What now?" Zeke asked.

Rachel stared at the wound. It bled, the stream of blood mingled with nasty yellow pus, which had a sick smell to it. "The more of the pus that comes out, the better," she said. "We let it bleed a bit, then I'll wash it. After that, I'll spread some honey over it, then make a paste of the comfrey and oregano. Then I'll cover it with that, let it dry – it should dry hard – then we'll wait."

An hour later, they had Boone back in bed, doctored and bandaged. The cot had been cleaned and returned to wherever it came from. Rachel begged a clean shirt from his brother and managed to wrangle it onto Boone, leaving it unbuttoned. Without more pillows, she improvised and rolled a blanket to put beneath the pillows, then propped him against them so his head would be higher. From that position, she thought it would be easier for him to drink and eventually eat. She used the soap and water to wash his face, hands, arms, and the uninjured part of his chest, too. Then she took her comb, wet it, and ran it through his tousled hair, bringing order to it. Last, she covered him with a bright quilt from her trunk, one she'd pieced herself. Ezekiel watched her with a frown.

"He'll feel better to be cleaned up," she told him. "He'll be hurting when he wakes, but in time, it'll feel good."

"How long till he comes around?"

She shook her head. "Laudanum can last four hours, maybe a little more. It's been at least half that long – I lost track of time. He's going to be very weak and sick, still for a day or two. What I did was hard on his body, but it had to be done."

Sweat dampened the back of her neck and dress. Rachel realized how hot the room had become and what a mess remained on the cot. "Would you open the window for a bit?" she asked.

"Then I'll clean the mess."

"We'll take care of that, Miss Rachel," Deacon told her. "It's the least we can do."

Until Zeke opened the window, she hadn't realized it was raining. The fresh, cool air that swept into the room helped remove the smell. In no time, the two cowboys had cleared away the cot, the stained towels, and the tools she'd used. The herbs were back on the table beside the bed, along with water and what remained of the willow bark tea.

It must be later than she'd realized because she could hear piano music from downstairs, and the saloon didn't open until noon. Her stomach ached with emptiness – she hadn't eaten since the day before and not much then.

"We're going to go back to the ranch," Deacon told her. "There's work waiting, and there's naught we can do here. We'll come back on Saturday to see how Boone fares – if anything happens, send the kid or someone for us."

After they were gone, Mary came into the room, quiet and slow.

"Well, you ain't killed him yet," she said in a half-whisper. "I'll send up something to eat and some hot water for you to wash."

"I'd appreciate that," Rachel told her.

The hot water arrived first, and Rachel asked Zeke if she could have time to change. He agreed and vanished from the room. She stripped off her sweat-soaked dress and apron, which was smeared with blood. Then she washed everything but her hair, which she water combed, then braided it again. She changed into a calico dress and a fresh apron with a sigh. Then she sponged her dirty garments and planned to take them down to wash at the first opportunity.

Graciela brought some tender beef cooked in gravy with biscuits, and when Ezekiel returned, he carried a wide-bottomed rocking chair. He scooted the straight-backed chair to the foot of the bed.

"Where'd that come from?"

He looked as weary as she felt, but he grinned. "I bought it off a lady," he said. "Used some of my wages so you'd have a comfortable place to sit, maybe sleep."

Rachel tried to protest, but he held up one hand. "Boone'd rather I spent the money on furniture than on wild women or drink," he said. "I'm hungry, let's eat."

"Thank you," she told him. "Bless you."

Her tired body sank into the chair, and she sighed with pleasure. They ate, saying little, and she kept a little of the beef for Boone, although she doubted that he'd feel like eating any time soon. Once he'd finished his meal, Zeke crawled into his bedroll and slept, snoring a little. Between that and the steady rain outside, Rachel grew drowsy and drifted close to sleep. She remained in the rocking chair, though, knowing she wouldn't rest beside Boone. Besides, she might hurt him, and the good Lord knew he had more pain now than most could bear.

After midnight, Ezekiel sat up with his brother, the straight chair dragged beside the bed. Opposite him, closer to the windows, Rachel drowsed in the rocker. She had almost drifted to sleep when the wind blowing in turned cooler, so she rose and shut the window. Shivering, she wrapped her shawl around her and then checked on Boone.

Zeke had fallen asleep and Boone had yet to wake. She touched his forehead, noting that he remained feverish, which she expected. He stirred a little beneath her fingers and moaned. His eyelids fluttered and then opened a little.

"Thirsty," he whispered in a low, raspy voice she could barely hear.

Rachel poured water into a tin cup and raised Boone's head so he could drink. He sipped the water and then shook his head, unable to drink more. She laid him back down and sat on the edge of the bed for a long while, holding his hand, hoping that she anchored him to life. The infection, the fever, and the removal of the bullet all weakened him, but now, he had a chance. Without her intervention, she had no doubt he would have died very soon.

He woke twice more, asked for water, then went back to sleep.

"How is he?" Ezekiel asked when he woke. "He doesn't look any better to me."

"He's awakened three times and drank a little," Rachel said. "He's very weak, but I think he's improving. He needs the rest for his body to heal."

"Doesn't he need to eat, too?"

She nodded. "As soon as he can, yes. I'll try to get him to take some broth when he wakes again."

"Beef?"

"That's all I have," she said. She had been keeping it warm over a small spirit lamp from her trunk, one designed to hold a cup of something over the flame.

"He'd rather chicken," Zeke said. "His favorite thing to eat in all the world is chicken and dumplings."

Rachel noted that for future reference. "I wish I had a chicken for broth," she told him. "But I don't."

Zeke stood beside the bed and scrubbed his face with both hands, to wake up more fully or to wipe away a few stray tears. Rachel suspected it was both.

"I know where to get some," he told her. "I'll go hunting as soon as it's daylight."

She envisioned him robbing someone's chicken coop and cringed. He could get shot in the process, which wouldn't help Boone at all.

"For *chicken?*"

Ezekiel stared at her and shook his head. "Prairie chicken," he clarified. "Reckon you can make some stock out of it for both broth and maybe dumplings later."

Rachel smiled. "I can if Graciela will let me in the kitchen."

The first fingers of light illuminated the horizon, and the rain, for now, had stopped. Rachel pinned her braid into a figure eight on the back of her head and pulled the rocker beside the bed. Zeke gathered his gear, including a Springfield rifle.

"It's Boone's, not mine," he told Rachel before she asked. "It'll work fine if I shoot them in the head, and I will."

"You're that fine of a shot?"

He nodded. "Boone taught me when I was small."

Boone moved his head, restless, and his eyes opened.

"Hungry," he whispered. "Dead men ain't hungry."

Ezekiel grinned. "And you ain't dead."

The faintest smile flirted with Boone's lips as Rachel pulled him into a sitting position and used pillows to prop him there. She took the mug of beef broth and grabbed a spoon.

"If you can take some broth, I have some," she told him.

His head moved in what she thought was a nod, so she spooned some broth between his lips. He took most of what was in the cup, one slow spoon at a time. She offered him water, and he drank a little.

"Thank you, honey," he said, his voice frail as an elderly man's.

Rachel touched his face. "You're welcome. You're still feverish."

This time, she was sure he nodded. "I hurt," he murmured. "Bad as being stomped by a colt."

Zeke's face lit up. "He's remembering," he told her. "Before he went off to fight the war, he got busted up pretty bad trying to break a wild colt. It put him abed for several days, longest I've ever seen him laid up till now."

"Devil's Mischief," Boone said. His voice faded until she could barely hear him.

"That's the horse," Zeke said. "He's coming around. I think he'll live."

Rachel smiled. "I know he will. If you're going hunting, it's daylight."

The kid touched his brother's hand, then gathered his gear and left. Rachel listened as his footsteps tramped down the stairs, then leaned forward to kiss Boone's forehead. His hand fumbled, seeking hers, and she took it. She kissed it, too, happy that he seemed to be on the mend and that her doctoring hadn't killed him.

Boone would live, and her soul rejoiced.

# CHAPTER SEVEN

Boone lay helpless as a newborn baby, hating every moment. Raising his head from the pillow took more strength than he could summon, but he could tell that Rachel thought he'd live. She smiled more often, for one thing. Adjusting to the notion he wasn't dying proved difficult, but he was glad. He had no idea how long he'd been bedfast, weeks and not days, but he chafed at it, eager to rise and go about his usual business. Someone had shaved him, but he didn't know who. Not Deacon or Mac because they had gone so it had to be Ezekiel or Rachel.

Rachel fed him, teas and beef broth that failed to satisfy his hunger. Then she spooned chicken broth into his mouth, and he grinned.

"It's chicken?" he asked.

"Your brother went hunting," Rachel replied. "It's prairie chicken. When you think you can manage it, I'll make chicken and dumplings for you."

On Saturday, the end of a very long week that began with Rachel pulling the bullet out of his wound, Boone grinned when he took the first bite of chicken and dumplings. After a steady diet of refried beans and beef broth, it tasted like manna straight from heaven.

"It's good," he said. "Tasty as Ma's ever was and that's saying a lot. Did you make it?"

"I did."

"It's one of my favorites."

She couldn't help but smile. "I know," she told him. "A little bird told me."

"The kid? I'm surprised he remembered."

"He dotes on you," Rachel replied. "You're like a hero to him, not just a big brother."

Boone couldn't argue. Ezekiel, headstrong as anyone he'd ever met, had left home in Kentucky and traveled all the way to Texas to join him last spring. He'd written their ma to let her know that's where the boy turned up, but he hadn't heard an answer yet. His mother wasn't much of one to write letters, though, and getting one so far took time.

"I reckon I look more like his pa than his oldest brother about now," Boone said. Although there wasn't a mirror to hand, he could guess that he must look haggard after his long ordeal. "He probably remembers me better; he wasn't but about three years old when our father died."

Rachel paused in feeding him and caressed his cheek with one hand.

"You look much better than you did," she told him. "How do you feel?"

He sighed. "I feel better enough to wish I felt good," he told her.

Her expression changed, and she laid her hand across his forehead, frowning.

"What's wrong?"

Rachel smiled. "Your fever's broke, Boone. You'll be out of bed in no time.

Those were sweet words to him, but he wanted up now. He'd never been one to lollygag or stay in bed.

"I want to get up now," he told her. "Today."

If he could, he'd not only climb out of bed, but he'd also

be outside. He'd be on his horse, Sprat, and he'd kiss Rachel on the lips.

The woman appealed to him in a way that no woman ever had. He'd found her pretty from the time she arrived in town. The coming of a new school marm had been big enough news that even a lowly cowboy was aware, he remembered. Boone had done no more than tip his hat when he met her in the street, figuring she was a social class – or more – above him.

Much of what happened after he was shot remained a feverish haze. He could remember most of it, but there were times he wasn't sure if his memory was correct. The one thing he knew beyond any doubt was that Rachel had been there for him from the moment she stepped onto the porch where he'd sat, certain he was dying. What prompted her to approach him, Boone would never know, but he was glad she had.

Without her, he would be dead or dying. That was a given. It had been her stubborn insistence that he wasn't going to die and her actions that saved him. Her hands had supported his weakened body, caressed his face, and cared for him in ways no one else ever had.

He depended on her, and that mattered. They'd never courted, never had a chance, but Boone wanted her. Like many men, he flirted with the idea of marriage and a family, but until now, it hadn't been something he thought he would have. In the war years, his focus had been to stay alive. Some of the men had women who waited back home, but the only girl he'd courted, Martha Allen, died of typhoid the first fall he'd been gone. He wouldn't have married her, anyway, because he liked her, but he hadn't loved her.

"I'd like to sit a spell in the chair," he told Rachel now. He reached out and took her hand in his.

"I don't know, Boone," she replied with a worried frown. "Your fever just broke, and you need to gain some strength back."

"C'mon, honey, help me," he said. With effort, he tossed back the covers and swung his legs to the side of the bed. That made his head spin, which he hadn't expected, but he was determined. In slow motion, he raised up until he sat perched on the edge of the bed.

Rachel steadied him with both hands, and he stood, legs quavering beneath him. She was smaller than he'd realized. She stood as high as his chest, but no more so he gazed down on her. She was smaller all over than he had thought.

"Boone, be careful," she fussed.

In answer, he put his arms around her and kissed her. It wasn't a quick kiss but a long, lingering one that told him everything he wanted to know and more because she kissed him back. His head twirled, and he thought he might well faint.

Rachel embraced him, her arms all that kept him from collapsing to the floor. He kissed her until his vision faded to nothing but brightness, and he knew he was near fainting. Boone pulled back, shaking, and said, "Chair."

She steered him the few steps to the rocker, and he sank into it, grateful for a solid seat in a spinning world. Rachel pushed his head down to his knees and told him,

"Don't swoon, Boone."

That took effort, but he managed not to, although he was breathing hard as if he'd run a footrace. Once the room stilled and he caught his breath, he grinned and began laughing, really laughing for the first time since he'd been shot. He'd tried before, but it had been a weak imitation. This was the real thing.

Rachel smiled back. "I'd say, judging by that kiss, you're feeling a lot better, Boone, but you nearly pushed too hard."

"It was worth it," he said. He ached to kiss her again but lacked the strength. "I haven't kissed many gals and none like that. My intentions are honorable, in case you wondered."

They were, after all, upstairs in a saloon, in a room

previously used by one of the ladies of the evening to conduct her business. The last thing he wanted was for Rachel to think he wanted anything immoral.

She blushed, and he liked that. It might be unconventional and socially shocking, but he'd marry her this very day if he had the chance. He would, however, want to be able to stand on his own two feet to do the deed. And come spring, he yearned to go home to Kentucky – if she was willing to go with him.

"I'd never think anything else, Boone," she said. She pulled the top quilt from the bed and tucked it around his knees. "Are you cold? I don't want you to take a chill."

He hadn't considered it, but he was cold. Before he could say anything, she draped her shawl across his shoulders.

"Coffee would be tasty if there's any way to get a cup," he said.

"I'm sure there's coffee downstairs," she replied. "I can go get some if you want."

Boone realized he didn't want her traipsing through a rowdy bunch of cowpokes and other assorted characters. "Where's Ezekiel? He can fetch it."

"Downstairs," she said. "He's taken a fancy to Peggy."

Before he could say another word, Rachel was out of the door, which she left open, and headed for the top of the stairs. Before she descended, he heard his brother's voice raised in fretful inquiry.

"What's wrong? Is it Boone, Rachel?"

"He's fine. His fever broke," she told his brother, who had pounded up the steps at top speed. "He's out of bed for the first time, but he's craving coffee."

"I'll bring him some," Zeke said.

The kid dashed into the room and stopped at the sight of Boone in the rocker.

"Glory be!" he exclaimed. "Do you feel better?"

"I do, some."

"I'm glad, Boone. Let me go bring up some coffee."

"Much obliged – thanks for the chicken, kid. Rachel makes good dumplings."

Zeke's smile lit his face, and Boone realized for the first time that he had their mother's expressions.

When he returned, Ezekiel brought the coffee pot, several tin cups, Peggy, plus a table from downstairs and two more chairs.

"What's all that?" Boone asked.

"We needed a table. There's no place to sit or eat," Zeke explained. "So I asked Mary if I could bring one up for now."

The kid might be young, but he had good sense, Boone thought.

He savored the cup of coffee, holding the cup with both hands, grateful for the warmth. Until now, he'd never realized that the room was chilly or that there was no source of heat.

The table crowded the small room, but it was necessary. The coffee pot sat in the middle of it, resting on a folded rag to keep from scorching the wood. Rachel drank a cup of coffee, too, sugaring hers, although Boone preferred his black.

Although the room was small, in an unsavory location, and despite the fact Boone felt weak and far from his best, he liked the hominess of it. It had been so long since he'd spent time in anyplace resembling a home, not since he'd left Kentucky. During the war, he'd slept rough like all the rest, lucky if they had a campfire for warmth and grub for their bellies. As a cowboy, he'd slept beneath the stars or under a wagon in rare instances. Even the bunkhouse at the Double B had been rudimentary at best, although there had been four walls, a roof, and a bunk where he could lay down his tired bones.

Here, in this room where he'd flirted with the Grim Reaper, there was an odd sense of comfort. He had coffee, a bed, good food, and a woman who gazed at him as if he were Christ resurrected. Boone had lived long without family near, now he had his youngest brother at his side and Rachel. He doubted he could walk across the room if he had to, but he now tasted happiness for the first time in as long as he could remember. He'd been mad, then glad when the kid arrived in the spring, but nothing compared to his current sense of contentment.

Sleet tapped against the windows, and the occasional burst of wind rattled the pane. Although without the blanket or Rachel's shawl, Boone would have been cold, but he appreciated the warmth and luxury of being indoors. He had ridden many a mile on Sprat through such weather and would rather not in the future.

At twenty-six, he wasn't old, but for the first time, he felt a desire to settle down. And although he hadn't minded leaving Kentucky behind when he went to war, now he wanted to go home. Boone had missed his family and he longed to be reunited. He didn't want to be a cowboy any longer – he wanted a home, a place to call his own where he could raise kids and grow old. Growing old had an appeal now that it hadn't before because old meant alive.

"Boone," Rachel said in the way she had that made his name sound like an endearment.

He glanced up. "Yes, honey."

"Do you want more coffee before it gets cold?"

Boone held out the cup. "I would, thank you."

The second cup was lukewarm, but it still tasted fine. He glanced across the room and saw Zeke sprawled out with his bedroll. "Do you reckon he's warm enough?"

Rachel looked and smiled. "I doubt it."

She gathered up one of the blankets and covered the boy with it.

"Tell me when you want to lie back down," she told him.

"I will, but not yet," Boone told her. "I want to sit up through my supper. Are there any chicken and dumplings left?

"I can go find out."

"Let Ezekiel go when he wakes."

"Why don't you want me to go downstairs?"

Boone groped for the right words to explain it, then just told her straight out. "You're a good woman, respectable. Those cowboys are a rough bunch, and since we're in a saloon, they're gonna think you're a different kind of woman. The rest of the customers are a rowdy lot, too. I don't want them taking advantage of you, and they will. Most of them haven't seen a decent gal for a long time. Some will want to marry you, and the rest will want to…."

"I know well what they'd want," Rachel said.

"So, stay up here," Boone told her. If there were any marrying to be done, he'd want to be the groom, but now didn't seem the time to tell her so. "I'd like you to be safe."

"Then I'll stay here," she said. Her cheeks flushed, and he wondered if she realized how much he cared or that he'd marry her without question. He hoped she felt the same, but Boone would wait until he had recovered to find out.

"Good."

Rachel picked up some sewing and sat near him, her deft fingers working the needle through the cloth. He liked watching the simple domestic task. After a time, she put it aside and came over to him. She brushed back his hair with a smile.

"I need to get the comb," she told him.

"I likely could use a bath."

Her grin widened. "It's possible, and I imagine it would feel good, but not yet. I wouldn't want you to take a chill, and this room is anything but warm. If your brother can find you some clean clothes, I'll give you a bit of a wash soon. He loaned you this shirt after the bullet was out."

"I ought to have a change of clothes in my gear, wherever it's at."

"Zeke said he wished he'd brought it when he came, but he was too worried you'd die to think about it," she told him.

Until now, Boone hadn't considered how afraid Ezekiel must have been, thinking Boone would die and he'd be left alone so far from home. When he first showed up, unexpected, he'd been a nuisance, although Boone had a deep affection for the kid and always had. It wasn't long until Zeke proved he was a hard worker, that he could trail cattle with the rest, and that he was responsible. Having someone of his own blood near after years of being alone proved to be important to Boone. He hadn't realized how much he missed his own folks until Zeke arrived.

"I ought to have some money, too, if no one's stolen it," he told her. "I had some saved and tucked into an old boot. I had my wages on me, and I was winning at faro right up till I got shot."

She nodded. "That money's safe. I found it and put it in my trunk with what money I still have."

At least he wasn't destitute, he thought. He had a little jingle in his pockets, he wasn't going to die, and things were looking up.

Now, all he had to do was get well, and then he could put his life back together again.

# CHAPTER EIGHT

Someone knocked on the door with three sharp raps that roused Ezekiel and brought Rachel to her feet. No one had ever knocked before, not here, but walked in without bothering to ask permission. Rachel tried to straighten her hair with her hands, then made sure her apron was in place. She opened the door with more than a little hesitancy and found a man standing there.

He looked as sober as a judge on hanging day, tall and lean with broad shoulders and a head of wild black hair that curled around him in a cloud. Although he wasn't dressed like a gentleman, he carried himself in a manner as if he were in charge.

He removed his hat and held it in his hand. "I'm sorry as can be to disturb you, ma'am, but I was seeking word about Boone Wilson. I'm Liam Rafferty, owner of the Bonnie Blue or Double B Ranch."

Ezekiel had joined her, his hair tousled after his nap, and stood at her left shoulder.

"Mister Rafferty," Zeke said. "Boone's here."

"Last I heard, he was fixing to die," Rafferty said. "I was right sorry to hear it, and since I was in town, I came to see how he's faring. I brought his gear, too, in case you'd want or need it."

"I'm not buzzard bait yet, Liam," Boone said from the rocker. Rachel noticed he managed more volume than he had thus far. "Come, light and set awhile."

"I'll be," the man said, astonishment spreading across his features. "I figured you might be dead and buried, but I'm glad you're not."

He walked across the room, skirted the bed, and sat in the chair Rachel pulled over near the rocker. Rafferty extended a hand to Boone, who shook it. "Have you seen Deacon and Mac? They told me you were in bad shape last they saw."

Boone shook his head. Rachel stood behind the rocker, her hands on his shoulders in a show of support. Ezekiel stood with her. "I likely was when they saw me."

"They were here earlier," Rachel said. "They said they'd be back on Saturday."

"That's today, although it's late in the day," Rafferty said. "First Saturday in November. We've been working with the horses, mainly. I figured the worst when the kid here didn't come back."

Rachel drew a breath. November? She hadn't realized, but she'd missed All Saints. Boone reached up and took her right hand in his.

"I'd rather have him with me than not," Boone said.

"Since you've managed to elude Death, are you planning to come back to the ranch? I'd take you on as top hand. There's that cabin you could set up housekeeping in should you want."

"I'm much obliged," Boone said. "I don't reckon I know yet what I'm gonna do, although I'd like to go home to Kentucky come springtime."

A strange look came onto Rafferty's face, and he twisted his hat over and over between his hands. "Have you heard from the folks at home? I fear they think you're dead."

Beneath her hands, Boone squared his shoulders. "I don't know why they would, Liam. I doubt they've heard the news."

"Well, they likely have, Boone, or will soon, and it's my doing," Rafferty said. "Everybody was so sure you'd die, so I sent them a letter – telling them you'd been shot and weren't expected to live. I inquired, too, if they wanted your young brother home. I see now I was hasty and should have minded my business, but it was well meant."

Boone drew in a harsh breath. "Did you hear anything back?"

"Not a word. I can send another if you like. I apologize, Boone, if I've caused you trouble."

"You likely broke Ma's heart," Boone said, in a small voice. "She'll take it hard, thinking I'm gone."

"She will," Zeke said. He sounded as upset as his brother. "So will Jacob, Moses, Garrett, and the rest. Lord, Boone, they'll be grieving."

"The road to hell's paved with good intentions," Rachel said, remembering a saying her Granny had used. "Letters travel slow, so they may not have heard yet. When was it sent?"

"Right after Boone here was shot, ma'am."

She calculated the time. "So, three weeks, give or take? Middle of October?"

Rafferty nodded. "I am sorry – I thought I was doing a good deed. I'll take my leave now. I imagine Deacon and Mac will be here before long. My offer still stands when you're back on your feet."

"He was very ill," Rachel said. "It's going to take some time before he'll recover."

Liam Rafferty bowed and found his way to the door. He shut it behind him, and she turned to Boone. He looked distressed and ill. His color had faded so that he was pale. A line furrowed his forehead, and his eyes, when he met hers, were dark with emotion.

Rachel took the empty cup from his hands before it clattered to the floor. Then she grasped his hands in hers. "Don't fret so, Boone."

"I can't help it," he said in a voice that sounded as shattered as broken glass. "My Ma and family think me dead and buried. She'll sorrow, worse than when my daddy died. I wish he hadn't done that."

"So do I, but I don't want you having a relapse," Rachel told him. "You're barely out of bed now, and your fever just broke. We'll send a letter today so they'll hear you're alive soon."

"It won't be quick enough to keep them from heartbreak," Boone said. "I just wish I could let them know."

Ezekiel stepped forward. "I'll go if you want, Boone. I'll ride hard for home and bring the news."

For a moment, Boone's face cleared. He released Rachel's hands and grabbed one of Zeke's. "I appreciate that, and I know you'd do it, but kid, how long did it take you to get here?"

"Near two months," he replied. "And that was riding hard as I could and fast, traveling alone."

"Winter's coming on," Boone said. "It's likely to take more than that."

"No telling how long a letter might take, though."

He sounded so upset that Rachel would have done almost anything to ease his mind. "You could send a telegram, a wire."

Boone lifted his head. "That is an idea," he said. "Not from here, there. It'd have to be from Galveston or San Antonio, which would be closer but still a fair ride."

"I'll go if you want me to," Zeke said. "I don't like to think about Ma weeping either."

"It's costly, though," Boone added.

"It would be worth it, though, for your mother's peace of mind," Rachel said. "Let's write a letter, though, and get it sent — then we can see about a wire."

She produced paper and pencil from her trunk, then seated herself at the table to write. "Tell me what you want to say."

Ezekiel sat on the floor at Boone's feet as he dictated the

letter.

*Dear Ma and family, I am well and alive. I was shot last October, but I didn't die, no matter what you've heard to the contrary. Ezekiel is with me, and we're still in Texas, but come spring, I plan to return to Kentucky. I am healing, and the fever broke. I'm still on this side of the grass and will see you as soon as I can. Your loving son, Boone Benjamin Wilson*

Rachel wrote, her penmanship large and neat, as he spoke. When he finished, he asked to sign it and scrawled "Boone" at the bottom.

"Without that, she'd never believe it was from me," he said with the shadow of a grin. "It will ease her mind when she gets it, but I still like the notion of a wire, though it'd take some effort to send."

"Your Mr. Rafferty should pay for it since he stirred up the trouble," Rachel said as she folded the letter and found an envelope for it. She handed it to Zeke, who scribbled "Mrs. Jemima Wilson, Hazard, Perry County, Kentucky" across it.

"I'll go get this in the mail," the younger man said.

Before he left, Deacon and Mac burst through the door, wild, loud, and exuberant.

"You're up!" Deke cried. "That's grand, Boone."

As they gathered around him, Rachel could smell tobacco, whiskey, and beer on them. She didn't mind it – they weren't drunk, just excited. She withdrew and picked up her sewing, hearing their voices but not listening. When she glanced at Boone, though, after a half hour or so, he looked weary.

"Gentlemen, it's time to let Boone rest a spell," she told them. "He's got a long way to go to be back on his feet, and we can't wear him out too much. He had a bit of hard news today."

"Aye, Liam wrote to his mother that he'd died," Mac said.

"'Twas a sorry thing to do, no matter how well-meant."

"We're gonna ride up to San Antonio and send a wire," Deke said. "I'll pay for it- it's the least I can do. The three of us, we lived through Sharpsburg together and a lot more hell in the war. Boone would do it for me, so I'll do it for him."

"Bless you and thank you," Rachel said, knowing what it would mean to Boone. "Zeke took a letter to mail, too, but a wire will get there faster."

Once the cowboys took their leave, promising to return when they could, Rachel came to Boone and stood before the rocker. "You look tired," she told him. "Do you want to lie down?"

He nodded. "I don't feel so good."

Boone leaned forward and put his arms around her, his head resting against her bosom. He began to sob, deep, ugly sounds that wracked his body. She held him tight as he wept and stroked his hair. When he finished, he pulled back, wiped his face with both hands, and sniffed.

"My poor ma," he told her. "It hurts me to think of her, weeping, sad, and lonesome while I'm not dead and gone."

Rachel kissed him, first on the forehead and then full on the mouth.

"She'll know different soon," she told him. "If I thought you were dead, my heart would be broken. Let me help you to bed, and you can rest awhile."

It proved more difficult to get him prone again, comfortable, and under the bedclothes, but she managed. By then, he looked wan and sick but so far, she didn't detect any fever.

"Do you want some chicken and dumplings in a bit?" she asked. "Ezekiel can fetch some when he comes back."

He shook his head. "I couldn't eat now – my belly's riled."

"Do you want some peppermint?"

"No."

"Try to sleep, Boone, and try not to fret."

"Stay with me, Rachel."

Boone reached for her hand and then held it tight in his. She moved the rocking chair beside the bed. "I will, Boone, I'm not going anywhere."

"My honey girl," he said, sounding sleepy.

Although she'd never thought she had much of a voice, she sang to him, old songs her Granny had sung to her, ballads that had crossed the water with her great-grandparents. Rachel sang until Boone closed his eyes, and his breathing shifted to a slower pace. Then she sat with him, still clasping his hand, as the room grew dim in the twilight until Zeke returned and lit the lamp.

"Is he worse again?" he asked.

"I don't think so – but he wasn't feeling very well, and he's upset about your Ma," Rachel said. "It's going to take some time for him to get well, but he will. His friends are going to send a wire to Kentucky, too."

"That's good," Zeke said. "Did Boone eat?"

"No, he wouldn't."

"Do you want something? I can fetch it up if you do."

Rachel was drained, and all she wanted was to watch Boone recover and then get married.

"No, thank you," she told him. "I'm good -I'll just be here with Boone."

It was the only place she wanted to be.

"He's taking this hard," Zeke said. "I got to thinking, though – Ma's awful stubborn, and she might not give up on Boone just because of a letter."

His words offered a faint hope, and she smiled at him. "Tell that to Boone tomorrow," she replied. "That might help him."

Lord, she hoped so.

# CHAPTER NINE

*Perry County, Kentucky*
*Near Hazard*

Jemima Lykens Wilson wasn't old, but she felt ancient. Since the letter came that told her that her oldest, Boone, had been shot and wasn't expected to live, she'd lost the faith and hope that had carried her through life thus far. She loved each of the children she brought into the world and the one who left it before he had time to live, but among them all, Boone was special. He'd been born when she was twenty, three years married, after losing another son, a little boy who lived less than a year before she lost him to diphtheria. Boone, born healthy and nine pounds, had been her triumph over that loss. As he grew older, he proved to be the most reliable and dependable of her children. After her husband died when Boone was not quite fifteen, he shouldered a lot of the responsibility. He cared for his siblings as more of a parent than a brother. Little Ezekiel had followed Boone around like a puppy dog, always wanting to be where he was at.

When Boone left to fight in the war, she'd hated it, but she didn't try to stop him. She worried and prayed for four long years, always afraid he might take sick or catch a bullet. When he returned home, still whole and sound with no more than a few scars, Jemima rejoiced, but it had become apparent he had changed. His eyes held an inner darkness, his face shadows that she could not illuminate. He needed to heal within, but instead, he'd left again for faraway Texas with some of the men he'd served with.

She thought he would come home once he finished sowing a few wild oats and recovered from the awful experience of war, but after five years, he hadn't. When Ezekiel lit out for Texas to join him, she'd shed a few tears, but she knew that Boone would take care of his brother. But if Boone died, as the letter seemed to think was certain, young Zeke would be alone more than a thousand miles from home.

Moses, the next youngest son at eighteen, came into the cabin, helped himself to a dipper of water from the bucket, and sat down across from her at the kitchen table.

"Ma, what's amiss?" he said.

Jemima blinked back a few tears and, with a sigh, handed him the letter she'd committed to memory. Moses frowned as he read it, then handed it back.

*Dear Mrs. Wilson – I take pen in hand with sorrow to write you regarding your son, Boone Wilson, who is in my employ. He was shot in the chest on Saturday last here in Laredo, Texas, and is not expected to survive due to the seriousness of the injury. He is a fine young man and has been a good employee. We served together in the war as well. I offer my condolences on his loss and inquire if you would like your younger son, also in my employ, Ezekiel, to return home due to his young age. Sincerely, Liam Rafferty, Bonnie Blue or Double B Ranch, Texas.*

"Do you think Boone's dead?" she asked.

"It doesn't sound too good, but I don't know, Ma. I hope not. Do you?"

"I want to think I'd know, here," she said and tapped her chest above her heart. "But that could be wishful thinking."

"Might be, might not be," Moses replied. "I don't feel like he's dead, myself, though he could well be. When did that say he got shot?"

"Middle of October by the date on the letter – three weeks ago, going on a month. Shot in the chest, it said, and that's as bad as it gets, near about. Do I tell the others or wait?"

Moses, who favored Boone a fair bit, met her eyes. "Surely, we'll hear something more, or Zeke will show up back here. How'd did this letter come?"

"Mail," she said. "Faster than I thought possible, but it probably came on a train part of the way."

"What happens now?"

Jemima, closer to her fifth decade than her fourth, sighed. "I don't know what to do, and that's the truth. I'd go down there myself to see and bring my least one home if it wasn't so far. I've never been farther than the next county – it would be too much for me."

"Ma, I'll go if you want me to."

"Moses, it's somewhere near 1400 miles from here to there. It would take a month and a half or more to get there and the same back. Three months or more to hear. I don't know that I could bear it."

"What about a train or a ship?"

"I don't reckon either goes all the way, son, and I've heard it's costly. I suppose we can write a letter, but to who? This Rafferty character, I suppose. I'd write to Ezekiel, but I don't know if he'd get it. We'll wait for now and hope to hear good news soon."

She'd trusted in the Lord all her life, and she decided she wasn't going to quit now.

"Are you sure? Ma, I'll do whatever needs done to find out Boone's fate."

"I am, for now. If I change my mind, I'll tell you. Let's keep this quiet – no need to upset the family. I won't accept Boone's gone unless I hear it for certain."

With the decision made, Jemima should have felt better, not worse, but she didn't. Instead, she moved through her days, always sending up a prayer for her son, ever hoping for good news, not bad. Her other children noticed her mood, but to their inquiries, she smiled and said all was well. She didn't admit anything else, not even to Garrett, her other bachelor son at home.

The week of Thanksgiving arrived. President Grant, formerly a general of the forces Boone fought against, declared it a national holiday. The Wilson clan prepared, and on the day before, with a hog ready to roast in the ground, a letter arrived.

Jemima didn't recognize the neat handwriting on the envelope, but the postmark, as best she could make it out, read Laredo, Texas. She held it in her hands for a long time, almost afraid to open it in case the contents confirmed what she feared most of all. She thought about waiting for Moses but then didn't, opening it with trembling hands. When the first words leapt from the page, she cried out.

*I am alive and well.*

Her eyes jumped to the bottom of the page. It was signed, "Boone". Except for the signature, it looked like a woman's handwriting, neat and precise.

*He's alive,* she thought, with a rush of joy. *Boone is alive.*

Moses was out milking the Jersey cow, but Jemima called his name, loud and he came running, milk spilling from the pail as he dashed into the house. He set the milk pail down in the kitchen and came to her.

"Ma, what is it?"

"Boone's alive," she said and began to cry happy tears. "He sent a letter."

Jemima handed it to her son, who sat down on the long bench beside the table as if his legs were about to fold beneath him. She watched as he read it, then read it again. A grin spread over his face.

"Told you he wasn't dead," Moses said with triumph. "I knew it!"

"He's healing," she replied. "Ezekiel is with him, and he's coming home. Thank the Lord."

"Amen," Moses added. "He said the spring – might take them until summer to get here, but he's alive and coming home."

She put her head down and cried. As she wept, Jacob and his wife, Sally Ann, came in. Her next eldest stopped and stared, looking from Moses to his mother and back.

Jemima wasn't one who cried often, and his expression became concerned.

"It's joyful crying," Moses said as he patted his mother on the back. "She got a letter from Boone. He's coming home in the spring and bringing Ezekiel with him."

"Glory hallelujah," Jacob said. "It'll be good to have him back where he belongs, the kid too."

Nothing would do, but Jemima wrote a letter back.

*"My dearest son – your letter brought me great joy. Though I worried you might well be gone, I held onto hope that you lived, and I am glad to know this is the case. I am happy you will return, your brother with you. We have killed a hog for Thanksgiving, and it does my heart good to know next year, all my children will be at the table. And rejoice for now. There is much to be thankful for. I wish you a continued recovery and a happy Christmas. With all my love, Ma, Jemima Lykens Wilson."*

Moses promised to take it into town on Friday. The knowledge that it would reach Boone perhaps by Christmas made Jemima glad.

On Thanksgiving, she and her sons, still in Kentucky,

gathered for a bountiful meal with roast pork, the last of the fall vegetables from her garden, pumpkin pie, breads, and more. Giving thanks had a bright, new meaning that year.

Four days later, a wire came, the first telegram she had ever received. It provided confirmation, although she no longer needed it. It read simply – "Boone alive. Stop. Wanted you to know. Stop. Boone's friends."

There was no doubt her son lived, and her heart soared.

This was a November she would always remember.

# CHAPTER TEN

Boone woke early, hungry, and for a moment, he was happy. Then he remembered Liam's visit and that his mother thought him dead. Despair hit hard, and he wanted to just close his eyes and forget. If he hadn't gone to town on that fateful October day to play faro, he wouldn't have been shot. But he realized that then he'd never have met Rachel, so there was some good in it after all.

Judging by the faint light in the room, it was barely daybreak. Beside him, Rachel slept in the rocker, her head cocked to one side. Boone started to reach for her, but his brother appeared at the foot of the bed.

"Let her sleep awhile, Boone," he said. "She sat up with you almost all night long in case you'd need her. She's worn out and worried you're about to have a setback. How are you farin'?"

Boone considered the question. "Fair enough, I reckon," he said. "I'm hungry. I could use some coffee."

Ezekiel snorted. "This ain't a fancy restaurant, but I can go see what I can round up. Can you sit up, or do you need my help?"

Boone used his elbows to scoot forward and then pull himself up higher on the pillows. It proved to be a struggle, but he managed, although Zeke assisted him to a comfortable position.

"Stay put," his brother told him. "I'm no hand at this

nursing, but I'll go fetch some coffee and grub."

He was gone a long time. "I forgot it's Sunday," he told Boone. "I made the coffee myself, so if it's bad, it's my fault. I got Graciela to make the mush, but if you want much else, someone's gonna have to cook it. I can go hunting or fishing afterwhile, and there's some stuff, but I reckon Mary will pitch a fit if we go to eating much of it."

"Mary's going to have to wait," Boone said. "I'll pay her if need be."

Boone cradled a cup of strong black coffee in both hands and sipped it with pleasure. It warmed him and lifted his dark mood a little. His brother also brought cornmeal mush, topped with a little brown sugar. Boone managed to eat it with a spoon, his movements shaky and slow, but hunger won, and he ate all of it. The simple fare rested easy in his belly. If he wasn't believed to be dead back home, he thought he'd be in a fine mood. He said something of the sort to Zeke, who shook his head.

"Boone, you gotta let go of that and quit fretting. I thought about it a lot during the night, sitting up with Rachel. Ma's stronger than you may remember – stubborner than a mule, too. I wouldn't be surprised if she won't accept it as true. During the war, she worried plenty, and after Sharpsburg, she heard there were many casualties, but she never gave up. Besides, she got Rafferty's letter, and she'll get yours too. Deke and Mac vowed they would send a wire – I believe they will. Ma will know you ain't dead sooner or later. In the meantime, you gotta remember there's another woman here, and you've worried her considerable."

"Rachel?" Boone said, surprised. "She knows I'm alive."

Zeke rolled his eyes. "'Course she does, but you takin' Liam's letter so hard, she's worried you'll take a turn for the worse. She's wearing herself to the bone, taking care of you. She's tired, and she's not eating all that much either. Did you know she's the one who dug that bullet out of you?"

He hadn't realized. "I figured it was Deacon or Mac. She did it?"

"She did. That took some guts, Boone, and nerve."

It had. An awareness that he'd taken Rachel for granted made him feel that he'd been selfish. "You're right – Ma will survive, and she'll know the truth, but Rachel's here, and I need to think about her."

"You do. I've grown right close to Rachel – she's like a sister to me. I know you've been bad sick and you plan to go home come spring. But that's six months from now – we cain't keep staying in this room over a saloon. For one, Mary won't abide it, and for another, Rachel deserves better, and it's too small, though it's not proper for her to live with us, she's got nowhere else to go. Soon as you're well enough, we need to find somewhere to stay. Maybe Liam would let us winter at the ranch."

Boone shook his head. "It's twenty miles out – I ain't up to riding yet, and it wouldn't be right, not when I couldn't work and don't plan to stay. You're right, though. I'll study on it and see what we can do. Look through my gear and see if I still have some money tucked in an old boot. If so, then we're all right for cash for now."

"I got my wages, too, Boone," the kid said. "And I may start working over at the livery stable. They asked if I might."

Rachel stirred and bolted from the rocker like a scared jackrabbit.

"Boone?"

He stretched out a hand to her, and she clasped it tight. "I'm right here, honey."

She put a hand across his forehead, checking for fever, and sighed.

"How do you feel?"

"Better than I did last night. Zeke brought me coffee and

some mush."

"Coffee's probably still warm if you want a cup," Ezekiel told her and indicated the table where the pot sat. "I can go down and get you something to eat, too, if you'd like."

"Coffee will do for now," she said. Rachel leaned down and kissed Boone. "You frightened me. I thought you'd take sick again."

In his newfound awareness, Boone saw how fatigued Rachel appeared. There were dark smudges beneath her eyes and frown lines in her face, and she appeared pale. Now, he was more than a little concerned about her, but he said nothing for the moment.

"You need something to eat, too," he said. "Come, sit here a spell, and let Ezekiel bring you something."

Without hesitation, Rachel sat down on the bed facing him. She accepted the coffee that Zeke poured and drank it. "I'm not really hungry."

Boone figured she hadn't eaten since the chicken and dumplings yesterday. "Honey, you gotta eat – if you get down sick, who's gonna take care of me, let alone you?"

She raised her head and met his eyes. "I never thought about that. All right, I'll eat."

Rachel managed to eat some mush and some applesauce, both of which Ezekiel brought from the saloon kitchen.

"That ain't enough to keep a bird alive," Boone said.

"It is for now," she replied. "I'll eat more later when you do. Try not to fret about your family thinking you dead."

"Ezekiel and I talked that over," he told her. "I'm not as worked up as I was – Zeke thinks our mother won't believe it so easy, and I hope he's right."

"She'll know you're alive when she gets the letter," Rachel said. "And if your pals send a telegram."

Boone nodded. "True enough, and ain't naught else I can

do about it."

Rachel reached out and took his hands in hers. "Would you like to get out of bed for a little while?"

"More than anything, but let me try it."

He didn't want to tax her strength supporting him, so he tossed back the quilt and then swung his feet over the side of the bed. So far, so good, he thought. Rachel stood up and stepped out of his way. She moved the rocking chair closer and waited.

Each movement took determination and a great effort to make. His head spun worse than a loco steer, but Boone managed. When he stood, he thought for a moment he might go down, but he focused. He made the three steps to the rocker and sat down, winded but victorious. She hovered, but he lacked the energy to kiss her again.

"I'm all right," he said in response to her anxious look.

Ezekiel stood from digging through their gear. "Boone, you should have asked me to help. I found the rest of your stash, though. You're good. Rachel said she'd already found a bit."

"Did you count it?"

His brother shot him a sharp look. "I did – your winnings too. It's all in that old boot till you need it."

Boone nodded. Knowing he could pay his way brightened his mood. "If Mary says anything, give her some money. I don't reckon any mercantile stores are open?"

"Not on Sunday. Why?"

"I thought with the saloon closed, maybe Rachel could fix us something if we had something to cook."

"I could," she said. "I'd be happy to, Boone. What would you like?"

He pondered the question. He'd enjoyed the chicken and dumplings, but he wasn't all that particular. The last few years, he'd had a steady diet of beans and bacon and biscuits. Beef had figured prominently on the occasions when he'd had meat.

"I'll eat about anything," he told her. "I don't want you to make a big fuss, though. You're tired."

"The saloon's closed, so I'll go down and see what there is," she told him.

Boone couldn't argue, so he nodded.

"Go with her, Ezekiel," he said. "She might need help."

"Are you gonna be all right alone?"

He wasn't at all sure, but he'd survived being propped on the porch when he was in much worse shape. "I reckon so."

The small space seemed to shrink once he was alone. Boone concentrated on remaining upright in the chair and resolved to ask his brother exactly how much money he had. He thought about trying to walk a few steps, figured he'd fall, and if so, that would upset both Rachel and Zeke, so he didn't. He was a little cold, and Rachel hadn't provided a blanket or quilt. Boone could almost reach one from the bed, but he realized he couldn't, not without rising.

They returned, after what seemed to be a long time, with a loaf of white bread, butter, along with some fried potatoes and ham slices. Boone struggled his way to the table, where he managed to eat with slow bites after Zeke cut up the ham for him. He savored the taste of the ham, the potatoes, and, most of all, the sourdough bread.

Rachel ate more than she had earlier, which pleased him, although she said little and seemed withdrawn. Zeke assisted his return to the rocking chair and then cleaned away the dishes.

"I'll take all this back down," he said. "Boone, if you need help, just ask."

Sated from the food, he nodded. "I'll do."

The other thing he craved was a smoke, but he was too drowsy and too fumble-fingered to trust he wouldn't drop it, so he didn't ask.

He let Rachel tuck a blanket around him, then sat,

somnolent, and listened to the rain fall outside. The sound increased his drowsiness, and he closed his eyes. He might have gone to sleep, but when he was almost there, Rachel made a slight noise, somewhere between a groan and a moan, that brought him fully awake.

Boone focused on Rachel. She sat at the table, and as he watched, she rubbed her forehead. Her sewing lay discarded, and she had a tight posture. The same sound came again. He tossed off the quilt and found his feet, then crossed the space to where she sat quickly.

He put one hand on her shoulder. "What's the matter, sweetheart? Are you sick?"

Startled, she jumped at his touch and whirled around.

"Oh, Boone, I thought you were asleep," she said.

"I almost was. What is it?"

"Nothing," she replied in a voice he'd never heard. "It'll pass. Go sit down before you hurt yourself."

He glanced around the room and found Ezekiel absent. He wondered where he'd gone, but for now, his attention was on Rachel.

"Tell me."

She scooted the chair around to face him, and he noticed how pale she'd become.

"I have a headache," she said. "It'll pass."

Worry fired in his gut. He clamped a large hand across her forehead, checking for fever, and sighed when her skin was cool. If she took sick, caring for him, he would feel responsible, and the last thing he wanted was Rachel to be ill.

"You're worn out," he said. "Come to bed and get some rest. It's my turn to take care of you."

"Boone –"

"I won't take no for an answer," he said. "If you don't come, I'll pick you up and carry you."

He said it with sheer bravado. He doubted he could manage to lift her, and he lacked the strength to carry her. She bought his bluff, though.

"Don't you dare, Boone Wilson." Rachel stood and took his arm. "I'll go sit a spell in the rocker."

"You're going to lie down proper," he said.

Boone put one arm around her as much to steady himself as her and propelled her toward the bed. Whatever Rachel needed, he'd do his best to provide it – or die trying.

# CHAPTER ELEVEN

Her head ached and pounded like a drum in a parade she'd seen once in Texas. Rachel did her best to ignore it, but the headache refused to go away and kept growing worse as the day continued. She couldn't remember ever being this weary, not even in the travels from Virginia to Mississippi to Texas and then to Laredo. More than a week of nursing, to Boone seemed much longer. She'd stayed at his side most of the time and worried over him every minute. Although she'd feared for his life, it had taken a deeper resolve than she'd known she possessed to dig the bullet out of his chest and nurse him.

Sleeping in the rocker proved to be an improvement from sleeping in a straight chair, but it was far from comfortable. She'd awakened with a slight headache after a brief rest. He'd been so distraught after learning his family had been notified he was certain to die that she feared he'd relapse. When she did awake, he'd been in good spirits, but she hadn't felt well at all.

Ezekiel remained gone after removing the dishes from their midday dinner, and Boone dozed in the rocking chair. Rachel tried to sew, but it made her headache worse, so she put the task aside. She rubbed her forehead as if that would relieve the pain and moaned a little. Boone heard, though, and startled her.

He'd walked from the rocker to where she sat and put his

big, work-calloused hand on her shoulder. "What's the matter, sweetheart?" he asked, his voice heavy with concern. "Are you sick?"

His kindness made her want to cry. She had always been the caregiver and alone for so long that it never occurred that someone else might worry or care.

"I have a headache," she told him. "It'll pass."

Boone refused to accept it. Instead, he threatened to pick her up and carry her to bed if she didn't go. That horrified her – because he might open his wound or otherwise hurt himself – but it also thrilled her. Rachel allowed him to lead her to the bed and crawled into it.

She settled onto her right side, and he pulled the covers over her, then sat on the edge of the bed.

"Sleep, honey," he said. "Get some rest."

Rachel couldn't relax. Her body remained as tight as an overwound clock.

He stroked her head and hair with one large but gentle hand. The repetitive movement calmed her.

"That feels nice," she said. "Granny used to do that."

"So did my ma," he replied.

"Boone, will you sing to me?"

He chuckled, something she hadn't heard him do before. "It's been said I have a good voice, though I haven't sung much in years, but I'll try. Mostly, I sing to the cattle at night."

"Sing to cows?"

"On the trail, sugar. Keeps them from gettin' too restless at night – all cowboys do."

Boone began to sing, his voice a rich baritone, a familiar song Rachel had heard often during the war. Some called it "Weeping, Sad and Lonely," others "When This Cruel War Is Over." Either way, the poignant lyrics hit home, and tears filled her eyes.

When one slid down her cheek, Boone wiped it away and stopped.

"You don't like my singing?"

"You're a fine singer," she told him. "But it's such a sad song. I don't want to be parted from you, Boone."

"You won't be." He sounded certain. "I was wounded, lonely, dying when I met you. It seemed fitting, but I'll sing another if you'd like."

"I would."

He sang a funny little song she'd never heard, something about roving down to Newry town that had an Irish lilt to the words. Then he sang a rollicking ballad about a highwayman named Willie Brennan. Rachel liked them both. The sound of his voice soothed her, and she closed her eyes. Boone switched to a Stephen Foster song, *I Dream of Jeannie With The Light Brown Hair,* except he changed it to Rachel. Then he sang some more Irish tunes, some of which were familiar to her and some were not.

As he sang, he continued to stroke her hair with an easy hand. She became drowsy but tried to listen. At some point, Ezekiel returned.

"Is she sick?" she heard him ask.

"No, she's just tired and had a headache," Boone replied, that tenderness still in his tone.

"Were you *singing?*" his brother asked.

"Yeah."

"You were singing some of Ma's songs."

"I was."

"Makes me kinda homesick, Boone."

"It does me too. But we'll be there when we can."

"What about Rachel?"

"I won't leave her."

"Then…."

"I mean to marry her when I'm well enough if she'll have

me."

That sentence pleased her, and she tucked it into her memory. That was the last she remembered, except for their voices soft and low, talking for a long time.

Rachel slept, and when she woke, it was dark in the room except for a single grease lamp that burned on the table. Disoriented for a moment, she roused to find Boone asleep in the rocker. He had pulled it beside the bed, and one of his hands rested on hers. From the opposite side of the room, she heard Zeke snoring. Her headache was gone, but she didn't try to rise yet. Instead, she savored the luxury of a bed, covers, a pillow beneath her head, and someone to hold her hand tight.

She dozed again and woke when she heard Ezekiel fussing at his brother.

"You're cold, Boone, I can see you shivering. You don't need to get down sick."

"I'm all right."

"No, you ain't. It's not even midnight, and it's likely to get colder still in here."

"I'll do."

It sounded like bravado to her, so she roused. "Boone?"

"Right here."

"Get in this bed and warm up." She had no hesitation. They'd already shared a bed for one night, and she trusted him.

"Honey, are you sure?"

Zeke interrupted. "You just heard her say to get in bed. Do you need help?"

"No." It turned out Boone did, a bit.

He crawled in the opposite side of the bed after she threw back the bedclothes and curled against her. With him spooned against her back, she felt how chilled he was.

Ezekiel pulled the covers over them both.

"You're like ice," she exclaimed.

"I might be a bit cold."

Although it was a challenge in the narrow bed, Rachel turned over so that she faced Boone. She put her arms around him and cuddled close, her head pillowed against his right shoulder. She used care not to get near his wound. He put his arms around her, too, and they slept the rest of the night, together.

Rachel woke early and, for a moment, couldn't recall why she lay in Boone's arms. When she did, she touched his face and found it warm, not feverish. In sleep, he appeared younger than he did awake. She traced the curve of his cheek with one finger, then let it travel down his nose. Rachel outlined his lips with a fingertip and stroked his chin. When he woke, his grey eyes met hers. He looked at her for some long moments, and she gazed back. As natural as breathing, he kissed her, his mouth soft and sweet against her mouth. Her lips melted beneath his, and she shivered, but not from cold. He kept kissing her until she realized that if they didn't stop, improper things might well happen, so she scooted back enough to end it.

"How's your head?" he whispered.

"The headache's gone, but now I'm hungry. Are you warm enough now?"

He nodded. "And I'm starving."

"It's early – the saloon won't be open for hours. I'll go down and fix us something."

"Let Ezekiel go with you. He can help you tote the food up here."

Venturing into the saloon always made Rachel feel like a trespasser. It wasn't her kind of place, and she knew it. Even closed, the place reeked of stale beer and spilled whiskey. The pungent scent of the patchouli and other fragrances that the gals wore hung in the air, too. The kitchen, however, was different, and she was comfortable there. Ezekiel sat down backwards on a chair while she collected the ingredients to make biscuits, one hand on the revolver he often wore. His presence guaranteed her safety, and although she'd fussed with Boone about it, she knew the things that could befall her. Once the biscuit dough was made, rolled out, and cut, she located some sausage and started frying it in a skillet. Biscuits and gravy sounded tasty, she thought.

"Exactly what are you doing in my kitchen?"

The sharp voice startled Rachel, and she nearly dropped the pan of biscuits. Zeke leapt to his feet, hand resting on his pistol until he recognized Mary. With a bravado beyond his years, he drawled, "Making some biscuits and gravy so we don't starve."

"You're stealing from me." This early in the day, Mary looked as rough as she was. Lines cut deep into her face, and she winced at the light as if she might have drunk too much.

"I paid you with a $20 gold piece," Rachel said. "I haven't used a quarter of that."

"And I'll pay more if needed, and so will Boone," Zeke added. "We're not thieves, Mary."

The saloon owner grunted. "I'll need more if you're staying and eating here. I let Boone stay out of the goodness of my heart when I thought he was dying only because he got shot in my place. He's not dead and now I got three of you under my roof. She's bad for businesses, being a respectable woman and all, and causing all kinds of talk."

Rachel's stomach twisted into a knot. "What talk?"

"What talk?" Mary mimicked in a falsetto voice. "Talk about an unmarried woman bunking with two cowboys over a saloon that offers sporting – both drink, cards and ladies. Some like that blacksmith want you run out of town."

"Kurtz?"

"That's his name. If he comes here again, I'm likely to shoot him myself," she said. "How's Boone anyway?"

"He's healing," Zeke stated. "But he's barely been out of bed yet. He's got a way to go."

"I need that room back soon," Mary told him. "I got a new gal who could be making me some money in it."

Rachel put on a proud face, but inside, she wanted to cry. Her chest hurt with unshed tears. She'd never had much but her pride and a reputation. She'd told Boone she wasn't a lady, and she had never claimed to be, but the gossip upset her. Thanks to the blacksmith, she'd lost her position as schoolteacher, a place to live, and her social standing. Although she'd never told anyone, Kurtz had an eye for her. More than a few times, he managed to brush a hand across her breasts or hip as if it were accidental. His apparent moral outage seemed to come from his disappointment that he hadn't got a chance to enjoy her favors. She had little future in Laredo but little money to return to northeast Texas or join one of her brothers. Without Boone and his brother, she had absolutely nothing. Boone made it no secret he planned to return to Kentucky in the spring, and though he'd kissed her and made her feel like he cared, Rachel wasn't sure what the future would bring. Boone seemed like a good man, a dependable, decent one, but maybe he wasn't. Maybe he thought he could take liberties with a woman who slept under a saloon's roof with two men. The possibility made her chest tighten even more.

The joy she'd had lying in Boone's arms faded, and embarrassment replaced it. She said no more as she finished making the meal. Ezekiel dealt with Mary and promised her that they'd talk about compensation, but she wasn't paying much attention. He helped her carry the biscuits, the gravy now thick with sausage, plates, and spoons upstairs. She'd brewed a fresh pot of coffee, knowing how much Boone liked it, and she carried that plus some cups.

"Figure out what you plan to do and let me know," Mary called after them in a shrill voice as they climbed the stairs. "And soon, you hear me. I'm not running a boarding house for wayward cowboys and schoolmarms."

Maybe Boone had an idea, Rachel thought, but she had none. Her options were few, and her future seemed both bleak.

# CHAPTER TWELVE

Boone managed to climb out of bed and stagger the few steps to the table. The simple act winded him, though, and brought home how very weak he remained. Recovering from the chest wound would take more time than he'd first thought, but he was alive, thanks to Rachel's efforts, and he would.

When she and his brother entered, laden with food and dishes, he sensed something had happened. Their tight, closed expressions warned him. He could remember times when a small Ezekiel got in trouble, the time he'd gotten into one of Ma's just-baked apple pies and eaten half, or the time he'd forgot to shut the henhouse door, and the birds escaped. That little fellow had worn an expression much like the one he did now, and his air of pretending to be innocent was familiar. Rachel wasn't smiling, and her eyes were brimming with tears.

"What's the matter?" he asked. "What happened?"

"Mary did," his brother replied in a tense tone. "She accused us of stealing, though Rachel paid her with a gold piece some time ago. She wants more money for us to stay here and keep getting grub, whether Rachel fixes it or Graciela. Wants the room back, too, said she only let you stay because she thought you were dying. And she said some things that hurt Rachel's feelings too."

Boone took in the information and cussed. He knew Mary

was mercenary, but he had money, and that could be handled. Rachel, though, was something different. "What did she say? Honey, tell me."

Rachel put the coffee pot down and dropped into the chair. "There's talk about me, that I'm not a respectable woman, not when I'm sharing space with both of you. There's gossip, and some, like Kurtz, want to run me out of town."

The tears she'd held back flowed down her cheeks, and the sight of them hurt Boone more than if they had been his. "Aw, Rachel, honey, don't fret. I won't let that happen, not ever. You're a good woman, and we know it."

"Maybe I'm not," she wailed. "She made it sound like I'm no better than one of the sportin' gals, maybe worse, taking both of you into my bed. I won't be able to stay here, and I don't have anywhere else to go."

Boone glanced at Zeke, who nodded. "It's all pretty much what Mary said, Boone."

He sighed and stood up with effort. Boone moved behind Rachel's chair and put his hands on her shoulders. "Don't cry, Rachel. Mary's bitter, and she's mean. She's likely jealous because you're young and pretty, and you got what she'll never have."

Her sobs slacked. "What could that be?"

"You have me," he said, surprised she didn't know. "C'mon, lift your head. I want you to see me when I say what I'm gonna say."

Rachel shuddered, then did as he asked. She sat up straight and turned to him. He sat back down before he swooned but pulled his chair so he faced her.

"Rachel, I'd rather say this standing on my own two feet, but at least I'm not in bed," he began. The words he wanted proved hard to find. "I ain't been trifling with you, honey. If you're willing, I want to marry you and bring you home with me to Kentucky."

She stared at him, her blue eyes so dark they almost appeared to be black.

"Why?" she said. "To save my reputation?"

The bitterness in her tone, like old hickory nuts, didn't fit her, he thought.

Boone shook his head. "No, because…I love you, Rachel. I figured you might know that, and I've hoped you might feel the same. I want to be your man, before God and for always."

The distress on her face faded. A faint smile flirted around her lips. "Is that true?" she asked in a broken whisper. "I heard you say something like that to Zeke, but I thought I might be dreaming."

He touched her cheek and wiped away a stray tear. "It's true, I swear to God, Rachel. It's like that bit from the Bible, from Solomon, 'I am my beloved's, and my beloved is mine.' Maybe you don't feel the same, not yet, but I hope that you will."

If she didn't, his heart might shrivel up and die. He'd never felt anything for a woman what he did for Rachel. Maybe she'd just been kind, he thought, with a sinking feeling. Maybe he'd been wrong as could be. Waiting for her to say something stretched into an eternity, and he'd almost begun to wish he'd died after all when she took his hands in hers.

"Boone," she said in the way that made his name sound like a caress. "Boone Wilson, I love you. I think I've loved you from that very first day on the porch. If you know your Bible at all, you might know this from the Book of Ruth, 'Entreat me not to leave thee, or to return from following after thee: for whither thou goest, I will go; and where thou lodgest, I will lodge: thy people shall be my people, and thy God my God: where thou diest, will I die, and there will I be buried: the Lord do so to me, and more also, if ought but death part thee and me.' That's how I feel, Boone, I'll go with you to Kentucky or to the moon."

He whooped with joy, and although he figured he might

end up on the floor, he pulled her onto his lap and held her close. Boone kissed her as she put her arms around his neck, his mouth claiming her as his as surely as if he'd branded her. He snuggled her tight and nuzzled her with a few more light kisses. The moment might have lasted forever or at least until he fell out in a faint, but his brother interrupted.

"I reckon that means you're getting married," he said. "I'm glad, but the food's gonna get cold, and Boone's gonna end up laid out on the floor."

Rachel's eyes met Boone's, and they laughed.

"You got that right, kid," Boone said. Rachel untangled out of his lap with a broad smile. "Rachel, woman, we're square?"

"We are," she said.

"Then let's eat."

The food remained warm, and he thought he'd never eaten anything as delicious. He ate his fill and then became so tired that Rachel insisted on tucking him back into bed. Her hands were gentle as she smoothed the quilt over him, and her lips soft as she kissed him. "Sleep awhile, my love," she said.

By the week of Thanksgiving, Boone found he could walk at a slow pace around the room, from bed or rocker to table or window. He had regained the strength to shave himself. He had yet to venture downstairs, although he now wore his brown trousers, worn and familiar with a shirt and often his leather vest. Although he put on socks, ones that Rachel had darned so that they no longer had holes, he hadn't worn his boots but twice.

He'd paid Mary, who had visited him twice with her hand out, $50 dollars to provide not only for food but to keep the room until Christmas. Ezekiel brought in game and fish, hunting almost daily and keeping a trot line on the river. On a few occasions, Rachel, with a borrowed basket and Zeke at her side, ventured out to one of the local mercantile stores to buy some things. His brother also worked at the livery stable as an extra hand when one was needed.

Ezekiel came in now. He seldom entered a room but burst into it with enthusiasm.

"Boone, I think I found a place where we can stay."

Interested, Boone turned around. "Tell me about it."

"It's three rooms above the saddler's shop, about two blocks from here," he told him. "Abernathy, who runs it, said he'd rent it for $15 a month."

"Why is it empty?" Boone had already learned, even without leaving the room, that places to live were at a premium in Laredo. If there was a catch, he wanted to know it now, not later.

"He was planning to get married, sent for his bride from across the ocean somewhere, but she married a man she met on the ship and ain't coming," Zeke said. "It's got furniture, too, a couple of beds, table and chairs, a stove and all in the kitchen."

"Have you looked at it?"

The younger man shook his head. "Not yet. Where's Rachel?"

"Downstairs, cooking, I hope," Boone said. "She ought to be back soon. You need to take her over to see it. If it looks decent and she likes it, rent it – get the money from my stash."

"I'll go down and find her," Zeke answered.

He returned with Rachel and the venison stew she'd made from a deer he'd killed a few days early. The hearty dish had chunks of meat, potatoes, carrots, and onions. Boone ate his first spoonful and grinned. He would love her if she couldn't boil water, but he liked that she could cook. "Best slumgullion I've ever had," he said. "I'll have my strength back in no time if you keep feeding me this good."

"I intend to do my best," Rachel said.

"Did the kid tell you about the rooms for let?

"He did – I'll go see them tomorrow. Do you want to try

to come along?"

He did, but he didn't dare. "I ain't quite up to it yet, I don't think. I haven't even gone downstairs, let alone down the street. If you like them, take them, and then we'll have a place to live once I can manage and we're hitched."

Her face brightened like dawn, beautiful and glorious. "I like the notion, Boone."

They had yet to set a date but Boone hoped to have the wedding around Christmas, then settle in with his bride until spring. He wasn't sure if the padre at San Agustin Church would marry them since he wasn't Catholic, but he thought a justice of the peace could, as long as Rachel didn't mind. He wanted vows and a ring on her finger before she changed her mind.

It was a wonder to him that she loved him, a woman like her. Boone had never expected to find anyone like Rachel, least of all to marry one and have her for the rest of his life. He'd thought she tended him out of compassion, out of mercy because she felt sorry for him, but from what she said, it started for her on that first day.

"Do you know you make me happy?" he asked, as they dined. "Happier than I think I've ever been in all my life."

Her lips blossomed into a smile. "I'm glad, Boone. You give me joy."

That pleased him so much that it was a surprise the buttons weren't busting off his shirt he wore. "I don't know how or why, but that's good," he told her, his voice gruff with emotion. "I hope you're gonna like Kentucky."

"It's not so far from where I was raised," she replied. "I'll like it well enough. Will you farm? What do you raise?"

Ezekiel looked up from his stew. "Boone, you never told her?"

"I hadn't," he said. "It's no secret, though. We grow tobacco and corn and garden things, but mainly, we raise Morgan horses. My horse, Sprat, is a Morgan from home, and so is Zeke's mount."

"I haven't seen your horse yet," she told him. "But I've heard of Morgans. Did you ride him through the war?"

Boone grinned. "I was a foot soldier. I got Sprat when I went home after the war ended. I'd raised him from a foal, and he remembered me. Zeke came to Texas riding Midnight."

"They're loyal and friendly," Ezekiel added. "Strong, too."

"Can you ride?" Boone asked Rachel. That was something he should have determined long ago. If she didn't, he'd need to teach her or procure a wagon, which might be the best option.

She nodded. "I can. I've ridden some horses and more mules, but if it goes, I can sit it."

"Sprat's probably near forgot me by now," Boone said with sadness.

"Aw, he ain't," his brother said. "But he misses you."

"Soon as I can get there, I'll go see him. Rachel needs to meet him, too."

Any notion she might think that silly vanished when he saw her smile.

"I'll save some sugar cubes for him or maybe a carrot," she said.

Boone laughed. "You do that, and you'll have a pal for life."

Ezekiel rolled his eyes. "I'm going hunting for a turkey."

He brought one back, a fine, large bird that would serve well as their dinner. On Thanksgiving Day Rachel parboiled, then roasted it to a brown perfection. On the side, she served sweet potatoes, light bread, carrots, and the ever-available frijoles, which she'd learned to prepare almost as well as Graciela. Deacon and Mac showed up in time to join the feast.

"It's good to give thanks," Deacon said. "But I hate that General Grant's the one who declared the day."

Boone, mellowed by the meal and the smoke he'd been craving, laughed. "The Yanks won, Deke, and that's the truth. I'm not fond of Grant, for he's a drunkard, but Lincoln, he wasn't so bad. After all, he was a Southerner at heart, born in Kentucky just like me and Ezekiel. It's a powerful shame he got shot."

"You got shot yourself," Mac stated.

"Yeah, well, thank the Lord it wasn't a head shot, or I would be as dead as Honest Abe."

"You came close enough as it was," Rachel said. "I'm thankful today and always that you're alive."

In front of them all, he kissed her and then held her close, well aware of the treasure he had gained with her.

# CHAPTER THIRTEEN

After Thanksgiving, with a month remaining until Christmas, Rachel found herself both restless and impatient. On the day after they dined on wild turkey, she accompanied Ezekiel to see the three rooms over the saddler's shop and rented them.

She liked the space, the large room that overlooked the street with a round table and four wooden chairs with a kitchen set up at the rear. There was a stove, shelves, workspace, and a large dish pan. They would need many things, but Rachel was confident that Boone could provide money to buy them. Off that large room, there were two bedrooms, both with iron beds. The smallest had a view of Laredo, and she thought it would work well for Ezekiel. The rear bedroom was a bit bigger, and in addition to a bed, there was a single chest and a washstand.

"I rented the rooms," she cried to Boone the moment she returned. "But we'll need some household things."

"We'll go buy what we need," he said. "I think by Monday I'll be able to make it to the mercantile, so make a list."

She noted that he wore his boots. "Are you going somewhere today?"

"I plan to go downstairs and play some faro with the boys," he told her with a grin. "Deke and Mac will be playing, and it's time I taught Zeke how to play."

Since the last time he'd gambled downstairs at the Out of

Luck, he'd been shot point blank and came near dying. Rachel was a little worried. She told him so, and he laughed.

"Mad Mike, who shot me, is dead," he told her. "It was just a bit of bad luck. I don't know why he shot me, and neither does anybody else. Likely, he was drunk and out of his mind. They called him Mad Mike for a reason."

"Still…"

Boone pulled her into an exuberant embrace. "Don't fret, honey. I don't look to get shot again."

His arms comforted her but failed to erase her concerns. After all, he'd never expected to get shot at all. She wanted to accompany him and sit at his side at the gaming table, but Boone refused. "Honey, they'll take you for the wrong kind of gal, and since you're my woman, I'd get more than a little het up if someone did. We don't need any trouble, Rachel."

It made sense, and she understood, but she didn't have to like it. On both Friday and Saturday nights, Boone made the trip downstairs to play. The first night, his brother stayed close as he descended, ready to provide support if needed. Well after midnight, they returned, Boone triumphant with victory and pockets filled with cash. He smelled like the saloon, stale beer, whiskey, and tobacco, although he didn't drink. Rachel didn't mind as long as he was tucked beside her in bed. Maybe they shouldn't share the bed but she figured if they remained chaste, it was fine. No one would think twice if Boone shared the space with his brother or even Deacon. They would be wed soon enough anyway.

On Sunday, Boone slept later than Rachel, weary from his gambling. She longed for church and so she convinced Ezekiel to walk with her over to San Agustin for the early Mass. To her surprise, he came inside with her and sat in the pew, respectful but not participating. Afterward, her spirits buoyed by the familiar rite, Rachel linked her arm through Zeke's as they made their way back to the saloon. The streets were muddy, even in December, and rough, so she appreciated his assistance. They had almost reached the saloon when Kurtz stepped out of a gap between two buildings.

Rachel had last seen him when he came raging to the room upstairs although Mary, the saloon keeper, had warned he wanted her run out of town. His face, never handsome, was twisted with a hostile expression. "There's the harlot," he shouted. "She's corrupting the boy, now, it seems. Too good for me, she was, but she'll lay down with any mounted saddle trash she finds."

Ezekiel stepped in front of Kurtz, one hand beneath his coat on his pistol. "Get out of here. I warned you once, and I won't again."

Although he spoke the words with determination and a lot more grit than Rachel had, Kurtz didn't seem affected. He reached past Zeke to grab Rachel's arm. A strand of hair trailed out from beneath her bonnet, and he pulled it hard. When she yipped with outrage, he backhanded her across the face with force. It hurt, and she screamed. Her reaction didn't stop Kurtz. He appeared to like it.

"Fight me, vixen," he told her. "If you like it rough, all the better because so do I. I mean to take a little of what you're giving away."

Then he pulled Rachel closer. Zeke tried to free her, and they had a tug of war over her. When Ezekiel wouldn't stop, Kurtz punched him hard enough to bloody his nose and then to knock him down on the street. *Of course,* Rachel thought, *he's strong – he's a blacksmith.*

She screamed again when Ezekiel fell to the muddy street. A crowd gathered around them, people on their way home from church like Rachel and others just out and about. With Zeke down, Kurtz began dragging her down the street with rough hands as she struggled against him. He slapped her twice, once hard enough to split her lip because she tasted blood.

Kurtz came to an abrupt stop so fast she almost tripped. Then she heard the unmistakable sound of a pistol being cocked and Boone's familiar voice.

"Let her go, or I'll shoot you dead where you stand. If you doubt I will just remember I spent four long years at war. Yours wouldn't be the first blood I've spilled."

Rachel had never heard such menace in his voice, but her heart leaped with joy to see him standing behind Kurtz with the barrel of his Griswold revolver at the back of Kurtz's head.

The blacksmith released her, his face red with fury. He lifted both hands to surrender. "This whore ain't worth dying for."

"My woman is worth the world to me," Boone replied. He hadn't moved or lowered the weapon. "My brother, there, means plenty too. The last time you came around, I was flat on my back, near death, but I'm alive and well. Get out of here, and don't let me see you again. You want to run her out of town, I hear, when leaving might be the best for your own health."

Her legs trembled, and she wasn't sure she could stand up until Ezekiel rose from the street and steadied her, although he was a bit shaky, too. Kurtz departed the scene, and Boone addressed the onlookers, "Go on, get. There's nothing more to see here."

He came to Rachel and put one hand beneath her chin. "Did he hurt you?"

She wanted to cry but didn't. "Not much."

Boone touched her lip with one fingertip. "Your lip's bleeding and your face might bruise. Does it hurt?"

"A little."

He turned to his brother. "Are you hurt?"

Zeke pulled out a bandana and wiped his nose, leaving the cloth stained with blood. "I'll live. I should have shot that stinking polecat."

"Better you didn't," Boone said. "We don't need trouble."

"Looks like we got some anyway," Ezekiel replied. "How'd you get out here anyhow?"

Boone narrowed his eyes. "I woke up, and y'all were gone. Then I heard Rachel scream and I came down the stairs in a hurry. I didn't even think about it."

Now that it was over, she thought she might faint. "Boone."

He turned and saw how pale she was. He wrapped his arms around her and held her close. "I'd carry you, but I doubt I can, not yet. Let's go to the room."

Since it was Sunday, only Mary saw them as they came through the saloon. She followed, frowning.

"What happened?"

"Kurtz tried to drag Rachel off," Boone told her. "He hit her and Zeke, too. And you know this – you were watching. I saw you at the door."

Her frown deepened. "You're a nosy cowpoke, Boone, but yeah, I was. What are you doing about him?"

"Nothing," he said, spitting the word out like a bad taste.

"Bad men like him, they don't quit easy," Mary said, her tone dire.

"He'd best, if he knows what's good for him."

Rachel touched her lip, and her finger came away with blood. "Boone?"

His arm around her waist tightened. "What is it, honey?"

"I might get sick." Her stomach was upset, and puking was a possibility, but her main goal was to get away from Mary. The saloonkeeper's vindictiveness carried a vile and bitter poison, something they didn't need.

"Let me get you upstairs," he said. "Ezekiel, can you fetch up some water or are you too hurt?"

"I can do it," the kid said.

He moved around Mary, who stood with one foot poised on the step to follow them up. "Is that a threat?" Mary asked Boone with a cackle that reminded him of a witch or laying hen.

"No, a promise."

Rachel sighed. She recalled Mary's boast that she'd shoot Kurtz if he set foot in the Out of Luck again. Loathsome as the man was, it'd be better not to, she thought.

Boone settled her into the rocking chair with gentle hands. "Would you rather lay down for a spell?"

"No, I'm not that hurt, just still shaking."

He poured water from the pitcher into the bowl and dipped a soft cloth in it. With easy motions, he washed her face, taking extra care with her lip. The cool water was delightful against her skin, and his touch soothed her troubled spirits.

"I won't let him near you again," he told her. "You should have woken me – I'd gone with you."

"I thought you could use the sleep." She still worried about him; always afraid he could relapse.

Boone folded his fingers against her cheek. "Honey, when I heard you scream, you scared the fire out of me. It's gonna bruise a little."

"It will heal, though."

He laid his hand across her abdomen. "How's your belly? Still got collywobbles?"

She shook her head. "It's better, it was just nerves, I think. Is Zeke all right?"

The kid rose from where he'd been sitting cross-legged on the floor and took a seat at the table. "I'm fine, Rachel. Don't you fret about me."

He had washed his face, and his right eye was swollen almost shut. Someone tapped on the door, and Peggy stuck her head inside. "I heard," she said. "I brought some ice up and some vittles in case you wanted to eat. Graciela made *pozole.*"

Still new to Texas, Rachel wasn't familiar with all the cuisine. "What is it?"

"Mexican stew," Boone said. "Pork, hominy, onions, garlic, cabbage and such. It's good. Tell her *gracias* or say thank you, please, Peggy."

The young woman smiled. "I will, she'll be glad."

Peggy wrapped a piece of the ice she brought in a clean, dry rag and carried it to Ezekiel. She put it over his eye and asked, "Does that help?"

He covered her hand with his. "Feels right good."

"Honey, come eat while it's hot," Boone told Rachel. "You've had a hard day so far."

The stew was as tasty as Boone had claimed, and Rachel finished a bowl. Her cheek stung where Kurtz had hit her, and when she chanced a glance in her hand mirror, it was beginning to show a bruise. It could have been worse, however, she reasoned. If Boone hadn't come, the blacksmith would have succeeded in dragging her away. He would have kissed her at the very least, a disgusting thought that made her want to wipe her lips even though he'd kissed them and likely worse. As much as Boone loved her, she wasn't sure that he or any man could get around their woman being taken by force. She knew without any doubt at all that Boone would have killed the man for it, too.

After dinner, Boone tried to coax her to rest with a nap, but she refused.

"I'd lay down if I wasn't well, but I'm fine."

"That yellow belly hurt you," he said and touched her cheek with the back of his hand. "And scared the tarnation out of you. It wouldn't hurt to rest a spell, honey."

She parted her lips to protest again, then stopped. Fatigue shadowed his eyes, and she realized that although he'd been more ambulatory, he wasn't yet restored to full health. Descending to gamble twice wasn't the same as bolting down the stairs to find her in peril or to defend her. Maybe she was being silly, but Rachel thought he looked pale and acted as if he wasn't very well. "You need to rest, too, Boone. I don't want you to wear yourself out."

He offered her his slow smile. "I could use it, I reckon. I'll need the strength to go shopping for house goods with you tomorrow. I'll lay down if you'll come lay beside me."

Rachel hesitated, but only for a few seconds. They weren't yet man and wife, but she trusted him. He'd never touch her in an intimate fashion until they were wed. Although she hadn't admitted it, the experience had rattled her, and she fancied a rest.

"I will, then," she told him.

Zeke picked up his hat. "I'm off to see to the horses."

She let Boone tuck her into bed and sighed with happiness when he joined her, her back spooned against him. He slept before she did, his breathing even. She loved this man so much and anticipated with joy the life they would weave together, first here, then in Kentucky.

# CHAPTER FOURTEEN

He didn't feel good, not at all. His body ached, and even his healing wound hurt a little. A headache pounded inside his skull, and if he could, without causing stress for his woman and brother, Boone would take to his bed and remain for a day, maybe more. He might have overdone it with his gambling efforts. Traveling the stairs had taken more out of him than he'd expected after more than a month convalescent. He'd stayed up too late and hadn't gotten enough rest, and the fear that clutched his chest when he heard Rachel's screams took a toll, too.

Boone had drawn on strength he hadn't regained, that he lacked to step in so that she wouldn't be hurt or raped. It was bad enough she would sport a bruise on her face and that her poor darling lip was split. His encounter with Harold Kurtz had been all bravado, although if he could, he'd beat the man senseless for what he'd done to Rachel. If Kurtz had fought back, Boone wasn't at all certain he would have prevailed, but he would have died trying.

Fatigue clung heavy to him like a blanket, and as soon as he stretched out beside Rachel, he became drowsy. The quilt over them provided both warmth and comfort, but her presence beside him provided some peace. With any luck, he'd feel better when he woke.

His head felt thick when he did, and he roused with

difficulty. It seemed as if there were layers of sleep to push through, but he heard Rachel's voice. There was a note of strain in her voice, so he made the effort to respond.

"Boone, it's tomorrow. Wake up, won't you? We're worried."

"Don't fret, honey," he said and opened his eyes. Sunshine streamed through the windows, and he blinked. The aroma of fresh coffee filled his nose, and he longed for a cup coupled with a smoke. He thought he also smelled food and realized how hungry he felt. "I'm awake."

He sat up in bed and found Rachel sitting on the edge of the mattress, Ezekiel behind her. His brother wore their mother's frown, his forehead wrinkled the same way she did when concerned. Rachel placed a hand across his forehead and cheeks, then sighed with relief.

"I ain't fevered," Boone stated. "I was just plumb worn out."

"You been asleep a good eighteen hours or so," Zeke said, his voice as dry as a drought in August. "We feared you might be sick."

"You're a pair. You ought not worry so much," Boone said. "Is the coffee still hot?"

Still fully dressed save for his boots, he sat on the edge of the bed beside Rachel.

"There's sickness going around. A lot of folks have come down with measles," Rachel told him. "And some with the grippe. And yes, the coffee is hot. There's also some biscuits and gravy I made in case you wanted to eat."

"I had measles when I was a boy," Boone said. "We all did, even the kid there, but he was a baby, and I don't reckon he'd recall."

He headed for the table and poured a cup, then paused before he took a sip.

"Have you had measles?" he asked Rachel. If she hadn't, he'd be the one worried.

She nodded and stood beside him. "Yes, I have."

Most of the time since the war, he wasn't one to pray, but now he said, "Thanks be to God."

Rachel placed her hands on his shoulders and rubbed them with a light hand. He shut his eyes to savor her touch, liking it and appreciating even more what it meant that she loved him.

"Are you feeling well, then, Boone?" she asked.

He decided to be honest. "I am, honey. Yesterday, I didn't feel so good, but I was tired, probably did a bit too much. I ain't sick, though, and right now, I'm fine."

She leaned over to place a kiss on his cheek. "I'm glad. I was worried."

Boone finished his first cup of coffee and tucked into a plate of biscuits covered with thick cream gravy and well-seasoned sausage. The delicious flavor filled his mouth, and he savored it. He finished a large portion and refilled his cup. The warm food in his belly made him feel very well indeed.

"Ezekiel, do I have any baccy left for a smoke?"

Zeke, midway through a serving of biscuits and gravy, glanced up.

"I reckon enough for one cigarette," he said. "I'll dig it out for you."

Once he had the makings in hand, Boone rolled his smoke and fired it with a match. He inhaled the fragrant tobacco with enjoyment and smoked it slow, sipping coffee. As poorly as he'd felt the previous day, he felt that grand and more now. The food had been tasty, the smoke was pleasant, and the company, his brother and his soon to be bride, was the best.

He watched Rachel as she made the bed, then fussed about the room, cleaning and putting things in order. She stacked the used dishes and such on a tray, and then Ezekiel carried it away. That reminded him he'd promised to take Rachel to the mercantile to buy the things they would need in their new rooms.

"Did you get that list ready?" he asked her.

She nodded. "I did, but it's quite a bit."

"Let me get my boots on, and we'll go."

Her expression faltered, and he reached out for her hand. "What is it?"

"I'm just a bit nervous," she told him. "I want to go, but I'd prefer not to run across Kurtz again."

"We won't." His confidence was bravado, but she didn't need to know that. "And you ought to know I'll keep you safe, honey."

"I do know that Boone."

"He's as likely to be out there tomorrow as today," he told her with a sigh. "We can't hide out from him forever. Let's go get your dishes and linens and such. I'd like to see these rooms you've rented too."

Rachel smiled. "I'd forgotten you hadn't seen them yet. Let me get my bonnet on and my shawl."

Boone slid his feet into his boots. Then he dug out his duster and put his hat on his head. He offered her his arm, and they descended the stairs like they were gentry folk.

Outside, it was colder than he had expected, and Rachel shivered. He made sure she walked on the inside, away from the mud and the potential to be splashed. The mercantile was north of the saloon by two blocks, so they strolled along. A few people nodded, and Boone returned the greeting, keeping Rachel close, her hand tucked into his arm.

At the general store, one that Boone had visited a few times during his visits to town, the clerk behind the counter looked askance at them until he pulled out a fistful of greenbacks and some silver dollars. "We're looking to set up housekeeping," he announced. "The lady and I will be wed soon."

"I beg your pardon," the man said. He was probably forty, more than a little heavy, and his hair had receded. "I took you for a cowboy, and I don't make much profit at all from such."

Boone couldn't resist a grin. His clothing marked him as a cowboy, and he couldn't deny it. "I've been a cowboy these five years since the war," he said, in his best Kentucky drawl. "But I'm retired now and planning to take my bride home come spring. She came here as the schoolteacher."

Recognition lit the man's eyes. "Oh, I've heard tell of you – you must be Boone Wilson, who was shot and thought to die over at the saloon, but you lived. And she's the teacher lady that the blacksmith wants run out of town. I heard about your encounter with the *Schweinhund* yesterday. They say you pulled a gun on the smith?"

"Guilty on all counts," Boone said. "But don't believe all the gossip you hear. Can you fix us up with some goods or not? I reckon there's another mercantile store at the other end of town."

"I can help you out. I'm Klaus Zimmerman, and this is my store. Tell me what you need, and if I don't have it, I sure can get it."

Glancing around, Boone had no doubt. The store appeared well-stocked, from the barrels of crackers, flour, and other dry goods to the household items that festooned the walls. He saw cloth ready to be cut, farm tools and implements, everything from stoves to baskets. From the gleam in Rachel's eyes, she liked the place. She took her list out of her reticule and they began the process of purchasing what they would need.

He'd known it was a long list, and he had the money, between his wages and what he'd won at faro, but as Boone watched the stack of items increase, he got more than a little anxious but did his best to hide it. He didn't want to rob the joy from Rachel as she selected a coffee pot, two frying pans, a couple of pots, kitchen utensils, a coffee grinder, a set of dishes, both loaf and cake pans, mixing bowls, a churn, spoons and spatulas, a washboard and tub, irons, silverware, and a few things he didn't recognize. Rachel chose cloth to make curtains and sheets, three blankets, and more cloth for towels. Then she moved on to food, choosing spices, cornmeal, flour, salt, sugar, lard, yeast, coffee beans, molasses, dried apples, pinto beans, and other staples. As the pile grew, he realized he had no idea how they would transport it from the mercantile to the rooms she'd rented and said so.

Ezekiel had joined them, and he solved the problem. "I'll borrow a wagon from the livery," he said. "Load it all up and drive it over there, Boone."

Zimmerman nodded with relief. "I was going to offer delivery, but if this young man has it handled, then that works."

"I'll wait on buying fresh food until we're wed," Rachel said to Boone's relief.

Boone added some tobacco and cigarette papers to the items, along with a few other things, including a basket of wood for the stove. After the storekeeper presented him with the total, he paid for it all, glad he had enough and a little concerned about how much it took of his savings. There would be rent, too, although if he remembered right, Rachel had paid the first month. Until he gained back his strength, he had few options for earning more, especially during the winter. Boone knew how to farm and to be a cowboy but not much else. They would need money and plenty of it to make the journey home to Kentucky in the spring.

Zimmerman and his brother loaded up the wagon Ezekiel fetched. Zeke helped Rachel climb into the seat, then boosted Boone up beside her. Unhappy that he needed help, Boone sat beside her, taking in the sights and sounds of town as they rode to the saddler's shop. He mounted the outside stair leading to the rooms without too much difficulty but Zeke carried in most of the purchased goods. Rachel brought up some of the kitchen items as well.

Once inside and he'd caught his breath, Boone walked through the rooms. He liked the arrangement, the second bedroom he'd share with Rachel after marriage most of all. Unlike their current situation, three people crammed into one tight room, there would be space for all of them, and that made him glad. He also appreciated the fact it came with a stove and furniture. If he'd had to buy those, too, he'd be broke.

Boone pulled up a chair to the table and surveyed the street below. He liked the view and, even more, the fact he could observe the goings on in town as well as see who approached. Other than Kurtz, he didn't know of any enemies he might have, but he still liked the ability to keep watch.

Rachel busied herself, putting away her new kitchen utensils on the shelves and cupboards provided. Ezekiel lit a fire in the stove, and the warmth soon spread through the rooms. Until now, with nothing but the street traffic below and Rachel singing as she worked, he hadn't realized how noisy it was living above the saloon. The quiet soothed his soul.

"Wish we could get moved over here now," Zeke said, joining Boone at the table.

"I figured we would wait till we're married," Boone said. They had talked about a wedding near Christmas, but it would be December in a few short days. "But maybe we won't."

"We won't what?" Rachel asked as she sat down beside him.

"Wait very long to get married," Boone said. "Do you want to pick a day?"

"If we wed in church, I'll have to ask the priest," she said. "That might take a while, though, since you're not Catholic."

"A judge can marry us," Boone said. "But if it matters to you, I can wait."

He'd rather not, but he kept silent about that. He'd marry

Rachel today if he could, but he wanted her to be happy with the ceremony.

"Boone, I want to be your wife," she told him. "I'd rather not wait any longer than we must."

A grin spread across his face. "Neither would I. You know what I'd like right now, honey?"

"I hope coffee," she said. "I just made some, first in our soon to be home."

He'd heard her grind the beans, so it came as no surprise. "Coffee will do," he said. "But I've a hankering for a good piece of cornbread. Could you make some?"

Rachel responded with a smile. "I could if I had two eggs and some milk or buttermilk," she said. "I'll go fetch some if you want."

After what happened with Kurtz, he didn't want her out of his sight. "Ezekiel can go," he said. "I've paid Mary enough – see if you can get both in the kitchen at the saloon, would you?"

The kid stood with a nod and grin. "Sure, I can. I need to take the wagon back anyhow."

He returned with eggs, buttermilk, some sausage to fry, a bit of butter, and some hominy.

"I recollected you like a good mess of hominy," he told Boone.

"I do," he told his brother. "Thank you."

Boone had breakfasted late, so the meal Rachel prepared would serve as both dinner and supper. She baked a perfect cornbread in one of her new cast iron skillets, fried up the sausage as patties, and heated the hominy. It was a fine meal, and he savored the taste, lingering over the table with a final cup of coffee before they headed back to the tight space above the saloon for a few more days.

He still longed to go back to Kentucky and would, but in the meantime, this place would serve as a pleasant home.

# CHAPTER FIFTEEN

Rachel spent her days sewing for the rest of the week, making bright calico curtains and hemming cloth into sheets for both beds. She also finished the shirt she'd been secretly making for Boone, based on one of his old ones. Made from a soft, grey flannel, the shirt would be warm, she thought, but also suitable for their simple wedding.

She planned to wear her best gown, a dark blue calico with light yellow flowers and buttons down the front with a small bustle in the back. Rachel hadn't had it out of her trunk since arriving in Laredo, but she thought it would suit her as a bride. She had some lace that she would add to the white collar and cuffs to fancy it up for the wedding. Her bonnet would be serviceable enough. Although she wished she could have flowers to carry, there were none in December.

They had yet to choose a day, but she thought she'd be finished with sewing and other preparations by December 10 or 12. The bruise on her cheek had begun to fade, and she thought it would be gone by the time they said their vows. Ezekiel would stand up with them along with Liam Rafferty, the ranch owner.

Each day, Boone healed a little more, and one day, Ezekiel brought his horse, Sprat, to him. Delighted, the horse nickered and nuzzled Boone, who gave back the same affection. The chestnut-colored stallion boasted a black mane and tail. When

Rachel offered him a sugar cube, he ate it from her hand, and she laughed with delight.

"Take him for a ride," Zeke said. "I've been riding him some, but he's missed you."

Boone mounted as Rachel watched him cantering through town. Until now, she'd never seen him on horseback, and he cut a fine figure. *He's come so far,* she thought, *from a pale, weak man sure to die wrapped up on the saloon porch to riding a horse, handsome and almost healed.* Love for him swelled her heart till she thought it would burst out of her chest.

He wore a grin when he returned, laughing a little. As he dismounted, he turned to her. "Soon, I'll take you for a ride down by the river."

"I'd like that," she told him.

The three spent more time in the new rooms than above the saloon already, with Rachel preparing meals there. Boone refused to allow her out alone in case Harold Kurtz might approach her so he accompanied her wherever she went. When she hung the curtains and made the beds, he helped. Boone accompanied her to church on Sunday, and if she decided she needed something more from the mercantile, he was at her side.

Liam Rafferty rode in from the Double B on the second Saturday in December, and without any fanfare, so did Deacon and Mac. All three men were friends and more, having served in the war together with Boone. On Monday, Rachel, who found she didn't mind the lack of attendants, dressed in her best dress and with Boone headed for the justice of the peace. The one person she wished could be present was her Granny, but she'd died years earlier. A letter to her sister and brothers would announce the news. None were close enough to come, and Rachel suspected they wouldn't have, even if they could.

The small office was close with Rachel and Boone, Ezekiel at his brother's side, along with Liam, Mac, and Deke. She carried a small bouquet of dried flowers that a kind woman from church had provided.

Boone faced her during the vows, his face more serious than she'd ever seen, his eyes dark with emotion. He held her hands as they spoke their promises, the traditional vows that each repeated. Rachel said hers first, "I, Rachel Rose Shaw, take thee, Boone Benjamin Wilson, to be my wedded husband, to have and to hold from this day forward, for better, for worse, for richer, for poorer, in sickness and in health, to love and to cherish, till death do us part according to God's holy ordinance. I pledge thee my faith, love, and life."

She met his gaze with her own as she recited. Boone's eyes brightened with unshed tears, and when he repeated the words to her, his husky voice broke more than once. Rachel gripped his hands tight.

Judge Ike Masters nodded when each had finished.

"By the power invested in me by the state of Texas, I pronounce you husband wife in the eyes of the law, by God, and before man. Bless you both. You can kiss your bride."

The others applauded and whooped as Boone bent to kiss her mouth with soft tenderness. His lips lingered on hers, their hands still clasped until he pulled her into his arms. He kissed her again and then held her tight against him.

"Let me see your hand," he said when he released her.

Rachel held up her right hand, and he shook his head, taking her left in his.

"There's one more part we didn't speak," he said as he slid a slender gold band etched with tiny roses onto her finger. "With this ring, I thee wed."

He surprised her. Until now, she hadn't wept, but now the tears came, moved by his sweet gesture. Rachel lifted her hand to admire it.

"It's beautiful, Boone. And it fits. Where did you get it?"

His cheeks flushed. "I might have had a bit of help getting it," he said. "I wanted you to wear my brand."

The men laughed with approval while Rachel put her arms around his neck and kissed him, deep and long. Then she locked her gaze with his and told him, "There's one thing more I want to say, Boone, and I mean every word."

"Tell me, honey."

She quoted from the Book of Ruth from memory, "Entreat me not to leave thee, or to return from following after thee: for whither thou goest, I will go; and where thou lodgest, I will lodge: thy people shall be my people, and thy God my God."

Boone's eyes shone with tears, and he nodded. "I like that, right well."

"Mister and Missus Wilson, there's a small party in your honor," Liam Rafferty said, clearing his throat to get their attention. "If you'll lead us to your new home and let us join you, we'd be honored."

"Boone?"

He shook his head. "I don't know anything about it, honey, but let's go. I'm awfully hungry."

They led the way and climbed the stairs in tandem. At the top, Boone paused and then swept her into his arms. He carried her over the threshold, then set her down as she protested. "Don't hurt yourself, Boone," she fussed. "I don't want you to overdo."

He silenced her with a kiss.

They dined on thick, fresh beef steaks, roast venison, fried fish, bread, fried potatoes, and tamales. Boone and Rachel sat at the table while the others held borrowed tin plates and sat on the floor or stood. Mary from the saloon was present along with Graciela, the cook, Peggy, and a few of the other ladies.

"Save room for cake," Peggy said with a giggle.

There was a heavy fruitcake and *polvorones*, small Mexican cookies that tasted like shortbread and were dusted with confectionary sugar. Rachel and Boone drank coffee, but some of the others shared a bottle of whiskey.

As they feasted, their other possessions, including her trunk, arrived from the saloon and were put in place. Although they weren't alone, Rachel and Boone never stopped touching. She held his hand or brushed back his hair from his forehead. He caressed her cheek and often leaned over to kiss her between bites.

Liam gave them a $20 gold piece as a wedding present and repeated the offer he'd made Boone weeks ago.

"If you change your mind about old Kentucky, there's a place for you on my ranch," he told him. "I'd hire you on for good wages as top hand, and there's a small house that goes with the position. I won't ask again, but I won't hire anyone else till late spring or summer, so if you decide you want it, tell me. It wouldn't be the worst place to raise a family, Boone, and your Rachel would have my Maggie for company."

Rachel waited to hear Boone's reply. She'd follow him to Kentucky or stay here – where he was, that was where she would be.

"I'm honored, Liam," Boone said. "And if I should change my mind, you're the first I'll tell."

"No hard feelings over that letter to your mother?"

"None at all. You did what you thought right at the time. We've rode too many miles together and had each other's back for too long to hold a grudge."

"Then we're square, and congratulations on your bride."

Deacon brought a guitar and played the unfamiliar instrument well. He sang, almost as nicely as Boone, old love songs, funny songs, and sweet songs. Boone sang some of the tunes he'd sang when she hadn't felt well and then added one she hadn't heard, a funny but sweet little tune called *The Stuttering Lovers*, then a hauntingly beautiful one about a castle in Dromore, and last, *Eileen Aroon*, the words straight from Boone's mouth to her, altering the old words to fit his bride, "Dear are your charms to me, dearer your laughter free, dearest your constancy, Rachel, *aroon*."

One by one, the guests departed until Ezekiel was the last. He hugged his brother, then Rachel. "Welcome to the family," he told her. "I'm gonna sleep at the stable tonight, but if you make breakfast in the morning, make plenty."

Rachel kissed his cheek. "I will."

Then they were alone, with the remainder of the feast, with the echo of music, and with love between them like a physical presence. Outside, the late afternoon sun cast shadows on the street, but it might well have been midnight to the newlyweds.

Boone stood, and she rose with him. She cupped his cheek with one hand, caressing the smooth skin where he'd shaved to be married. He put his larger hand over hers, and then he kissed her with a gentle fire that ignited new feelings that tingled through her blood.

"I love you, woman," he said. "This is the best day of my life so far."

"Mine, too," she whispered back.

"I want to love you," he said. "I don't want to hurt you or scare you, but I need you, all of you, Rachel."

She heard the desire in his voice, and she felt it. "I want it, too, Boone."

A figure-eight knot made of a braid crowned her head, and he reached up to pull the pins from it, one by one. Then he undid the braid, releasing her hair to swirl down her shoulders to her waist. Boone let his fingers ruffle through it, then buried his nose in it. She'd washed it the day before with castile soap, so it should smell sweet, she thought.

"Pretty," he said. "The door is locked, and the curtains are closed, wife. Let's go to our bedroom."

There, he cherished her in every way. His hands were light and gentle as he undid the buttons on her dress, then pulled it down over her arms. She removed the chemise she wore beneath it and let the dress fall to the floor. Boone never hurried, his mouth slow and sweet as he kissed her in many places. His fingers stroked her in light, easy ways that made her bold enough to undo the buttons on his shirt. Together, they pulled it free.

When they came together, it wasn't clumsy or frightening but somehow right. There was a short span when she experienced a fleeting pain, but it passed as Boone taught her that this act could bring a joyful pleasure. Afterward, they cuddled close, her head against his chest, the sound of his heartbeat steady and comforting. It was just evening, and now that she knew what to expect, they did it several more times, then they slept.

At some point, she rose and lit a single candle to illuminate their bedchamber, then returned to her husband. In the flickering light, Rachel traced the scar left by his wound, the skin puckered as she expected it always would be. It was so near to his heart, she thought, that a few inches would have killed him on impact. But it hadn't and the wound had healed over. She thought he still experienced an occasional pain, but the infection was gone, and he would live. Theirs might not have been a conventional courtship, but she was happy.

Rachel slept the night in his arms. His embrace provided a cocoon where she felt protected and safe. In this room, in their bed, in his arms, nothing could touch them or hurt them, she thought. This was sanctuary and home.

It had been so long since she had a home of her own. After her parents died, Granny provided a home, but once she was gone, Rachel spent time with one of her siblings as the beloved aunt who did as much of the work as possible. Then she'd become a schoolteacher, boarding with different families. Sometimes, she'd been fortunate to have her own room, often just a bed like at the Kurtz's.

At the thought of the blacksmith, some worry crept in, and she hoped they'd seen the last of him. Nothing should shadow these early days of her marriage, nothing. Never a fan of winter, she didn't look forward to more months of cold and the possibility of snow. The season could be a time for illness, which she feared but didn't expect. Rachel pushed the anxious thoughts away and snuggled tighter against Boone. Without waking, he held her closer and murmured her name. That brought a smile – she had no doubt he loved her, and it'd been a long road. She'd thought for a while she might be a spinster schoolteacher, but she was glad she wasn't. Rachel had little desire to return to the classroom, and she wanted to start being Boone's wife.

She thought a little about Liam's offer and wondered. The Double B Ranch was no more familiar than distant Kentucky, so it was hard to envision either, she thought. They had time, though, months to decide. Life could be capricious, and there was no telling what could happen.

In time, she slept well and without dreams, waking with delight beside Boone, who greeted her with a smile and kisses. Now, their married life would begin. He had recovered, and she believed life would be good now.

# CHAPTER SIXTEEN

He woke happy, still a novelty but one he liked. Boone watched his wife sleep, and when she woke, he kissed her.

"Good morning, honey," he said. He'd be waking up with her for the rest of his life, and that made him even happier. Someday, he hoped there would be some children, and he looked forward to growing old with Rachel.

She returned the kiss. "Are you hungry?"

"Honey, I could eat a full-grown steer. We never had supper last night."

Rachel blushed. "We got busy."

"I reckon so."

He enjoyed watching her dress, brush, and braid her hair and add an apron. As soon as she finished, he rose too. By the time he joined her, she had coffee made and poured him a cup. Boone inhaled the bacon frying, and his appetite increased. She had just served them each a plate with bacon, eggs fried over easy in the bacon grease, and biscuits when he heard his brother dashing up the stairs.

Ezekiel burst into the room, winded. "Boone, Kurtz is dead! They found him dead behind the saloon, shot one time in the head. They think it happened last night, or someone would've found him afore now."

Boone swallowed a bite of biscuit. "I'm not one to rejoice a man's dead. But I can't say I'm sorry to hear the news. He won't be bothering Rachel anymore."

She rewarded him with a tiny smile.

"But Boone," Zeke said, his voice distressed. "Boone!"

His fine breakfast soured in his gut because his brother's tone indicated something was amiss. He sounded upset. "What's wrong, Zeke?"

"Boone, they're saying you killed him."

Across the table from him, Rachel paled. Her fork dropped onto her plate.

Boone let the words settle into his brain with disbelief. Not this, not now, he thought. He didn't need any accusations as he started married life. "Who says?"

"It's the talk all over town," Ezekiel said. "I heard it first at the livery stable, then on the street."

"I didn't kill him nor anyone else," he stated. It was the truth, but he felt a few qualms about it. Innocent until proven guilty didn't always play out.

"I know that Boone," his brother said. "But they're saying the Sheriff is out for you. I hear he's a Yank, and he hates anyone who wore gray."

Boone had heard the same and dismissed it. Back when he was a cowboy on the Double B Ranch, Laredo had just been a place to go, and he knew he could go elsewhere if the climate turned sour. He'd seen the man often enough and didn't like him. Sheriff Barnabus Johnson walked with a swagger and a mean sneer on his face. He carried a Starr Arms double revolver on each hip and used them often. Sometimes, he bashed someone over the head. Other times, he shot without remorse. If Boone hadn't known for a fact that Mad Mike shot him, he would have suspected Johnson. It had been Johnson who dispatched Mike with a rope before any questions could be asked or answered regarding why he shot Boone.

He'd steered clear of the Sheriff, and since his recovery, he hadn't seen him except for the two nights he played Faro at the saloon. He wasn't the enemy anyone would want to have, but until now, Boone had no idea that the man didn't like him on a personal basis.

The jail lay in an adobe structure not far from the main district in Laredo. It had a dilapidated air about it, and Boone had seldom passed it.

"He can't accuse me of murder because we fought on opposite sides in the war," Boone said. "Sit down, kid, have some breakfast. There's coffee, biscuits, and more bacon. If you want eggs, Rachel can fry some."

Ezekiel dropped into a chair. "I'll eat what's cooked. A letter from Ma came – I was bringing it when I heard about the blacksmith."

That lightened Boone's mood. "Let's have it – I been waiting to hear from her."

He read it, then read it aloud. "Sounds like she's glad I'm alive. She'll be happy to hear I've got a wife, too. I'll write her back and get it mailed. I doubt she'll have it by Christmas, but maybe for the new year."

Rachel stood and fixed a plate for Zeke. She moved with slow steps, almost as if she'd been wounded. She handed him the food and coffee, then sat down, but she ate little of her own breakfast.

"Rachel?" Boone asked.

"I'm afraid," she said. "What if he arrests you for it?"

He shared her concern but said, "I doubt he will, honey. Don't let it spoil our day. Eat. These are good biscuits. Let's get this letter done."

Boone dictated to Rachel, who wrote it, although it was not in her best penmanship since her hands shook.

*"Dear Ma – I received your letter. Ezekiel and I are well. I have a piece of news – I am married now to a schoolteacher named Rachel. I trust you and all the family are well, and I wish you the best of things in the new year to come. Love, your son, Boone."*

"You didn't tell her about this murder," Ezekiel said.

"And I ain't," Boone said. "No need to worry her again. She had enough when she thought I was dead. Don't you write her about this nonsense, neither, you hear?"

The kid nodded, but he wore a glum expression.

After the meal and once the letter had been written, Boone poured a fresh cup of coffee and lit a cigarette. From his vantage point, he watched Laredo, noting more activity than normal on the street below. He saw his friends approach, so he was ready when Deacon and Mac came through the door, wild-eyed.

"Boone, have you heard?" Deke said. "If you want to light out, I can get your horse ready, and we'll go."

Boone took a long drag from his smoke. "Boys, I didn't kill the blacksmith, so I'm not running. I got a wife to think about."

"I'm thinking about her too – won't do her good to see you hang, would it? We can head over to Galveston or even into Mexico for a spell till it blows over."

"They won't hang me," Boone said, but his throat felt tight, and he didn't dare look at Rachel. "I told you, I ain't killed no one, least not since the war ended."

"That Sheriff Johnson, he's coming after you," Mac told him, his Scots accent more pronounced than ever.

"Liam's on the way, too. He headed for the ranch, but I rode after him to tell him, so he's coming back," Deacon said.

Boone's early contentment vanished, and his stomach ached. He was about to be accused of killing a man who deserved to be dead, but he had no part in it. He'd seen men hung during the war and since. It was a brutal way to die. Most didn't go quickly – they strangled slow and often soiled themselves in the process. He'd beat a wound that should have been mortal – he didn't want to face another challenge.

Rachel put her trembling hands on his shoulders. He reached back to put his hands over hers. "Don't fret, honey."

"I can't help it," she said. Her voice was harsh with unshed tears. "Boone, maybe you should listen to your friends and go."

That turned him around and brought him to his feet. "I'm not running, Rachel. I'm not leaving you, and they won't hang me. I didn't kill the man – don't any of you believe me?"

"I do, Boone, but I couldn't bear it if…anything happened to you."

He took her in his arms and held her close. "It won't, Rachel."

Liam arrived with his black leather duster swirling about his knees.

"You didn't kill him, did you Boone?" he asked.

"You know I didn't, Liam. Man, you were at my wedding yesterday."

"Then I'll stand with you and do whatever I can," he replied. "Your brother didn't kill him either, did he?"

Everyone swiveled to stare at Zeke except Boone, who said, "He didn't. And they'd best not try to pin it on him either."

He didn't say it aloud, but he'd swing for a crime he didn't commit before he let them hang his youngest brother.

"I didn't," Ezekiel said. "I swear I didn't."

"Then you didn't," Liam replied. "And that's the truth."

Boone sat down and pulled Rachel onto his lap. She clung to him, as frightened now as she had been passionate during their wedding night. He wanted to comfort her, to assure her that nothing would come of the ridiculous charge, but he couldn't promise it would be so. He put on a gambler's face, a bland mask that hid his turbulent emotions and his own fear.

They sat and waited in silence but with solidarity tempered with fear.

* * *

Sheriff Barnabus Johnson sat in his office, fingers drumming a tattoo against his desk. He had a dead man, the local blacksmith, found behind the local saloon with a bullet through his skull. His questions had yielded no answers, and no one seemed to have heard or seen anything in Laredo between sundown last night and dawn this morning. Kurtz was not well-liked, and the Sheriff knew that well. But in the war, the man had worn Yankee blue, the same as he did, and he'd had words with a known Johnny Reb, that troublesome cowboy Boone Wilson. Wilson had managed to get shot playing cards but didn't die as expected. Instead, he'd healed and found a woman, the very woman that Kurtz had some history with, or so Johnson understood.

They'd been living above the saloon in one of Mary's rooms, something he found both sinful and suspect. If she were a righteous woman, wouldn't she have objected to the arrangement? Besides, she'd shared the space with both Wilson and his young brother, as well as several cowboys who came and went at will. For all he knew, she'd been intimate with them all or earning a few extra dollars on the side as a prostitute. Such things did happen. Once, he'd enjoyed a few favors from the ladies but since coming to Laredo and serving as Sheriff, the gals steered clear of him. None of Mary's doves flirted with him and barely spoke. He'd also heard that the teacher was a Papist, another black mark in his personal book. Mary had nothing but disdain for the lawman and wouldn't tell him much. She refused to answer any of his questions, although she did provide one key bit of information.

From the saloonkeeper, he learned Wilson had married the wench and that the pair had taken up housekeeping over the saddler's shop. Such wedded bliss wouldn't last, Sheriff Johnson vowed, and he would take pleasure in destroying it with an arrest.

It took a few hours, but he finally got someone to sing long and loud about the recent encounter Wilson had with the dead man. Doc Smitty, the town's only physician, drank far more often than he practiced medicine. Already far gone into a bottle of whiskey despite the early hour, Smitty was delighted to tell him all about the incident. He described how Boone Wilson had placed his pistol against the blacksmith's head and threatened to shoot him dead. There were other choice words and threats, too, more than enough to make Johnson decide Wilson would do as scapegoat for the killing. And Smitty was only too willing to act the scene out for Johnson. He could have joined a traveling troupe of actors, Johnson thought, as the man repeated the things both Wilson and Kurtz had said. Doc did indicate that the smith was trying to haul off the former schoolmarm, and although in any other circumstance, that might have made a difference to the Sheriff, he didn't care. He needed someone to blame for the killing and to hang for the crime. There didn't need to be any questions other than the ones he'd been asking.

He ignored the accounts that described how Kurtz had tried to drag the woman away for unsavory purposes or that he'd bruised her cheek and split her lip. Nor did he take any stock in the fact that the younger Wilson got knocked down and suffered a black eye in the process. What mattered was that the blacksmith was dead, and he now had a killer to blame. Whether or not he was guilty didn't matter in the least, at least not to Johnson, who had his reasons to find someone to take the blame.

First, he went to the Out of Luck Saloon, but the proprietor, Mary, another woman he loathed, cussed him out and sent him on his way without answering any of his questions. She wouldn't even speak with him save to tell him Wilson no longer bunked under her roof. Apparently, Boone Wilson had married the wench and set up housekeeping over the saddler's shop. Sheriff Johnson grabbed his deputy, a thin, mean-spirited man called Deuce, and headed to arrest Wilson for the blacksmith's murder.

Johnson marched down the street with purpose, then mounted the stairs to the rooms where he would find Boone Wilson. He kept his hands on his revolvers. If Wilson happened to resist arrest or try to fight him, he'd be only too happy to dispatch the former Confederate to the hell he should have been in long ago. If he didn't get there today, Johnson had every intention to make certain that Wilson would join the devil at home soon enough.

# CHAPTER SEVENTEEN

Rachel couldn't be still. She moved through their rooms with restless energy, pacing from one to another. Boone had provided a temporary refuge by holding her on his lap, but she worried too much to stay there very long. His arms holding her and his body beneath her had been tense and hard. This day should have been joyful, the start of their life together, but it had turned into one of anxiety. After his first comments, Boone had fallen silent. If she didn't know him so well, she'd think he was calm, but his expressionless face equaled bravado. She'd never watched him play cards, but she thought this must be the way he looked when bluffing during a game of faro.

She brewed more coffee and offered to fix more food, but no one was hungry. Rachel busied herself by washing up the dishes and skillet from breakfast, the task failing to keep her mind from the imminent trouble.

Despite Boone's assurances that everything would be fine, she knew it wouldn't be, judging from the grim features of every man present. As she walked or worked, she prayed. Boone rose from his seat and leaned, gazing out the window. When she passed by, he snagged her hand and pulled her to him. Rachel huddled against his chest, taking comfort from his embrace. She buried her face against the shirt she'd made him to hide her tears.

"Sheriff's coming, Boone," Ezekiel cried. "He's got that

deputy of his with him."

"I see them," Boone said in a flat voice. "Rachel, look at me."

When she lifted her head, he kissed her hard and soundly. "Honey, you need to step away and let me take care of this business."

She wanted to remain at his side. "Boone –"

"Whatever happens, I love you," he told her. "Remember that, and it's all gonna work out. I got no idea how long this might take, but I'll be back home with you just as soon as I'm free."

Rachel, against every instinct she possessed, moved aside, heart pounding, legs trembling beneath her skirt.

Boone stood near the windows like a statue. He could have been carved from marble, she thought, pale and yet staunch. His eyes were harder than she'd ever seen, and his mouth was set in a firm line. He appeared capable and more than a little dangerous.

Rather than bust down the door or knock, the sheriff rapped three times with his fist against the wood, then entered. "Boone Wilson, you'd best come with me. You're wanted for the murder of Harold Kurtz."

He jangled a pair of handcuffs with one hand while the other remained on one of his pistols.

"I'm innocent," Boone said in a calm, clear voice. "I have witnesses here who will vow it."

"I don't give any nevermind about *these* witnesses," Johnson growled. Behind him, Deuce drew his gun and held it at the ready. "They'll say whatever you want, I have no doubt. It's the ones who heard you threaten the blacksmith's life that count."

"I won't deny it," Boone told the man. "He hurt my wife and my brother and tried to haul her off to do unspeakable things. It wasn't the first time. I protected my own, but that's no crime, and I didn't kill anyone."

The Sheriff stared at Boone as if he were a venomous snake or spider. "That's a black lie, and you know it, Reb. You were in the war, so you must have killed many."

"A few," Boone replied. "But on the battlefield, it's different, which you well know since you wore Federal blue. War's over, Sheriff."

"I lost a brother at Antietam," Johnson said. "Were you there?"

"At Sharpsburg? Yeah, I was along with thousands of others," Boone replied. "I'm sorry for your loss, but I'd think it would make you understand why I wanted to protect my youngest brother here."

"All I understand is that you're a killer, and you might be the very Johnny Reb that took Timothy's life," the sheriff responded. "Unless it's your brother who took Kurtz's life?"

Boone sighed and stepped forward with his hands held out for the cuffs. "It wasn't, and you're not pinning that on the kid. Take me to jail, then, but you'll learn I'm innocent. I ain't murdered no one."

Johnson laughed, and it was a harsh, ugly noise. "Jail? I'm gonna start building some gallows so I can hang you, Wilson. You're no more innocent than John Wilkes Booth was of killing Lincoln."

The handcuffs snapped shut around Boone's wrists, and Rachel moaned. Boone didn't flinch or look at her. If he did, she'd break, and she figured he knew that.

Liam Rafferty stepped forward. "You'll not hang a man without a trial or due process," he said. "If you take Boone to jail, I'm coming along. I read law in my younger days back in Memphis before the war. You can't hang an innocent man, not even in Texas. Deacon, head to San Antonio to wire Governor Davis for me. Tell him what's happening here and sign my name to it. I bet a hundred people can tell you where Boone was yesterday and last night, including Judge Masters, who married him to Miss Rachel yesterday morning. And if you ask witnesses about that incident with the blacksmith on the street, I believe most will tell you the truth – which matches what Boone said. If you're going, let's go – but you're not getting shed of me."

If looks could kill, Rachel had no doubt that the Sheriff's evil glare would have smote Liam where he stood. "Then come on because I'm taking him now. Get a killer off the streets of Laredo."

Boone paused to look at Rachel. Without words, his glance told her how deeply he loved her. She ached to run to him but managed to stand in place, her heart breaking.

"Mind Rachel for me, Ezekiel," he said. "I'll be home as soon as I can. Take care, kid, and stay out of trouble."

Rachel couldn't go to Boone, but she offered Zeke her hand, and he took it. He held it tight, and she saw the tears that stood in his eyes. She watched as the sheriff roughhoused Boone down the stairs, then along the street to his office and jail. Liam Rafferty, true to his word, trailed behind them. Rachel didn't take her eyes off Boone until the lawmen took him inside, and she couldn't see him. She staggered to the table and sat down hard in a chair. Ezekiel followed and sat beside her, still holding her hand.

Her stomach clenched hard and tight like a fist. She'd held her sobs because it would have upset Boone if she cried, but the pent-up grief made her chest hurt, too. If she didn't cry, at least a little, she thought she would explode. A single sob burst between her lips, and once it was out, she put her head down on the table and wept. Ezekiel sat with her, no longer holding her hand but patting her back as if she were a colicky baby.

It took a while to realize that he was talking to her, too, and when her sobs slowed, she heard what he said.

"Boone wouldn't want you to take on so," he told her.

"You're gonna make yourself sick if you keep on like this. He'll be back – he said he would, and Boone always keeps his promises. Besides, Liam will see that it all works out, and he's as book-smart as anyone I've ever known."

Rachel wanted to be positive, but inside, she had a dark, brooding feeling it wasn't going to be that simple. "I hope so," she said, scrubbing at her face with both hands. "I thought everything would be good, now. We got married, and I thought we'd wait the winter, then go home to Kentucky since that's what Boone wants."

"Is that what you want?"

His question surprised her. "I suppose it is – I want to be where Boone is, and he seems set on going home. Don't you want to go back?"

Ezekiel grinned. "I'll go if he does, but I left that place behind to come here. I like it here, despite all that's happened, Boone shot and now in jail. Ain't nothing wrong with Kentucky, but there's a lot of Wilsons already getting their living from the farm – it's not so big. Boone never cared much for dirt farming, growing tobacco, corn, and garden stuff. He likes raising horses. And odd thing, when he come back after the war, he didn't stay. He didn't seem very happy to be home at the time and lit out for Texas afore long."

"Isn't there enough work to go around?" If nothing else, the conversation diverted her thoughts from the current situation.

"Well, there is, and there ain't," Zeke replied. "Jacob and Garrett do most of the farming. Moses is like Boone – he works with the horses. Jacob and Moses live there with Ma. So did I before I left. I reckon Boone plans to build a cabin too if he gets back home, but I'm just telling you how it is."

"Boone never told me any of that," she said.

"Well, he's been gone from home for what is it – near nine years now," Zeke replied. "He did come back after the war and stayed for a couple months, then lit out for Texas. He never seemed keen on going back till I showed up, and then he vowed he'd take me home. From there, he got the idea that maybe he wanted to go back to stay."

"And then he thought he'd die, so home sounded like heaven," Rachel stated, thinking out loud.

"I reckon so. I hope I ain't turning you off Kentucky. It's a good place, right enough."

"I wasn't raised that far away," she told him. "I imagine I'd like it well enough, but I could stay here too. It'll be up to Boone."

"He'll go where you want," Ezekiel said. "He'll have time to study on it before spring."

That reminded her of Boone's current location, and she sighed. "I hope so, Zeke, I do."

Rachel had no appetite and no desire to do anything but rush to the jail to see Boone. She didn't think he'd like that, though, and so she started cooking in hopes he'd be back before the day was out. She baked a pan of gingerbread, then started a pot of pinto beans seasoned with bacon and onion. If Boone returned in time for supper, she'd bake cornbread, too.

The day stretched out, slow and endless, but Boone didn't come home. Deacon Lee and Mac came to visit, but the news they brought wasn't the best.

"Sheriff said he's keeping him locked up," Deke told her. "Liam, though, is staying put. He rented a room at the new hotel, and he'll sleep there, but he says he'll spend the rest of the time at the jail."

"How's Boone faring?" she asked.

Deke wouldn't meet her eyes. "He's down in the mouth, that's for sure. And he's at sea - cain't understand why the law's trying to pin this on him. He's missing you, Rachel, and that Johnson is being anything but kind. If it weren't for Liam,

I wouldn't doubt he'd strung Boone up from the hanging tree already."

The hanging tree, a huge live oak down by the river, was familiar to Rachel. She'd heard the name but had never experienced a hanging there and hoped she never would. Deacon's report made her concern deepen, and the fear inside grew larger.

"We're riding out in the morning for San Antonio," Deke told her. "We're gonna send the wire to the governor that Liam wants, then come back."

Ezekiel came to his feet. "I want to go with you," he said. "I'm sending one to my brothers about Boone."

"But he said don't write and tell them," Rachel cried.

"I know that, but I'm gonna," the kid said with steel in his eyes that enhanced his resemblance to Boone. "They need to know."

Late in the evening, after Liam had stopped by on his way to his hotel room and the other two had gone to sleep before their long journey, Zeke turned to Rachel and asked, "Will you be all right while I'm gone? It shouldn't be more than a day and a half, maybe two. If you won't, I'll stay."

She stirred through the bowl of beans she hadn't been able to eat. "Go. I'll be as good as I can be until Boone is free. Kurtz is dead now."

"The Sheriff's not," Ezekiel said. "Boone's some worried he'll try to get you involved in all this."

*More to worry about,* she thought. "He won't as long as Liam Rafferty is here, and I mean to go see Boone tomorrow."

"Don't tell him where I went," the young man said. "He'll be mad if he knows."

"I won't – I'll just say you're working at the livery, maybe."

He nodded. "Just be sure you go when Liam's there too, Rachel. Boone won't be able to stand it if he thinks you're in any danger, and that sheriff will be on any weakness he sees like a duck on a June bug."

Although it was December, thunder boomed during the night, and a storm pounded Laredo with heavy rains and hail. Lighting forked through the sky, and Rachel watched it from the window, unable to sleep. It struck somewhere not too distant. She heard the loud crack and smelled the ozone. She watched as some men dashed through the streets to see and opened the window to hear their report.

"It blasted the hanging tree," she heard one man call out to another. "The thing's ruint – split in half and splintered. It's still smokin', too."

"I reckon that Boone Wilson is innocent," another gent said, a cowboy by his dress. "Looks like the hand of God smote that tree so he cain't be hanged."

A small smile flirted with Rachel's lip as she eavesdropped, hearing the first small thing that gave her any hope after the day that had been a waking nightmare.

# CHAPTER EIGHTEEN

Boone sat on the edge of the hard cot in Laredo's only jail cell, an iron cage that he suspected the late blacksmith might have made. It sat in the corner of the small adobe one-roomed building that housed the sheriff's office and provided no privacy. The bars stretched from the floor almost to the ceiling, probably seven feet tall, but within, there was room for the single cot on the right side. There were no other furnishings but a bucket intended to serve as a slop jar. He would have laid down, but he suspected that the bedding, consisting of a single blanket and a dirty sheet, was infested with lice.

Since being locked into the space that morning, Boone had said little. Liam Rafferty had been present, and his support was the sole thing that kept Boone from going crazy. He ached to smash his fists against the bars, to beat his head against them, and to see if he could spread them wide enough to bolt. It wasn't possible, and he knew it, but that didn't change what he wanted.

His left eye hurt where Johnson had punched him, and he knew it had to be black. Boone's head ached, too, and his belly cramped hard. He hadn't eaten since Rachel's breakfast that morning. Johnson had served him a tin cup of coffee, but when he had it in his hands, he caught the rank smell of piss and poured it into the bucket. Either the sheriff or his deputy had ruined it, and he wasn't going to drink it. After Johnson left for the night, the deputy, Deuce, handed him a piece of stale bread so old it had greenish mold at the bottom. Boone tossed it, too.

When the sheriff accused him and marched him to jail, he'd hoped it would be straightened out by noon, then by evening. Boone had thought he would spend the night at home with his bride, but it didn't happen. He couldn't even imagine how Rachel must feel and wasn't sure he wanted to know. But he thought of her constantly. Her image, the memories, was all that kept him from a black despair.

"Boone, I'm heading out for the night."

He glanced over to see Liam standing at the door to the cage.

Boone nodded, his throat dry and uncertain of what words to say.

"Do you need anything before I go? A smoke or some coffee? Something to eat."

"Naw, I'm good." His voice rasped as he spoke. The things he wanted – Rachel's loving hands, her tasty food, and freedom were beyond Liam's ability to provide. "I reckon I'll be here come morning unless…"

"Don't you say it, Boone." Liam's voice held a warning note. "That won't happen."

He managed a dry laugh that had no mirth but reminded him of rattling bones.

"I hope not," he said. "Liam? If you see Rachel…"

"I will."

"Tell her I love her."

"She knows."

"Still, tell her."

Liam promised that he would.

Boone sat upright until his back began to ache, and he longed to lay down, so he did. It was probably too late to think he wouldn't pick up some lice from a sitting position. He'd had a few during the war and hated them with a passion, but at the moment, the vermin were the least of his worries.

During the long night, it stormed with a fury that he could hear but not see. A leak dribbled cold rain from the ceiling onto the floor near his bunk and across the room, the deputy snored with a rattling noise that put Boone on edge. He saw the keys to his cell tossed on the desk and contemplated how difficult it would be to snare them. They were out of reach, and he had nothing to use that might bring them closer, but he spent a half hour considering what it would be like to unlock the door and walk away before Deuce woke. If he did, Boone vowed he'd get his horse and woman, then make tracks away.

It wouldn't work, even if he tried, and he knew it.

He dozed a little from sheer exhaustion but woke startled, cursing when he realized where he was at. His brief dream had been pleasant, so the reality slammed down hard in his brain. Morning came, and the rain ceased. The sheriff returned, boots loud on the hardwood floor. He'd brought a quirt with him and used it to swipe the air as he walked. When he realized his deputy was asleep, he used it to strike the man who woke.

"Sleeping on duty," Sheriff Johnson said. "I should mark you with this more than I have. Get out of here and sleep today so you'll be awake tonight, else I can't have you guard a dangerous prisoner."

He slapped the whip against the bars, but Boone didn't react since he wasn't asleep. That angered the lawman who used the quirt to poke at Boone through the bars.

"I planned to hang you today," the sheriff said. "But lighting blasted the hanging tree, so I'll have to build a gallows."

"You can't hang me without a trial," Boone answered, his emotions a wild mix between trepidation and relief. He'd have to mention this to Liam as soon as the man arrived.

"And who's going to stop me, pray tell?" Johnson asked

in a hard voice.

"That would be me," Liam Rafferty said from the doorway to the street. "And if you try, I'll have your badge, sir, before I'm done, and you may well face a trial of your own."

The sheriff sneered. "You're back. I hoped you'd gone back to your ranch and left this worthless yellow-bellied dog to die."

Boone rose to sit on the bed and then to walk toward the bars. He opened his mouth to greet Liam and then stopped when he saw who stood behind him. Rachel wore her best dress, the one she'd married him in, and a bonnet. She carried a basket, and across the room, he could smell the bacon. With the grace of a lady and the proud walk of a queen, maybe Esther from the Bible, she crossed the room to stand beside the cell.

"Rachel, you ought not be here," he said. "It's no place for you."

She stretched her free hand through the bars and touched his. "Whither thou goest, I will go, Boone Wilson. I came with Liam to bring you some breakfast, bacon, and fried cornmeal mush."

"He'll eat what we give him, nothing more," Johnson announced in a thunderous voice, but she paid no mind.

Liam did, however. "There's no harm in it, Sheriff."

"Honey," Boone said. "Oh, Rachel."

She touched his lips through the bars with a single finger. Then she pulled out a piece of fried mush and handed it to him. He took it and ate it. It tasted like manna straight from heaven, he thought, and she followed it with a slice of bacon.

"My hands are filthy," he said. "I wish you'd brought some coffee."

Her smile was triumphant. "I did," she said and fished a bottle from her basket. He couldn't tell if it had previously held patent medicine or whiskey, but he didn't care. She passed it to him, and he uncorked it, then drank. Bit by bit, she gave him the food she'd brought, and he felt better with it in his belly.

"You ought not be in this place," he said again. "But I'm glad you're here."

Rachel twined her fingers through his, and although he held onto her for a few moments, he released her. "Honey, I'm likely crawling with lice."

"I don't care, Boone."

Across the room, Liam and the sheriff bickered. Deuce had taken his hat and bolted. With their voices as cover, Boone said, "Listen to me, Rachel. Take what money there is and hide it good. Somewhere nobody will look for it. Have Ezekiel help you, but don't tell nobody else."

"I will. Are you sick? You look awful, and you have a black eye."

He touched it, remembering.

"Naw, I may not feel so good, but I ain't sick. And yeah, he belted me one on the way over here. I won't eat or drink what they give me, so you saved my life. I'm better now, Rachel. I'd kiss you if I could."

As if to prove it, he kissed her fingers, and she closed her eyes.

"Don't you come without Liam or at least my brother," he told her.

"I won't."

The acrimonious voices ceased, and Liam approached.

"The tinhorn sheriff says you can have your wife come once a day only and bring food one time and stay no more than half an hour," he said. "It took some talking to convince him, so you'll have to abide by what he says. I'll walk you home, Rachel, and come back."

Boone's eyes stayed on her face, and when he read the question in her eyes, he nodded.

"You'll have to go now, honey, but come back tomorrow. Bring me something hot to eat – there's a slot built into the door that I think a plate will pass through. You take care, Rachel, you hear? This is bad, but it won't last long, I promise."

"I love you, Boone."

"And you know I love you."

She touched his hand one more time, then turned and was gone, leaving the scent of the soft lavender fragrance she favored behind. Boone inhaled it with longing and with sorrow, then sat down on his bunk. Johnson rallied above women and wives in his jail, but Boone didn't listen. He savored the brief time with his wife for as long as he could, then endured the unpleasant reality he now faced.

One day passed into another with no change. Each morning, Rachel arrived either early or late with a meal for him and coffee in a glass bottle. He spent that precious thirty minutes with her, scarfing up the food she delivered with the appetite of a hungry man. Boone refused anything that the jail provided him. If it wasn't tainted or spit in, it usually looked stale or spoiled. When Rachel realized that she brought larger portions and often some biscuits or something he could tuck back to eat later, as long as the sheriff or deputy didn't notice. If he became thirsty enough, he would drink a cup of water but even that usually tasted brackish and suspect.

On limited rations, Boone became lean and lethargic. Watching Rachel each day hurt him, too, deep within. She wore a worried frown that seldom left her face, not even during the precious moments spent together. He thought she seemed thinner as well and worried that she wasn't eating enough. Sometimes, Ezekiel, after the first few days, accompanied her, but even the kid looked haggard. He didn't say much when he was there, but neither did Boone. After all, what was there to say except the same things over and over?

When Zeke didn't come for a stretch of four or five days, Boone asked his whereabouts, and when Rachel admitted the young man had fallen ill, he grew concerned and fretted till Zeke returned with her. Although he seemed pale to Boone, he swore he was fine after a few days, running a fever with a cough. Illness could so easily turn severe and fatal that Boone couldn't stop being anxious about his brother and fearful Rachel too could fall ill.

The week before Christmas Eve, which was on Saturday, Johnson and his deputy began whistling Christmas carols and were more jovial than usual. Liam told Boone he planned to spend Christmas at the ranch with his wife, Maggie, and daughter, Grace.

"I'm heading home on Friday," Liam said. "I'll be there for Christmas Eve and Christmas Day, and then I'll be back. I don't expect even Johnson would hang you over the holiday."

"I wouldn't put it past him," Boone replied. The mention of Christmas brought sorrow, not joy. He'd had ideas of how he'd spend their first holiday together with Rachel but never dreamed he'd be in the hoosegow. "You ought to take Rachel and the kid with you. It's not gonna be very merry around here."

"I've asked them both, Boone," Liam answered. "They'd be welcome. In fact, I've tried to persuade your wife to come stay at the ranch for a spell till all this is over. Maggie would be glad of the company, and I do think it'd do Rachel some good. She's pining hard for you, Boone, and that's a fact."

The selfish bits within made Boone want to reject the idea, but he didn't. Love won over his own longing, and if Rachel could spend a pleasant holiday at the ranch, he wanted her to go. When he suggested it, however, she said no.

"Boone, I can't leave you here like that," she said. Her voice sounded thick with unshed tears. "You wouldn't even eat if I was gone."

"I could figure out something," he replied. If he didn't have this short time each day to see her and hear her voice, he'd be sad, but he wanted her to go. "Maybe Zeke could get Peggy to bring something over. If he's not going, he can bring some grub himself and visit me."

"Don't you want to spend Christmas with me?" Rachel asked.

The question broke Boone's polite façade, and he answered with complete if savage honesty. "I do, more than anything on this earth, honey," he said. "But we won't be spending Christmas together – I'm in jail, you're not. Even if the sheriff decides you can stay longer, we won't be together for Christmas, and you know it. I wanted to go with you to church, to hear all that pretty Latin I don't begin to understand, to sing Christmas carols and eat the fine dinner you'd cook. But it's not happening this year, Rachel, none of it. It can't. I want you to go have a good day at the ranch. You've never even been there – it's a pretty place, and Liam's family are good people. I want to give you this, sweetheart. Next year, we'll spend Christmas and every other holiday together. I vow we will."

When she began to weep with harsh sobs, it broke Boone's heart, and he wished he'd said nothing at all until she raised her head, reaching her hands through the bars to grab his. "You're right, Boone. I'll go to the Double B if that's what you want, but I'll miss you so very much."

He took her hands and held them, then lifted them as best he could to kiss them, one at a time, with lips that were cracked and dry. Without her daily visits, he would be like a man in the dark, without any sun or hope. Rachel was the sole light in the darkness of his despair in jail.

Boone hoped – and prayed as his Ma had taught him – that he would endure this and survive the experience.

# CHAPTER NINETEEN

Many things in her life had been difficult, Rachel reflected. The loss of her parents wasn't easy, but she'd been so young it hadn't impacted her as much as Granny's death did later. She'd prepared her grandmother for the grave and mourned her, both painful as well as hard. Once she became a schoolmarm, and what family remained was far away, Rachel adapted. She'd taken pleasure in her faith and in the children that she taught, but there had always been an emptiness that couldn't be filled.

When she first met Boone, fevered and with a bullet lodged in his chest, she'd fought to save him and won. Those days battling his injury and infection, then removing the bullet had taxed her capability, but she'd stuck with it, stubborn and certain.

Her wedding day had been a happy one, but when Boone was arrested for a murder he didn't commit, her joy faded, and she now faced the most formidable challenge of her life.

Each morning, she rose after a night with very little sleep and many tears to face another day. Rachel washed her face, dressed, and cooked, using all her culinary skills to make dishes that would feed Boone. Then she summoned up all the strength within, prayed hard, and forced a smile to go visit him in his spartan jail cell.

Ezekiel returned from his journey to send a wire to his

family in Kentucky, and he helped her in many ways. He toted water up the stairs each day, offered a shoulder to lean on and an ear to listen, and shared her worries over Boone.

As if having her husband in jail with a sheriff who threatened daily to hang him wasn't enough, Zeke fell sick. The weather had been cold, with gray skies and rain or snow almost every day. He'd trudged back and forth to his job at the livery stable and, most days, went with her to visit Boone. Ezekiel spent what spare time he had hunting or fishing, bringing home meat for the table.

On a blustery evening, when a chill wind buffeted the windows and smacked sleet against the panes, Zeke stirred their simple supper, a rabbit stew with potatoes, carrots, and onions. Rachel thought it tasted fine, although her appetite had diminished with each day Boone spent in jail, but usually, the kid devoured whatever she served.

"Is something wrong with the stew?" she asked.

He glanced up, eyes too bright, and shook his head. "Naw, it's fine, but I ain't hungry. Rachel, I don't feel so good."

She shook off her preoccupation and noticed what she hadn't – he was pale, but his eyes glittered with fever, and he had two red spots, one on each cheek. He looked weary but also just sick. His eyes drooped, and so did his shoulders. As he laid down his spoon, he shivered, and Rachel leaped into action.

"You're sick," she stated. She rose and put one hand flat across his forehead, finding it hot. "You've got a fever. Let's get you into bed."

Ezekiel nodded, then coughed hard enough to shake his body.

By the time she had him settled beneath the blankets, wearing long johns, and dosed with some willow bark tea she'd steeped, Rachel was exhausted. Although ill, he didn't appear to be dangerously sick. He was cold, however, and kept shivering, so she heated a brick, wrapped it in flannel, and tucked it near his feet. She debated whether or not she should sit up with him, her mind racing with all the different diseases it might be.

It could be pneumonia, she thought, or any of a dozen fevers. It didn't seem like smallpox or typhoid or typhus. It seemed late in the season for malaria or yellow jack, so she ruled those out. She hadn't heard of anyone suffering the measles recently and besides, she recalled Boone saying he and Zeke had already had them. Her best guess was that he had a case of la grippe, the fever that came on so quickly but was often mild. Unless he grew worse, she decided she would try not to worry, but she did leave a lamp burning low in his room and the door between the bedrooms ajar so she'd hear him if he called out for her.

He remained in bed for five days, most of the week, but although miserable, he never appeared to be in danger. Rachel nursed him with a kind hand and coaxed him to eat a little and to drink the teas she made. Some helped, some didn't. She continued to cook for Boone and go visit him despite the fact she feared she might bring Zeke's illness with her. She didn't want Boone to fall ill but she couldn't bear not to see him. When he asked why his brother had been absent, she told him and watched the worry lines furrow deep in his face.

"He's not bad, Boone," she told him. "He'll be up and around in a day or two."

"I hope you're right," he replied. "Our father died of a fever."

Liam invited her to come to his Bonnie Blue Ranch to spend Christmas. Rachel had never visited a ranch, and although the notion had some appeal, she told him no. Her place was to stay near Boone, she thought, and to attempt to keep Christmas for his young brother. Maybe Boone would be free by Christmas day, she thought.

Ezekiel recovered, just as she predicted. He said he

wouldn't go to the ranch even if she did and encouraged her to go.

"Liam's wife is a peach," he told her. "You'd like her, and you could use a friend. Their little gal is about two, and she's sweet as molasses, stubborn as a mule."

Rachel almost gave in when she heard about the child. She wanted a baby, Boone's baby, very much, but she wanted a home, a real home, too. Their rooms were nice, and she liked them, but a house would be an improvement, whether it was in Laredo or the wilds of Kentucky.

The week before Christmas, she changed her mind about spending Christmas with the Rafferty family because Boone talked sense into her. Boone had mentioned something about a present, but Rachel didn't ask. She had nothing for him, and all she wanted was for him to be freed. On the day before Christmas Eve, she packed a small bag. Although they left early, just after daybreak, she insisted on stopping to see Boone. She'd made molasses cookies as well as some chicken pie for him.

He hid the cookies and ate the hot pie. During his jail time, he hadn't been able to shave, and stubble covered his face. When he did his best to kiss her through the bars, it tickled her face, but she didn't laugh. And when she told Boone she would be riding his horse, Sprat, to reach the ranch, he didn't laugh either.

Rachel didn't mention that she planned to don a pair of his britches, tightened up to fit, to ride. She'd learned to ride astride with her brothers, and she figured it would be the way to reach the ranch. At the livery stable, she changed in a stall while Ezekiel kept watch and then tucked her discarded dress into her bag. Zeke grinned. "You do beat all, Rachel, sometimes."

"Take care," she told him. "And look out for Boone for me, too. I'll be back on Monday."

He nodded. "It's a long ride, sister. Liam's gonna want to move quick and ride hard, so take care."

Moved by his concern, she nodded. "I will."

She rode with Liam across the flat terrain. Sometimes, there was a road, and sometimes, he struck out across the country, but she kept up, although, after the first hour, her muscles protested and hurt. Liam talked as he rode, and she struggled to pay attention, her focus on staying mounted. Sprat was a good horse, and he proved easier to ride than she'd feared.

It was late afternoon, almost evening when they reached the Bonnie Blue. Rachel was bone weary, clinging tight to Sprat to avoid pitching off the horse. She wasn't sure she'd be able to walk more than two steps when she dismounted. On the way in, once they'd reached ranch property, they'd passed a herd of long-horn cattle. Rachel's experience had been primarily with milk cows in the past, and she marveled at the sight of so many beasts. It'd been one thing to know Boone helped drive a herd north to sell each year but another to see them on the hoof.

Although there had been few trees in the open country they'd ridden through, other than clustered around a creek or small stream, where there were trees. The main house sat under several, a pretty frame farmhouse with two entrance doors on a covered front porch. Dormer windows above overlooked the yard. To the left of the house, a dog trot cabin sat. The name came from the open dog trot space that divided the two halves. Several barns lay down the hill from the main house with several corrals. Not far from it, a long, low bunkhouse sat near a small pond. Several cowboys emerged from it, and she recognized Boone's friends, Mac and Deacon.

Deacon Lee approached and helped her off Sprat.

"I'll tend him for you," he told her. "It's good to see you. Is Boone still locked up?"

When she nodded, blinking back tears at the reminder, he added, "I'm sorry to hear it. There's Miss Maggie – she's probably looking for you."

Rachel turned to see a blonde woman about her age in Liam's arms. He kissed his wife and held her tight, then released her, and the woman walked toward Rachel. She wore her hair in a long, single braid, and when she spoke, Rachel caught the slight German inflection.

"Welcome, Rachel," she told her, hands outstretched. "I'm Magdalena Rafferty – everyone calls me 'Maggie.' I'm glad you came. Liam has spoken well of you, and Boone is one of the best men I've known in this country. You must be worn out riding all day – come in, have something to eat, and I'll show you where you'll sleep."

They entered from the back of the house into a spacious kitchen. At one end, a big round table that must seat at least eight and maybe more took up much of the space. At the other, the stove cast heat. The room was warm and welcome after riding so many miles in the winter air. Something smelled delicious, and Maggie indicated Rachel should sit at the table. Without asking her preference, she brought a cup of coffee to the table and dished up a plate of beef stew.

"It's *marsch*, German beef stew. On Christmas Day, we will have roast pork, and I'll roast a goose even though we mostly eat beef with all the cattle. Tomorrow, we'll have carp from the pond. Liam's the son of Irish immigrants, me, I'm the daughter of German immigrants."

Once she'd eaten, Maggie took her on a tour of the house. The two front doors from the porch opened into two rooms. One was a large bedroom that Rachel assumed was the Rafferty's because, in addition to a spool bed, there was a cradle. Beside it was a trundle bed. The other room was a parlor, and both boasted a fireplace. The parlor had a small cedar tree decorated for Christmas, in the German custom, tied with lace bows, some fruit, and other pretties. Rachel wondered how far they'd had to send to get the tree, but before she asked, Maggie explained.

"Liam had some of the hands head up into the hills to get the tree for me," she said. "I know it's probably silly, but I like a Christmas tree. I'll put a few candles on it Christmas Eve, too."

Maggie led her up a narrow, steep, covered flight of stairs. The upstairs was more of an attic or loft, divided in two, but in one corner close to the chimney, there was a bed, a chest of drawers, and a chair.

"It's not very good for a guest room," Maggie said, her accent making the word more 'gut' than 'good.' "Eventually, we will make bedrooms for the children up here – right now, it's just little Grace, but we plan for more."

"It's fine," Rachel said. She was relieved she would have a bit of privacy since she anticipated the holiday might make her weep.

"Go ahead, go to bed if you want," Maggie said. "Is that the only bag you brought?"

Rachel nodded. "It is – thank you. I am very tired."

Although she hadn't thought she'd sleep easy, she did and didn't wake until after dawn when delicious aromas wafted upward. Rachel put on her dress and came down to find a breakfast spread. A few of the hands, including Deke and Mac, were at the table, too. Once she'd eaten, Rachel offered her help, and Maggie accepted it. The two women cooked through the day and then sat down to feast in the evening. Miles from any town or church, there was no Christmas service, but Liam read from the Bible at his wife's request. Those present sang Christmas carols and a few hymns. As promised, Maggie lit a few small candles on the tree, and the simple thing became lovely.

Rachel held her tears until she was alone, then wept, missing Boone and sad because he couldn't be present. On Christmas Day, there was more feasting, more singing, and more happy times, but Rachel, despite the chill wind that blew, had to walk outside for a little while. She needed the solitary time to deal with her emotions. It had turned sharply colder, but she wrapped her shawl tighter and walked. After an hour, Liam joined her.

"See the dog trot cabin there?" he asked, just as if she wasn't wandering alone on an unfamiliar ranch on a blustery winter day. When she nodded, he said, "That's where the top hand lives, at least on one side of it. Should he have a bigger family, they'd be welcome to both sides. It's where you'd live if Boone changed his mind and took the job."

That piqued her interest. "Is it?"

"It is indeed, and the top hand doesn't often have to hit the trail with the rest of the cowboys. I go because I'm the boss, but the top hand runs things here at the ranch. That's one reason I need a good man because I leave him to watch over my family as well as everything else."

"I thank you for helping Boone in his current situation," Rachel said. "All bosses should care as much as you do."

Liam paused in his stride and faced her. "If I hadn't, that sheriff would have hung him by now," he said. "He's got some personal beef with Boone, and I don't understand why, though, I mean to find out. But, Rachel, it's not because I'm his boss that I'm doing this – it's because Boone is one of the best friends I've ever had and because he's saved my life more than once."

That surprised Rachel, although it shouldn't have. "I wasn't aware."

He laughed. "Boone's one of the humblest men I know – he wouldn't mention it. But he took a bullet for me during the war. It wasn't nearly as serious, thank the Lord, as his recent wound, but he got hit in the thigh after he pushed me out of the way. That's the first time. On the trail, he doctored me after I got stuck with a mesquite thorn – they're poison, you know, and then another time, I got bit by a big rattler, and he tended me then, too. That's three times I might've died but didn't, thanks to

Boone. He's more than a friend to me—he's like a brother even though he's got plenty of those."

Rachel accepted the information. It explained a lot, she thought.

"Let's get to the house. We'll head back to Laredo early come morning."

She nodded and returned, her heart and mind brimming with emotion. If Boone were here too, she thought she'd be happy just to stay on the ranch, but he wasn't, and that was that.

# CHAPTER TWENTY

On Christmas Eve and Christmas Day, Boone's spirits were as low as they'd ever been. He missed Rachel with a deep ache that brought an emptiness nothing could fill, and he longed for Liam's company. The man was cheerful in the face of any adversity, and his presence had saved Boone some measure of humiliation and persecution. In his absence, both the sheriff and his deputy stepped up their rude ways. His brother's daily visits were all that kept Boone from spiraling into a dark abyss of despair, and without Ezekiel, he wouldn't have eaten a bite and done anything but lie on his cot, brooding.

"Boone, I brought tamales," Zeke said on Christmas Eve. He'd come later than Rachel usually did but that didn't matter since he was here. "And those frijoles."

He could smell the spicy aroma, and his stomach growled with hunger as he took the plate. "Thanks," he said as he dug into the food. "Are you feelin' okay? You look peaked to me."

Ezekiel shrugged his shoulders. "I'm awright, Boone, a bit tired, that's all. Being down sick took a lot of starch out of me. Don't fret about me – you need to save your strength, man. To tell the truth, you probably look worse than I do."

That might well be true, Boone thought. He didn't feel well, suffering from frequent headaches and the occasional pain in his gut. His back ached from the hard cot.

"I'll be right as rain once I get out of here," Boone said, as he scarfed down the food. "I'll be better once Rachel's back."

As a small Christmas indulgence, Deuce allowed Boone to shave under scrutiny but not to wash. Ezekiel argued, but the deputy shut him down, what goodwill he'd shown vanishing in the face of adhering to the Sheriff's unceasing cruelty.

He endured both the holiday and the constant badgering from the lawmen. He developed a deep cough that made his chest ache.

To pass the time, which moved at a sluggish crawl, Boone thought about the Double B Ranch and imagined Rachel there. He could envision her at the main house, maybe helping Maggie bake or cook in the kitchen or at the table in the adjacent space. He wondered what she'd think about the tall trees that circled the house or the dog trot cabin where they could live if he decided to accept Liam's job offer. Boone wished he could watch her with the cattle and was curious what she would think about little Grace. He figured she liked kids. After all, she'd been a teacher, but someday, he hoped to raise a family of his own. The food would be tasty and plentiful, he knew. They always served goose on Christmas Eve and plenty of roast pork on December 25. He longed to be able to join Rachel there, but the reality was that he couldn't.

On Monday, he woke early to the sound of hammers at work and soon learned, because the sheriff shared the news with glee, that a gallows was under construction.

"Lighting may have blasted the old hanging tree," the sheriff told Boone with a wicked grin. "But we're building a gallows. Town needs one, and you'll be the first to swing. I doubt it will take them long to finish it. Without any luck at all, I'll see you hanged by the end of the month."

"I'm not guilty," Boone said, his tone weary and his body taut. "You can't hang me without a trial."

Johnson laughed. "So you say, but I say different, and I'm the law."

If it wouldn't show weakness, Boone would have wept with fear and frustration. Instead, he turned away and lay on his cot, one hand over his face. His faint hopes faded away, and for the first time, he thought he most likely would be hanged. Rachel would be left a widow, Ezekiel alone in this frontier town, and his body buried in Texas soil. He wouldn't make it back to Kentucky or see his family there again in this life.

Construction halted by noon because it started snowing, a heavy, uncharacteristic event in Laredo. Although it could and often was cold, it rained during the winter more often than it snowed, and usually snow was light. This time, by all accounts, the snow came down heavy and fast. When Ezekiel arrived, his coat and hat were covered in snow. He stopped at the door to stamp snow from his boots and then, with permission, advanced to the cell.

He handed Boone the plate of beans and sighed, "It's snowing like crazy out there, and the wind is sharp."

"That's what I heard them say," Boone replied, cocking his head toward the lawmen. "Do you think it will keep Rachel from getting back?"

"I don't know, but if it's as bad out at the ranch as here, I hope they wait," Zeke said. "Boone, they're building gallows out here."

Boone snorted. "Yeah, they made sure to tell me so and that I'll be the first to be hanged."

As soon as he spoke, he wished he hadn't because his brother's face crumpled, and the kid looked ready to cry. "I can't bear it if they do," Zeke said, his voice anguished. "You ain't guilty. How can they?"

"They won't if Liam has anything to say about it," Boone replied with more bravado than he felt.

"You should have lit a shuck and gone before you were arrested," his brother said.

Maybe so, but Boone still didn't regret it. Living as an outlaw had no appeal, and he wouldn't have dragged Rachel along. If he'd known what was coming, he wouldn't have married her either, but he was still glad that he had.

"No, that was never a good idea," Boone said. "It'll be all right. Ma always says it'll all come out in the wash."

His words didn't seem to reassure his brother, and they didn't do much for Boone. He longed to have a view outside and worried about Rachel riding through the heavy snow. Sprat, though, was sure-footed in all weathers, but he couldn't stop being concerned. Liam had promised to return on Monday, with Rachel, but he wouldn't have any idea that the snow would come.

It was almost dark when the door into the sheriff's office flew open, and two figures entered. Boone rose from the cot with speed when he recognized Liam, but he didn't know the man at his side.

"Where's Rachel?" he asked, standing at the bars. "Where's my wife?"

"Boone, I'm here," the second figure said, and he looked again. Rachel wore a pair of britches, he noticed, and her clothes were covered in snow. "I'm back."

He reached out through the bars to grasp the hands she offered. "I was worried, honey. That snow…"

"It's a mess, and we had a long, hard ride," she said but with a smile. "Sprat brought me home safe, though. I missed you, Boone, very much."

"Whose pants are you wearing, woman?"

"Yours, although they're much too big," she said, blushing. "I can ride better astride than not, Boone."

"I thought you were a boy or a young man when you came in," he told her. "But you're prettier. I like you better in a skirt, though."

"I'd rather wear one, and I'll change as soon as I'm home."

Boone coughed and asked," What did you think of the ranch?"

"I liked it," she replied. "It's a pretty place."

"It is. I bet the food was larruping good, too."

She nodded. "I wished every meal you were been there to eat, too."

"Ezekiel's been keeping me fed."

"I'll bring you something better tomorrow," she told him.

"I'll be glad of it, but right now, let Ezekiel get you home and get out of those wet clothes," he replied, fussy as a mother. "I don't want you to fall sick. Get warm and dry, honey."

"I will." She caressed his cheek through the bars. "You shaved."

"On Christmas."

"I love you, Boone, and I'll be here tomorrow."

"I'll be here, honey, though I wish I wasn't."

Their few precious moments together warmed him body and soul, but once she'd gone into the night, he was like a man without a fire in cold, open country. The stove the sheriff used to warm the place was beside his desk, and little of the warmth reached the cell. Boone shivered as he pulled the ratty blanket over him. Rachel was back and safe. That should have relieved his fears and brought a little happiness, but it didn't. All he wanted was out of jail and to be with her, free and away from this place.

His brother left with his wife, but Liam, who had to be also weary, wet, and cold, remained. He approached the cell, and Boone said, "Thank you for having Rachel for Christmas and getting her back through the weather."

Liam laughed. "That woman of yours would ride through hell if you were on the other side," he told him. "You've got a rare one, there."

The praise made his heart ache. "I do for all the good I'm doing her now. They're building gallows outside this place, Liam."

"I saw that," his friend commented. "Don't get your drawers in a knot just yet – it's not built yet."

"When it is, Johnson will hang me, innocent or not."

Liam must have caught the note of despair in his voice tempered with resignation.

"I wouldn't give up yet, Boone. There's got to be a reason he has an ax to grind with you. It's personal, and for the life of me, I don't understand why, but I'm trying to find out. I also want to know who really killed the blacksmith – if we can figure that out, then I can get you out of here. I'm also starting to think that Mad Mike shooting you wasn't an accident or that he was drunk. I think maybe it was planned."

The notion shocked Boone. "You don't think it was random?"

"I don't. I've given it a great deal of thought. I know I wasn't there, but Deacon Lee was, and he told me that Mike just walked up to you and fired. He couldn't have missed if he tried, and afterward, Deke told me Mike was worked up, thinking he'd killed you, kept saying, "I liked ol' Boone, he was my pard, I didn't have no beef with him. I shouldn't have done it."

Boone shrugged. "He could still say all that, and it been an accident. He weren't called Mad Mike for nothing."

"True enough, but the way to get you free is to figure this all out," Liam said. "I'm working on it, thinking hard."

"I wish I knew."

"Give it some thought, Boone. You might recollect something you haven't. I'm gonna sit over here by the stove and get warm for now."

Boone thought until his brain wanted to quit, and he had a headache. He went over the events in his mind again and then again. He'd ridden into town to play faro, mostly for the break from the work routine and to win money to finance taking his brother back to Kentucky. He hadn't let the kid come, figuring he was too young to spend time in a saloon, even though Boone didn't plan to partake in either wild women or hard drink. He had been winning when Mike strolled up, lifted his revolver, and shot Boone in the chest. There hadn't been time to anticipate it or even react. He'd been bleeding on the floor, his chest on fire with pain before he hardly understood what happened. His memory grew sketchy after that. Boone recalled hearing that he'd die for sure. He knew Deke and Mac had carried him upstairs, and then afterward, he begged to be out in the sun and fresh air to the porch. He'd been fevered and hurting, but he did remember the day Rachel came up onto the porch and changed everything.

Now he wondered if someone had put Mad Mike up to shoot him, maybe even paid him. The man hadn't been right in the head since the war, he'd heard, and Boone never had a chance to ask why he'd shot him. The sheriff had strung Mike up and hung him the day after he'd shot Boone. It seemed odd now because Boone wasn't dead, although there had been no doubt Mike shot him. Maybe Liam was on the trail of something, he thought, but he had no clue what. Johnson had talked about Sharpsburg and mentioned he had a brother who died there, but if Boone's shot killed him, it wasn't deliberate during the battle. It wasn't very likely either. There must be more to this story, Boone thought, and if he could figure out what, then maybe he wouldn't stretch a rope after all.

What they needed, however, was time, and he wasn't sure how much they had.

Sheriff Johnson seemed hellbent on moving forward with both the gallows and Boone's execution. The winter weather had halted construction for now, and although Boone trusted Liam's persuasive and stubborn efforts, the lawman wouldn't wait forever.

He couldn't sleep, trying to figure it all out, desperate to find that missing bit of information that could change his fate.

Boone hoped he could.

# CHAPTER TWENTY-ONE

The new year came without celebration or fanfare for the Wilsons. Rachel plodded through each day, weary and heartsick, as she cooked for Boone. Each day, she rose, prepared a dish that she would then take to the jail, and then served the remainder for supper. Most nights, Ezekiel and she were alone at the table, but at least once a week, sometimes twice, Liam joined them. If they were in Laredo and not out at the ranch, so did Deacon Lee and Mac. Rachel had little appetite for what she cooked, but she would eat what she could, listening to their long discussions and debates on how to prove Boone innocent.

"There's got to be somebody who knows more than we do," Liam said one evening over a plate of fried potatoes and sausage. "Someone killed Kurtz, and it wasn't Boone."

"And you still think that Mad Mike shooting Boone was more than it seemed?" Ezekiel asked.

"I do," Liam replied. "I think perhaps this sheriff had something to do with it. It's just I don't know how to go about proving it."

Rachel listened but said nothing as she stirred food around her plate, so queasy she feared she might have to leave the table to puke. Since around the first month anniversary of her marriage, she'd been feeling sick, and her stomach had been out of sorts. She suffered from frequent nausea, which sometimes led to vomiting. So far, she'd been able to keep Ezekiel or anyone else from knowing. There were times her stomach hurt, too, but she chalked it all up to stress over Boone's situation. As January waned, her fatigue increased until she often had to force herself through each day.

If she were ill, she didn't want Boone to know because he'd worry. Rachel ruled out cholera and dysentery since she had no diarrhea. Without fever, she thought it couldn't be anything too serious. Smells or sights could set her off, she noticed.

Ezekiel kept them in meat, mostly game, so she could cook for Boone. One morning, when he brought a brace of rabbits, cleaned, and gutted to her, the odor of blood and death brought on immediate nausea. Rachel had stuck her nose into her sleeve and carried on.

A few mornings later, though, she woke with her stomach so riled she barely had time to roll over and take the lid off the slop bucket before she retched into it. Her stomach turned inside out as she puked, unable to stop. When she finished, her eyes were streaming, and she gasped for air.

"Rachel, what's wrong?" Ezekiel stood beside her bed, face hard as stone, arms crossed.

"I'm sick to my stomach," she said and then retched again with nothing more to bring up. "Maybe something I've eaten didn't agree with me."

"We ate the same," he replied. "So did Boone and Liam. Have you been puking a lot?"

She thought she'd fooled him, but apparently not. "Some," she said. "Don't tell Boone, though."

Ezekiel put the lid on the slop bucket. He shook his head and went to the washstand, where he wet a cloth and brought it to her. "I reckon he would want to know he's gonna be a daddy," he said, his tone soft and even.

Rachel laid back against her pillow after she'd wiped her

face and stared at him. "What are you saying?"

"I'm saying it's likely you're in the family way, Rachel."

He blushed as he said it, and she realized he might be right.

"Why do you think that?"

"Jacob's wife Sally Ann has three young 'uns," he told her. "I might be the least one, but I ain't stupid. I've seen how gals that are gonna be a mother get sick and all."

Rachel put her right hand against her belly. She knew that, she thought, but it hadn't come to mind. Her fatigue was another common symptom of pregnancy, and she'd noticed that her breasts had been sore as well. All the small pieces fit together like a puzzle, and she smiled. "I do believe you're right, Ezekiel."

He brought her a cup of water and a few crackers.

"Maybe you ought to stay in bed," he said.

She shook her head. "No, being sick passes. I need to cook Boone's food and take it to him."

"I can carry it over."

"No, he'll fret if I don't come," she told him. "Don't tell him, not yet. I'll tell him when the time is right, but not now. It'll just eat him up if he hears while he's in jail."

Rachel hugged the knowledge tight. There would be a baby, she thought, a product of their love. By her reckoning, it would be born in September. From a large family, she knew very well there were risks. She might lose the child, or she might die during birth. It happened too often, but she wasn't afraid. As she got up and dressed for the day, she imagined a baby with Boone's gray eyes. Although still worried about Boone, fearful he might hang, there was joy in her heart.

At the jail, Boone was in low spirits, but he managed a small smile when she walked in.

"It's later than usual," he said. "I thought you weren't coming. I got worried you were sick or something."

*It's like he knows, somehow,* she thought, *he feels it because we are bone of our bone, blood of our blood, heart of our heart.*

"I had to wait for the dumplings to get done," she told him. "Ezekiel shot a prairie chicken, so I made you chicken and dumplings."

He took the plate and inhaled it. "Thank you, honey. I never thought I'd still be locked up in here come February."

"You'll be out and home soon," she said and prayed it was so. "The weather's kept the gallows from being built."

If it wasn't snowing, it rained and remained cold, so the progress on the structure hadn't advanced the way the sheriff had hoped.

"Liam's not found out anything new," Boone told her as he devoured the food. Rachel could see he'd lost weight, but she didn't mention it. He continued to eat what she brought and nothing more, not trusting the lawmen to provide decent grub. He'd said they spit in the meals or drinks, and she believed it.

"He will, though," she replied. "He has to."

"If anything happens to me," Boone told her, "Let Ezekiel take you back to Kentucky, you hear? Don't stay here – I don't trust the Sheriff not to bother you."

"Boone, don't talk like that," she said. His gloomy words made her stomach hurt, and she almost told him about the baby. She didn't, though. It needed to be happy news, not delivered in a moment of despair.

"Rachel, honey..."

He moved as close as possible to the bars, and she caught the rank, unwashed odor of his body. It wasn't his fault since Johnson refused to let him take a bath, but the smell turned her stomach. She put one hand over her nose and stepped back, gagging. She held off puking through sheer force of will.

"What's the matter? You *are* sick," Boone said, eyes narrowing with concern.

"No, I'm fine. I am."

He didn't look convinced, but he held her hands through the bars and kissed them.

"Take the plate and go home," he told her. "Get some rest, honey. You don't look well, Rachel. I'll see you tomorrow."

She didn't want to go but did because almost as soon as she stepped outside, she bent and vomited again. Hoping that the sound didn't carry so that Boone heard, Rachel leaned against a corner of the building before she headed home. Someone took her arm, and she jumped until she saw it was Mary from the saloon.

"You're breeding," the woman said with her usual blunt manner.

"Did Zeke tell you?"

Mary laughed. "No, he didn't, but I've eyes and can see. Besides, I remember it too well."

Shock replaced Rachel's nausea. "You have children?"

"Don't sound so surprised, but yeah, a daughter. I got knocked up when I was young and green and had her when I wasn't but seventeen. She's near grown now."

"Does she live here in Laredo? I don't remember seeing her."

"I wouldn't have her here," Mary replied. "I sent her to the Sisters of Charity in Galveston as soon as she was born. She don't know me, and I don't know her. It's for the best that way. But I remember carrying her, and I can tell you a few tricks that will help. If you ain't worried for your reputation, come over to the saloon for a spell."

Rachel snorted. "I don't have a reputation to worry about, and you know it."

At the saloon, not yet open, they sat at a table and Mary had Graciela make a pot of tea. "Tea'll help soothe your belly," Mary said. "So will sucking on a peppermint stick. I've been wanting to talk to you, Rachel."

She had never been one of Mary's favorite people, so she asked, "Why?"

"I heard Rafferty is trying to find someone to say who really killed the blacksmith and if Mad Mike was put up to shoot Boone."

"He is, but so far, no luck."

Mary poured them each a second cup of tea. "He should've asked me, but he hasn't."

Rachel sat up straight in her chair. "What do you know?"

Mary shrugged. "I was here when your Boone was shot. I saw it happen – I was tending bar that night."

"And?"

The saloon proprietor smiled, although it was a sick, weak grin. "Before Mike walked right up to the card table and shot Boone, he was talking with Sheriff Johnson. I don't know what was said, but that does seem odd, doesn't it?"

A tendril of hope curled within Rachel's heart. "It does."

"And although I don't know, maybe someone does."

"I'll tell Liam," Rachel said. "Thank you."

"Don't thank me yet – your man could still swing," Mary answered. "And I have one more bit you can share with Rafferty. I saw Kurtz the night he was killed. He'd been in here, drinking, which was not his habit. When he left, he left with that deputy, the one with dead, mean eyes they call Deuce."

"Johnson's deputy?"

"The very one. He's an odd one, not been in Laredo much longer than you have and he's only been a deputy since November, I believe. I've heard talk that the only reason the sheriff took him on was that he was a Yank, too, in the war and I don't know. But I do know this – Kurtz came from New York state. That's where he wore his blue, and so did Deuce."

"Why would the deputy kill Kurtz?" Rachel wondered

aloud. The blacksmith had been a despicable man.

"That's the question without an answer," Mary said. "But maybe Rafferty can find one. I like your Boone, though, he's too good for my taste, too honorable. If I can help him not to hang, I'm glad to do it. You look like a wet, dirty dishrag. Go home and rest awhile, Rachel. You want that baby to be born healthy next autumn, don't you?"

"I do."

On the way back to their rooms, Rachel met Ezekiel. He took her arm and hugged her on the street. "Where you been?" he asked. "I been looking everywhere 'cause I heard you sicked up outside the jail."

"Mary took me back to the saloon for tea," Rachel told him. "Zeke, she's got information that might help Liam save Boone."

The kid steered her up the stairs and got her settled at the table. "Do you want something to eat?" he asked. "You look worn out, Rachel."

"I'd like some coffee," she said with a shiver. It had turned cold again.

He brewed some and sat with her to drink it while she shared with him what Mary had said.

"We don't know enough, but that's more than we've had," he said. "I'll tell Liam to come to supper. Is there plenty of those dumplings to go around?"

Rachel nodded. "There is, and I'll make some biscuits."

He reached across the table and took her hand. "After you rest a spell, Rachel," he told her. "Boone's asked me to look after you, and I mean to do it all the more now that you're carrying his child."

His devotion to Boone – and to her – made Rachel smile.

After a much-needed nap, she rose to stir the pot of chicken and dumplings, then made biscuits and more coffee. Liam arrived after dark and when she shared what Mary told her, he grinned.

"That puts us closer than we've been," he said. "I should have gone to talk to her, I suppose, but I'm not much of one for saloons. I will now, though, and I'll start asking around. I sent Deke and Mac back to the ranch to see to my family, but when they're back, I'll have them do the same. Zeke, you can, too, but take care. The last thing we would want is to spook the sheriff or killer.

"Did you hear back from the governor?" Ezekiel asked.

Liam sighed. "I did, but he's waiting for more information – maybe now we'll get it."

Rachel touched her belly and hoped they would. She wanted her husband out of jail so they could begin their life together.

# CHAPTER TWENTY-TWO

Moses Wilson's horse gave up the ghost about a hundred miles from San Antonio. It wasn't surprising, really, since he'd ridden the animal hard for more than a month, and it was a long way from Kentucky. He traveled light, but in his breast pocket, he carried a much-folded telegram the family had received in December, one that had cast a shadow over them all. He no longer had to read it – he had memorized the message weeks ago.

"Boone in jail for murder," it read. "He's not guilty, but the sheriff wants to hang him. Ranch boss trying to get him free. Thought you ought to know. Ezekiel Wilson."

This time, his mother, Jemima, didn't hesitate but urged him to head to Texas.

"Go to Boone," she told him.

"Do you want me to go or Garrett?" he'd asked. After all, Garrett was older.

"You ought to go. Garrett's more settled in his ways, but I know you'd welcome the chance to ramble as well as see to Boone."

"Do you want me to bring him back?"

"I don't rightly know, son. He's married, he wrote, and he's welcome if he comes. I don't know if there's much here for him now. It's changed since the war, and so has he. I need to know how he fares, though, son and young Ezekiel likely needs help. He's just a boy."

Moses had left before Christmas and rode hard, stopping at night but sleeping rough. He'd bunked in more than a few barns when it was too cold or wet. When his horse, Whiskey, named for the color of his coat, died, it broke his heart. He'd raised him from a foal and didn't doubt he'd pushed the mount to his death. Moses lacked any tools to bury the horse, and it bothered him he'd leave the carcass in unfamiliar country. He pondered the problem but found no solution. Still, he had to go on, so he gathered up his belongings, including his saddle, and set out afoot toward Laredo.

The load was heavy, and the traveling on foot was slow. Light sleet fell from gray skies, and a wind chilled him to the bone as he plodded onward. His best guess was that Laredo lay fifty miles or more in a southwest direction, a long walk even on a good day. He imagined he'd have to stop when it grew dark and camp, then make it into Laredo the next afternoon. Moses was weary and had no idea if he'd find his brother alive or dead.

His gear, especially the saddle, were burdensome, and his shoulders ached from the weight. Moses paused, aware that no one in the world knew his current location, and if he fell the way Whiskey did, he'd be a goner. With a sigh, then a muttered oath, he kept walking in the late afternoon, on the lookout for a place to stop for the night.

He heard two horses galloping toward him and halted. Two men rode toward him, whooping aloud and calling out Boone's name.

"Did you bust out?" the first rider called. "Or did you get free, and where's Sprat?"

"Aye, and where be your wife?" the second said in a voice burred with the flavor of Scotland. "What are ye up tae?"

Still mounted, they blocked his path, and Moses squinted in the dim light to see them. They seemed to think they knew him and that he was Boone.

"I'm on my way to Laredo," he told them. "My horse died away back, so I'm on foot."

"Jumpin' Jehoshaphat, you ain't Boone," the first man said with surprise. "I thought sure you were our buddy Boone Wilson. From the back, you looked just like him."

If they mistook him for Boone, then maybe his brother wasn't dead. "I'm his brother, Moses," he told them. "I've come from Kentucky. So, he's still on this side of the dirt?"

"He is or was last we heard," the man said. "I'm Deacon Lee, and this is Mac. We all work for Liam Rafferty on the Double B Ranch, and we all served in the war together. Liam's in town, doing his best to see Boone don't swing for a killing he didn't do."

Moses' tired mind took in the information and tried to make sense of it.

"Where's Ezekiel?"

"In Laredo," Deacon said. "He's been a hand here at the ranch, too, or was till Boone got shot. Zeke's been in town since, working at the livery and watching out for Rachel while Boone's in the hoosegow."

Relieved to hear that his younger brother was safe, Moses asked, "Who's Rachel?"

Both men shot him a sideways glance. "Boone's wife."

Although he'd known his brother had married, he hadn't known the name of his sister-in-law.

Fatigue settled over him like a heavy blanket, and he sighed. "Reckon, I need to find a place to camp for the night," he told them. "I'll go on into Laredo tomorrow."

"Come wi' us, man," Mac said. "Ye can bunk with us and get some grub at the ranch house plus the loan of a horse to get ye there."

"They won't mind?"

"It's nae bother to them," Mac replied.

"You'll be welcome even though Liam's in town. He's fond of Boone and young Zeke, too."

The two cowboys split his gear between their horses, and Deke offered Moses a hand up to ride double on his mount. It was nearly dark by the time they reached the ranch, but once they stowed Moses' gear in the bunkhouse, they took him to join the other hands for supper.

His rations had been scant during his long journey, so the sight of biscuits, fried chicken, mashed potatoes, and cream gravy looked like manna from heaven to Moses. He ate his fill, and the warm food made him sleepy. At the bunkhouse, he would have slept on the floor, but the men insisted he take Boone's bed, so he did. He slept longer and deeper than he had in more than two months with a comfortable bed beneath him and the knowledge that, for now, Boone was alive.

In the morning, after breakfast, they saddled a little paint mare for him to ride and escorted him into Laredo. To his Kentucky bred eyes, the town seemed more than a little raw and crude on the edge of the river. "Where's the jail?" he asked. He needed to see Boone.

"It's beside the gallows they're building, and we'll get there," Deacon told him. "First, let's go to the livery and stable the horse. Ezekiel's likely to be there this time of day, and you can meet up with him first."

At the livery stable, Moses dismounted and led the paint into the shadowed interior. He paused when he heard his brother talking to a mare he combed. His eyes stung at the sound. He hadn't seen Ezekiel for almost a year, so he watched. The kid had filled out and grown a couple of inches, he noticed, and he moved more like a man. He'd lost most of the gangly awkwardness he'd had when he left home.

"Ezekiel," he said in a quiet voice.

Zeke stopped, and the curry comb fell to the ground as he turned.

"Moses?" he cried. "You came!"

Ezekiel flung himself onto his brother and hugged him hard.

"I left as soon as we got your wire," Moses told him. "I didn't even stay for Christmas, and I been riding hard since. Whiskey up and died on me somewhere past San Antonio, but two cowboys happened on me."

"'Twas us," Mac said, entering the stable with a grin.

One question mattered the most, so Moses asked it. "Boone still in jail?"

His brother nodded. "He is, but we've got some leads now, so hopefully, he'll be free soon. He's down in the mouth, being locked up so long. The sheriff arrested him the day after his weddin'."

Moses left the paint horse at the livery, and his brother toted his gear, except the saddle, up to their rented rooms. Ezekiel promised he'd catch up, so Moses started down the muddy main street toward the jail, hat brim pulled low. He hadn't gone far when he heard the familiar sound of a cocked pistol and a voice that growled, "Don't know how you busted out, but you've made it simple for me. I don't have to wait to hang you now – I'm gonna shoot you right now for trying to escape."

This had to be the sheriff, he thought, as the gun barrel pressed against his back, and Moses didn't dare draw breath, or he might be shot. He considered lifting his hands in surrender but thought the volatile sheriff might shoot him for it.

"Are you out of your head, man?" someone said and, in one swift move, grabbed the lawman's gun hand. As he did, the pistol fired, but the shot went wild. "That's not Boone."

"I'm no fool – it's Boone Wilson, as I live and breathe."

Ezekiel ran up, panting. "No, it's not. It's our brother

Moses."

With a snort, Sheriff Johnson holstered his weapon and gave Moses a long, hard stare. "I'll be darned if it's not Boone. You favor your brother a fair bit, all the more from the back."

"You came near to shooting an innocent man in the back," the man who'd stopped the lawman said. "I plan to have your badge anyway, but that would do it, aside from what you've done to Boone."

"Mind yourself, Rafferty," the sheriff said with a snarl. "I'll lock you in beside him."

Then, without another word, he pushed past the three men and moved toward the jail.

"Moses, this is Liam Rafferty," Ezekiel said. "He's our pard, and he owns the ranch where we've been working. He's been standing for Boone since he got arrested."

Moses extended a hand to shake. "Then I owe you thanks, man, for your help to my brothers and for your hospitality. I spent last night at your ranch, and I'm riding one of your horses."

Rafferty shook hands. "You're welcome to it. Boone will be glad you're here, although he may yell at the kid first."

"He told me not to let the folks at home know," Ezekiel added.

"But he'll be happy you came – his spirits are low, and this should raise them, I hope."

"Is he all right?"

The ranch boss shrugged. "He eats once a day, only what his wife brings him. He doesn't get to wash or shave, so he's filthy, stinking, and crawling with lice. He's been locked up for near two months now, and he misses his wife. Listening to men building gallows to hang him don't help either. Some days, he's about lost hope, and I can't say as I blame him."

Moses' gut clenched hard and tight. "So, you reckon he will hang, then?"

"No, no, I don't. I've spent weeks trying to put together what really happened. I think the man who shot Boone last fall was paid to do so by this sheriff, but what I don't know is why. If I can find someone to come forward and speak up, I'll have his badge and his job. He'll be the one locked up if I can prove it. As for the murder of this blacksmith, I have an idea that the deputy killed the man, but I've no notion why. I mean to find out, though. Go see your brother, Moses. We'll talk more later. Come to Rachel's for supper."

At the jail, Boone sat on his cot, head in his hands, looking dejected. Even across the room, Moses could see how dirty he was. His hair had grown longer than he'd ever seen it, to his collar and past. Whiskers hid his face, and Moses winced, knowing how Boone preferred to be clean shaven. He'd lost weight, too, Moses noted.

"Boone," he said as he approached the cage with Ezekiel at his side.

His brother glanced up, then shook his head with disbelief. "I must be seein' things," he muttered.

"You ain't – it's me," Moses told him.

"Why'd you come?"

Surprised, Moses said, "For you, Boone, and for Ezekiel."

Boone met his gaze, and he saw the tears glistening in his brother's eyes. "I'm glad to see you, Moses, though I wish it were a happier circumstance. If they hang me, promise me you'll see the kid and my wife safe."

"You know I will, but I don't intend to stand back and let them hang you," Moses said. "First thing, though, I'm gonna see you get washed, shaved, and your hair cut, along with some clean clothes. Those you have on can probably stand up on their own and say howdy by now."

Boone's lips curved in a small smile, and Moses decided the long journey from Kentucky and losing his horse had been worth it all.

Among the Wilson brothers, Moses was known back home as the one who could charm the birds from the trees. He could convince the most miserly farmer to buy a horse when nothing else would. As a boy, he'd talked his way out of many a scrape with his words and manner. He had little fear when it came to facing authority, and he'd learned that a sweet tongue could accomplish things that a bitter one never would.

Moses stepped over to the sheriff and said, "I'm gonna need some hot water, some soap, a good razor, and some scissors."

The lawman laughed, a bitter dry noise that reminded Moses of leaves in an autumn wood. "I hear people down in hell want ice water, too, and they don't get it."

"The devil didn't nearly shoot them down in cold blood, mistaking them for someone else," Moses said. He locked his eyes on the man's face and stared hard. "That didn't show much good sense nor judgement. Word gets around. There's some who won't respect a trigger-happy sheriff without wisdom. I'll ask again."

Behind him, he heard Ezekiel gasp, but Boone laughed, a little.

Johnson's mouth turned downward, and his gaze could have cut diamonds. "I ain't letting your brother out of that cell, not for love nor money."

"Then let me in the cell," Moses said. "You can lock it if you want as long as you let me out when I'm done."

After a very long pause, the sheriff nodded. "Fine. He'll hang, clean or dirty, but if that's what you want, I'll allow it."

For the first time since he'd arrived in Texas, Moses Wilson grinned.

# CHAPTER TWENTY-THREE

By the time dark fell, Boone was clean, shaved, and dressed in fresh garments, ones that belonged to Moses. They used to be the same size, but he'd lost weight, and the clothes were too big. His hair had been trimmed, then combed. Moses, God bless him, had also picked the lice from his hair and killed each one with a fingernail. He'd had Ezekiel take the mattress out and beat it until it was vermin-free, then sent the kid to fetch clean blankets and a different pillow. Then, after consulting Liam, he asked Ezekiel to bring food from the saloon. Boone dined for the second time that day, something he hadn't done since being locked up, on Graciela's tamales and beans.

Johnson had gone home, but Moses persuaded Deuce to allow Rachel to come for an extra visit. Ezekiel went to fetch her, and he wondered what he would tell her so that she would come. He'd been some worried about her because she'd been acting what he thought was strange and different.

Moses was back outside the cell when she rushed in without a bonnet.

"Is something wrong?" she cried. "Zeke said I should come quickly."

Moses stood a few steps from his cell, and she ran to him. "Boone? Are you free?"

"Honey, it's my brother, Moses," Boone called from

behind the bars. "Rachel, he came from Kentucky."

She halted where she stood and stared, first at Moses, then at Boone.

He reached his hand toward her through the bars. "Rachel."

"You shaved," she said in a soft voice. "You're washed, and your hair's cut. Boone, you look so handsome."

Then she closed her eyes and crumpled, her legs giving way as she went to the floor. Ezekiel caught her before she landed hard and picked her up in his arms.

Boone's heart stopped beating. "What's wrong with her?" he yelled. "Rachel!"

"She's swooned, Boone, that's all," Moses told him, but he could see by the furrow in his brow that Moses was also concerned. "Deputy, open the cell so we can lay her on the cot till she rouses."

When the lawman hesitated, Moses's eyes turned dark. "Do it, or I'll rake everything from the Sheriff's desk and let Ezekiel lay her there."

When Zeke put Rachel down on the cot, Boone knelt beside her. It was the closest he'd been to her in months. He took her limp hand in his and kissed her as if that would wake her.

"She's not Sleeping Beauty," Moses said, referencing the old story Ma used to tell them. "You ain't gonna wake her with a kiss."

Boone heard him but paid no mind. He couldn't stop touching his wife, holding her, caressing her cheek, and putting light kisses on her mouth. When she stirred and opened her eyes, he could breathe again.

"Boone?" she whispered.

"Hush, honey. You're fine, just fainted with the shock of seeing another of my brothers or seeing me shaved and clean," he told her and hoped that's all it was. "Rest a spell."

She shook her head from side to side. "I must be dreaming, Boone."

"It's no dream, Rachel. Moses got them to let me clean up, and even the cot's clean, or you wouldn't be laying on it. Are you sick?"

Her mouth stretched into a smile, and she blushed. "No, Boone, I'm fine."

"You wouldn't be laying on my bunk in jail if you're fine, honey."

She twined her fingers through his with one hand and touched his face with the other. "Don't fret, Boone, I swear I'm not sick."

"You'd best tell him," Ezekiel said from outside the cell. "He's gonna worry if you don't."

Fear clutched his chest like a fist. "Tell me what?"

Maybe she was sick, he thought, maybe with something bad like consumption. She hadn't acted herself for weeks, and he'd noticed.

"This isn't where or how I wanted to tell you this, Boone," Rachel said. "I wanted it to be just the two of us and you free."

"Honey, say it. Whatever it is, say it."

"I want to sit up first," she told him, then swung her legs across the cot. "Come sit beside me, Boone, and I will."

He thought his belly might reject the tamales he'd eaten, and his hands trembled as she faced her. He took both her hands in his. "Rachel?"

"Boone, I'm with child," she said, her voice so low he could barely hear it. "I'm carrying our baby. It'll be born next September."

Her eyes met his, and he read the truth of it in their depths. For a moment, he forgot he was locked in jail and that he might hang. The wonder of it filled him with a wild joy, and he wrapped his arms around her and held her close. She leaned against him with a sigh. He'd needed this more than the wash or the food, Boone thought. He'd needed Rachel in his arms.

"She's roused, so she can come out now," Deuce stated. "If the sheriff comes in and finds her in there, I'll be hanging right after you."

"Leave them be," Moses said. "Another few minutes ain't gonna hurt."

Boone put his hand flat over her stomach. "We're gonna have a baby."

She nodded. "We are."

"Weren't you gonna mention it?"

"I was, but I hoped to tell you after you're free," she told him. "Nobody knew but me, Ezekiel, and Mary. Your brother figured it out almost before I did, and Mary, she just knew."

He came to his feet and raised her with him. Then he kissed her, arms locked around her, with a slow, sweet tenderness. Boone touched her abdomen again, and then he grinned.

"Honey, I love you," he said. "You're gonna have to go, though. I don't have the fancy words to say what this means to me, Rachel."

She rested her head against his chest. "I know, Boone, though."

He kissed her one more time, then let Ezekiel take her from the cell. Boone locked gazes with his brothers. "You both take care of her," he said, with a fierce passion. "You treat her like she's made of glass or like she's a flower. Until I get out of here – and God willing, I will – you hafta care for her. Promise me."

"Boone, we will," Moses told him. "You know that."

"I already am," Ezekiel said.

"Take her home, kid," he said. "Honey, I'll see you tomorrow."

Rachel reached out and stroked his cheek. "I love you, Boone."

He watched her go, aware of each movement she made, willing her to go steady and not fall. The news settled through his brain, and he realized everything had changed. When – and he vowed it would be when and not if – he walked out of the jail as a free man, he would be not only a husband but one with a child on the way. He wondered how his money had held out for her and realized he'd need more to provide for a family.

Moses remained, and as if he read his thoughts, he said, "It makes a difference, don't it?"

"It does," Boone said. "How'd you know to come to Texas?"

"Ezekiel wired me."

Boone chuckled. "I told that scamp not to let anyone know, but I can't be mad. I'm glad you're here, Moses."

His brother smiled. "So am I, brother, so am I."

"You must have near flown to get here this quick."

Moses' smile faded. "It was a long, hard trip," he told him. "Rode my horse to death getting here. Traveling in the winter made it worse."

As he spoke, Boone realized something – Rachel couldn't make the trip, not in her current state. It would be much too difficult and dangerous for her. Nor could they travel so far with a tiny baby. For the first time, he thought maybe he wouldn't be going home to Kentucky, but he had no notion what he might do.

"You'll have to tell me all the news from home," Boone said. "I wrote a letter that I got married, but I'm guessing it didn't get there before you headed out."

"No, it did. Boone, we got to get you out of this place."

Boone nodded. "You'd best go. You must be wore out from riding so hard. We've got rooms, and there's a place for you there. Rachel will have something to eat, too."

"I'm going. Liam's supposed to come, and we'll talk about how to get you free. Tomorrow, I'll tell you all about the family."

"I'd like that."

"Boone?"

"Yeah?"

"The kid's gone and grown up, hasn't he?"

Boone smiled. "He makes me proud, Moses. He's a fine young man, and I'd trust him with my life. He's got plenty of sand and iron."

Ezekiel came to the door and gestured at Moses, who laughed. "He's back to guide me to your place, Boone. I'll be back tomorrow."

Boone looked around his cell. "I'll be here."

Once he was alone, save for the deputy, who dozed at the desk, Boone sighed. Thanks to his brother, he felt human once again and like a man. Although he'd seen Rachel each day he'd spent in jail, those moments when he'd been able to hold her close and kiss her filled his soul with joy. When she'd collapsed, he had been terrified, scared enough that he had thought he might be sick, but when she shared his news, he had been struck dumb with happiness and pride.

He'd filled her and made a baby on their wedding night. There was no doubt, for it was the only time they had come together in the flesh. The reality of her pregnancy made him want to holler out loud with delight, and it brought home the fact he had to get out of jail. He had to live – he couldn't hang and leave her a widow with a child on the way.

With two meals in his belly, a vermin-free cot, and the novelty of cleanliness, Boone slept through the night for the first time since being locked up. If he dreamed, he didn't remember it at all but woke with a renewed sense of purpose and hope. And he had family.

Since the day he'd ridden off to fight in a war he still didn't begin to understand, Boone had left his family behind. He'd grown up with plenty of love, but during the war, he'd been alone. His fellow soldiers had been the closest thing he had to kin. They had become his surrogate brothers, especially Liam, Mac, and Deke, who remained in his life.

The war had been terrible most of the time, and he'd suffered, as had they all. But when he returned to Kentucky, Boone felt like he no longer fit within the family. He'd become the outsider, the stranger who looked on and might be loved but wasn't part of the life they led. He hadn't been there when people were sick or hurt. He hadn't struggled with them to put food on the table or fought the elements to save a crop. They continued to weave the fabric of their lives without him. He had planned to stay but hadn't.

Boone had changed, too. A man who'd fought for four long years, killed men in battle, and bled couldn't be the same good-natured farmer he'd been before. He'd been restless at home, edgy, and seeking something he couldn't quite find. When Deacon Lee found him and talked him into heading to Texas, he'd gone, although he still figured he'd return one day.

Five more years had passed, and he'd settled into a new life that centered around cattle. He trailed cattle to Dodge City and Abilene in Kansas, a few times to Colorado or other places. Then Liam started a ranch, and he went to work for him year-round. Boone had written a few letters home and received some in return, but he'd been settled in his ways. He never worried about if he was happy or content and never gave a thought to the future. Boone existed, and that had been enough.

Some of the war wounds, the ones that didn't show, healed in those years through hard work, but he had forgotten how much he lacked until he'd been shot and Rachel came into his life. Without her, Boone had no doubt he would have died, and her tender care evoked something he'd never known before, love for a woman. As a young buck at home, he'd courted a bit, but he'd never felt for any girl what he did for Rachel.

She brought biscuits and gravy in the morning, and he ate them, still as hungry as if he hadn't eaten for days. Although he had to remain within the cell, her presence pleased him, and he held her hands through the bars.

"Do you feel well, honey?" he asked, scanning her face for any sign that she didn't.

"I do, Boone," she replied. "I get sick to my stomach sometimes, but that's part of it."

"Where's my brothers?"

"Ezekiel's at the stable. Moses went to see if he could get someone to talk to him about things," she told him.

If anyone could get the straight story about his shooting or the blacksmith's murder, it would be Moses, Boone thought, and his hope increased. He thought of a hymn his mother favored, one that sang about saving a wretch like me. Boone was that wretch, he thought, and maybe between his brothers, Liam and Rachel, they could save him from the hangman's noose.

# CHAPTER TWENTY-FOUR

Rachel thought once Boone knew about the baby, she'd be able to settle down and be content. But, since she hadn't planned to tell him until he was free and since he was still in jail, she remained restless. Getting Boone released, not hung, was the main worry she carried, but there were others. Money was another. She'd paid a month's rent when she rented the rooms, and before their wedding day, Boone paid another four months. He'd urged her to hide what money he had with Ezekiel's help, and they had tucked it into the lining at the bottom of her trunk. When they hid it away, there had been some of his last wages along with his faro winnings, but it hadn't been as much as before. Furnishing the rooms had taken more than half of it, by her reckoning.

The needs of their household were simple. Ezekiel bought most of the food with his wages from the livery stable and hunted a lot of the meat. He gave her money to buy other things, like soap when needed, but she worried about running out of cash. Her small stash had been spent before she married.

On the first night that Moses Wilson shared their supper table, he broached the question of finances. "How are you fixed for money?" he'd asked Rachel over the fried rabbit dinner she served with potatoes and beans.

"Boone had a bit," she told him. "But we spent a great deal of it furnishing this place, for we needed everything from pots and pans to linens."

"Is it all gone?"

Ezekiel spoke up. "No, it's not, Moses. I been spending what I can from what I earn over at the livery. Are you in need?"

Moses shook his head. "No, I have a little, enough for my needs and some skill at cards. I can do some work, too, if need be. I just wanted to know how y'all are fixed."

"Don't be worrying about money," Liam said. He had joined them for the meal, so there were four at the table. "I've got enough scratch to help if need be. We need to get Boone out of that hell hole, though."

His words encouraged Rachel, and she managed a smile.

"Fill me on what you think happened, both with some madman shooting my brother and the deputy killing this blacksmith," Moses said. "I need all the details you have, then I'll go out digging for the truth."

Liam provided the information which Rachel had heard several times. It was apparent that Sheriff Johnson had a grudge against Boone, although no one knew exactly why. When he'd mentioned the battle at Sharpsburg, where his brother had died, the Sheriff seemed to suggest that Boone was responsible. Rachel thought there was more there as well, but she didn't know what. Nor could she figure out why the deputy would have killed Kurtz, although she knew firsthand what an unpleasant man he'd been. He had few friends.

"You'd best go wary," Liam told him. "If you spook the sheriff, he'll take it out on Boone or hang him. That gallows gets closer to done every day despite the weather."

The talk of the gallows upset Rachel, and since everyone had finished eating, she cleared the table and busied herself with the dishes. Her back ached, and so did her head. Fatigue crept over her, and she longed to finish so she could sit down again or, even better, lie down.

A pair of hands reached from behind her and picked up a dish to scrub. "Let me help," Moses said.

His offer surprised her. "It's women's work," she said.

"My Ma has more sons, not daughters," he told her. "We all learned early to help. I've helped Ma many times in the kitchen. Go sit down. I promised Boone I'd watch out for you."

Rachel almost refused, then decided to accept his help. She dried her hands and turned to him. "Thank you. I shouldn't – you must be tired yourself. You came a long way to get here."

"I spent last night at the Double B," he told her. "The rest of it was very long and very hard, but today wasn't a bad ride."

She nodded. "I liked the ranch very much."

"It's a fine place."

Standing beside him, she remarked on what she'd noticed before. "You do favor Boone, don't you?"

To her eyes, he stood as tall and was built much the same. From the back, she would have taken him to be Boone, she thought. His face was similar, even more so than Ezekiel's, with the same eyes and a solid chin.

Moses laughed. "I do, for my sins, the most of any of us, I reckon. Ezekiel does, too, but maybe not as much as me. Jacob, back home, does the most. That sheriff mistook me for Boone when I first hit town."

No one had told her. "He did? What did he do?"

"Threatened to shoot me for escaping until Liam and Zeke showed up," he told her. "That's why he let me get Boone cleaned up."

As he spoke, he washed and scrubbed dishes, then pans, his hands buried in the water she'd heated. She'd expected him to be clumsy, but he was efficient. Rachel watched for a short time, then decided he was doing a good job so she sat down at the table with a sigh. What she really wanted was to go to bed, stretch out under the covers, and sleep until morning. Instead, she listened to the men talk as they spun theories about how to free Boone until she became drowsy.

"Rachel," Moses said, his hand on her shoulder. "Go to bed. You're falling asleep in the chair. I'm going myself."

"I will, then," she told Moses. Rachel wanted to be up early to cook for Boone, a process which now often took longer if she had to stop and be sick. She had venison to cook, thanks to Ezekiel's hunting and more mouths to feed. Most of it hung in a smokehouse where he'd wrangled space, but there was a haunch to prepare, one that would feed them all.

Liam had gone back to the hotel the night before, and Ezekiel, after bringing up two buckets of water from the communal pump, had gone to the livery. Moses remained asleep, snoring, which Rachel liked. It made her feel less alone. As dawn unfolded over Laredo, she busied her hands, preparing a meal she would first deliver to Boone and then share with the others later in the day.

Cooking usually brightened her mood, but this time, the meat smelled gamey and of blood, which turned her stomach. She vomited twice before she got it seasoned, browned, and roasting. Moses rushed into the kitchen as she puked for the last time in the farthest corner away from the food.

She heard his footsteps and managed to say, "Don't fret, I'm all right."

"I'd rather not answer to Boone if you're sick," he said.

"It's the shape I'm in," Rachel replied, alluding to her pregnancy. "From what Ezekiel said, you ought to be familiar from your sister-in-law."

"I wasn't told to watch out for her," he told her with a chuckle. "Boone may have been gone from the family a long time, but he's still my brother. When our daddy died, he took on the responsibility of us all, and he worried plenty. I can see you mean the world to him and I promised to see to you until he can."

"I'd say you know him well," she answered with a smile.

"You likely know him better," Moses said. "Ezekiel more than me now 'cause he's been here longer. But Boone is still Boone – more now than when he came home from the war. When we first got that wire that he'd been shot and was expected to die, it hit us hard. I near about came then, but we figured – Ma and me – that he'd live or die long before I could get here. He's in a poor place now, but I cain't hardly imagine how bad he was then."

Rachel didn't like to think about it, even now. "He came close to dying," she said. "But I could fight that. I can't do anything about whether or not he's hanged, and that scares me."

"I'll do everything I can," Moses assured her. "I told our Ma he wouldn't die from being shot, and he didn't. I'm telling you now that he won't hang, either."

His optimism pleased her and lightened her heavy heart a small fraction.

"I want to believe that."

"What are you cooking with the venison?"

"I thought I'd do potatoes, carrots, and onions," Rachel told him.

"If you made noodles, Boone would be over the moon," Moses said. "It's one of his favorites."

"Ezekiel said his favorite is chicken and dumplings."

Moses laughed. "It is, but he fancies noodles, too, and I doubt much he's had any for some time. Fact is, I wouldn't mind a bit of them myself."

Noodles were simple to make, so Rachel did, with nothing more than eggs, flour, and salt. It would take a little longer since they'd have to dry first, but she didn't mind and figured if the meal arrived a bit later, Boone wouldn't care either.

It was almost noon when she set out for the jail with Boone's dinner and a bottle of hot coffee. Moses accompanied her. Boone stood at the bars, waiting, his forehead creased with a worried frown, but when he saw Rachel, he smiled.

"I started to fear you weren't coming," he told her. "Are you well?"

She nodded and handed the plate through the narrow slot. "I was cooking. It's venison – Ezekiel got a deer."

He lifted the checkered napkin from the plate and grinned. "Venison and noodles!"

"It was my idea," Moses told his brother. "She was gonna make taters and carrots."

"That would have worked," Boone replied. "But I've had a hankering for noodles. What's the day? Is it March?"

Although there was a calendar hung on the wall, Rachel saw it was probably out of Boone's line of vision.

"It is, today's the third of March and a Friday," she told him, wondering why it mattered. It meant that on the 13th, Boone would have spent three long months behind bars and most of their marriage.

"Zeke's birthday is the 5th," he said. "I reckoned since it's the first time I've been near him on the day in years, we might ought to do something to mark it."

"I could cook one of his favorites – what does he like?"

"He's fond of pudding," Boone said. "Or pie. Maybe you could take a bit of money and get him a gift, maybe a pocket knife. Man can always use one."

Rachel nodded. "I can do both, most likely. He'll be sixteen?"

"He will, and I recollect when he was born – makes me feel like an old man."

She laughed. "You're not, Boone."

Although he was thinner and despite being clean as well as a bit worse for wear, Boone remained more cheerful than he had been, she thought, but the sheriff was in high spirits, and that concerned her. Johnson sat at his desk whistling off-key with an odd look on his normally stern face. Although he hadn't spoken when they arrived, Boone had barely finished his meal when Johnson rose and came over to stand within a few feet of Rachel.

"He's eaten, so you need to go," he said. A weird grin touched his lips. "I can't have you hanging around the jailhouse. Besides, Mrs. Wilson, your husband will swing soon – the gallows is almost finished, as you might have noticed."

She hadn't, but his words caused a sharp dismay. She bit her lip hard in her effort not to reply to avoid providing him any additional ammunition. Her throat ached with unshed tears, but Rachel refused to give him the satisfaction. Boone's expression shifted, and he handed her the plate.

"It tasted fine, honey," he said, but from the look on his face, he might have well as eaten barbed wire or ground glass.

"Might as well tell her what you want for your last meal," the sheriff said. "Give her time to plan it all out. I don't expect to wait past next Friday or Saturday at the latest. Saturday hangings usually draw a crowd."

If she hadn't reached out to grip the bars with one hand and Boone's fingers with the other, Rachel would have fallen to the floor. She schooled her face to remain calm, for Boone's sake.

"That ain't happening," Moses said, although he had gone pale. "My brother will walk free before then."

Johnson laughed, but there was nothing merry about the sound. It was dark and bitter, like rotten walnut hulls. He said no more, having spewed his poison and spread his damage, but returned to his desk and began to whistle once again. This time, although still out of tune, Rachel recognized it as "John Brown's Body," a Union song, so she knew it was chosen on purpose to devil Boone.

"I was at Antietam, too," he remarked. "That's where my brother fell and where you killed him, Reb. The day I watch you hang will be sweet vengeance."

"Vengeance is mine, I will repay, saith the Lord," Moses quoted from the Book of Romans. "Best you not forget that, lawman."

If a look could kill, Moses would have dropped dead onto the floor with the power of Johnson's glare.

"Don't mind him, Boone," he said in a quieter voice. "We'd best go, but it ain't over, so don't lose heart."

Boone stared at them both with anguish in his eyes. Rachel managed to touch his cheek through the bars. "I love you, Boone Wilson," she said. "Remember, *entreat me not to leave thee.*"

A single tear escaped from one eye. "I love you, honey," he said, his voice cracked and broken. "But it'd be best for you and the child if you did."

# CHAPTER TWENTY-FIVE

Moses escorted Rachel away from the jail with all the manners and care he could muster. Inside, fear gnawed at him with such power that he had pains in his belly. His confidence that they could prove Boone innocent remained, but with a time limit, he worried he might not find the truth in time to save his brother. He refused to give up, however, and he would fight to save Boone up until the moment his brother mounted the first step to the gallows platform. Moses entertained the wild notion of breaking Boone out of jail but dismissed it. The sheriff would ride them down and kill both him and Boone, he reckoned. After that, he'd seek retribution from Ezekiel, Rachel, and even Liam, and that couldn't happen.

Rachel stumbled as they passed the rickety gallows, built with such speed that it rocked in the slightest wind, so Moses caught her. She began to weep then, and he steadied her as he led her home.

"Save your tears," he told her. "It's not gonna happen. Boone's not gonna hang."

As he said it, he prayed it was so.

"If that lawman has his way, he'll hang in a week's time," Rachel wailed.

Moses stopped in mid-stride and turned her to face him. "I don't intend to let that happen," he told her. "Neither does

Ezekiel or Liam or Boone's friends. I should have started sooner, but I'm asking around, and I won't quit till I find out the truth. You gotta stay strong, Rachel, for Boone and for that child. And you can't give up on Boone."

Her eyes narrowed as she watched, and then she did a quick nod.

"I won't," she told him.

He saw her safe home, then headed for the hotel to find Liam. He interrupted the man's late breakfast with his news and included what Johnson had said about Antietam.

"I was at Sharpsburg, too," Liam said, wiping his lips with a napkin. "Same place, different names depending on if you were Yank or Rebel. If Boone killed his brother, which I doubt, it wasn't intentional – it was in battle. Besides, it's highly unlikely, for that's where Boone took a bullet for me. He was wounded in the thigh, which the sheriff wouldn't know. We were in the cornfield, the first part of the battle. Casualties were high for both sides, and I believe they still call it the bloodiest battle of the war. Nine long years ago, Moses."

Moses did the arithmetic and realized Boone had been eighteen, the same as he was now. He figured Liam to be older but probably not by much, guessing him to be thirty or thirty-two now, in his twenties during the battle. "Will your word be proof enough Boone didn't kill Johnson's brother?" he asked.

Liam spread his hands wide. "I've no idea, but it should be. Deacon and Mac were there too, and their word should be good. I wouldn't doubt we can find a few more soldiers who fought there as well, right here in Laredo. It may help, but Boone's to be hung for the blacksmith's murder, so that's the mystery we must solve. Johnson holds a grudge, tis' true but he can't hang Boone for Sharpsburg."

"I reckon he had him shot for it, though," Moses said. He'd thought about it since hearing how Boone had been shot and factoring in what Mary had told Rachel.

"It's likely," Liam replied. "And if I find it's true, at the very least, I'll see him finished as sheriff. But right now, we must find out who killed Kurtz, or your brother will hang for it, and that's not an option. Boone saved my life three times. I'll do everything I can, short of breaking the law, to save his, and I might even consider it."

"I intend to find out who killed the blacksmith," Moses stated. "I may not have seen my brother for near about five years, but I know it wasn't him. Why did the sheriff think it was?"

Liam rose and paid his bill. "Let's take a walk, kid."

Moses figured the man might not want too many ears listening in as they headed for the river, where they walked along the water. Liam paused to skip a stone, then sighed.

"It's a long story, but I'll make it short if I can. Rachel came here to be the schoolteacher, and as such, she boarded with the Kurtz family. She hadn't been here all that long when she saw Boone. He'd been shot, and his friends would carry him out to the saloon porch every day to take the air. Everyone, including Boone, figured he would die, but Rachel, she saw it different. She took up with Boone, fed him when the rest had been too afraid to feed a fever, and started nursing him. 'Twas Rachel that dug that bullet out of his chest and Rachel that tended him. Ezekiel came in from the ranch when he heard Boone was shot and dying. Rachel sent for her things to the blacksmith's house, and Kurtz came screaming to the saloon, calling her names, and carrying on till Boone threatened to shoot him from his sickbed and Mac laid him out cold. That was bad enough, but then he spread rumors about her all over town."

"He's a sorry excuse for a man, then."

Liam laughed. "He was. Then he tried to grab Rachel on her way home from church one Sunday, and when she wasn't inclined to go, he hit her hard enough to bruise her cheek, and when Ezekiel stepped in, he blacked his eye and knocked him down. By then, Boone was well enough that he heard the commotion and came down, gun in hand. He threatened to shoot the blacksmith if he didn't let go of Rachel and suggested he might want to leave Laredo."

"Can't fault him for that."

"I'd done the same if it'd been my wife," Liam said. "But when Kurtz turned up dead a bit later, the sheriff figured Boone had done it, and if not Boone, then Zeke. There wasn't a shred of evidence, and the night Kurtz was killed was Boone's wedding night, but Johnson has his ax to grind, so he arrested Boone. He's held him in jail ever since – almost three months now. I've spent more time in town than on my ranch to make sure he doesn't hang Boone, and I sent a wire to the governor, who didn't do much of anything 'cause he wants more information. I figure that means evidence, which we don't have."

"Then we need to get some and fast."

Liam shook his head. "We need a confession, I think. Johnson's not going to listen to reason or consider evidence. But you're right – we need it quick."

A chill wind blew hard from the west and rippled the water. Moses shivered but continued to walk at Liam's side. "Who do you think killed him?" he asked, and when Liam started to shake his head, he added, "I reckon you got someone in mind."

"I thought at first it might have been Mary at the Out of Luck," he answered with a sigh. "She hated Kurtz, but she's fond of Boone – not like you're thinking, though – and she'd never let him rot in jail over this. Mary has no love for the sheriff either. Kurtz had many enemies. He was a rude man and wasn't liked. I figure whoever killed him had a personal reason, but I'd say they knew well it would get pinned on Boone. Whoever did it is walking around Laredo, I reckon, while Boone's in jail and the gallows was built."

It could be anyone he passed in the street, Moses realized. That made his task difficult. He envied Ezekiel, working in the livery stable where he would hear all the talk of the town and meet many of the locals. Since he resembled Boone so much, Moses figured most folks would know that they were brothers, but he wasn't sure if they might make them more willing to talk or less. He could hang around the mercantile store or the saloon, both places where people gossiped.

"I reckon I'd best go find this killer," Moses said.

Liam nodded. "I'll ask around, too. I'd planned to go out to my ranch this weekend, but I won't now. Time is short to prove Boone's innocence."

They headed back to town, then parted ways with an agreement to meet later for a supper featuring the venison Rachel cooked. Moses considered stopping by to see how she fared but decided he wouldn't. At the livery, he shared the latest with Ezekiel, whose cheerful expression wilted like a candle too close to a roaring fire.

"How'd Boone take it?"

"Poorly," Moses told him. "Rachel took it hard as well."

"This ain't right. Boone never killed that blacksmith, but it looks more and more like he'll swing for it."

"I don't intend to let that take place," Moses told him in a harsh voice. "We gotta figure out who killed him. You keep your ears open, kid, and I'm going to do the same. I'm heading over to the general store now, then after we gather to eat with Rachel, I'm going to the saloon. Someone knows who killed the man, and I mean to find out."

Ezekiel gave him a glum nod, and Moses embraced him.

"I'm going now – I'll see you at supper."

Moses had seldom smoked tobacco, though they grew it back home, but he craved a cigarette. If he did, he reckoned Boone, who'd smoked from an early age, must, too. At the mercantile, he bought fixings and then returned to the jail. The sheriff was not at his desk, but the deputy was.

"You already visited today," he told Moses.

"And I'm visiting again," he replied. "Gonna have a smoke with my brother if you don't mind, and even if you do."

"Sheriff Johnson won't like it."

"He ain't here."

The hard-eyed deputy nodded. "Go ahead, but if he comes back, I'll vow you didn't ask."

"Boone," Moses said as he stepped over to the cell. He rolled two cigarettes and fired both. "Brought you a smoke."

Boone gave him a puny smile and took the smoke. "Thank you."

He drew hard on it and inhaled the rich tobacco.

On impulse, Moses turned to Deuce. "Deputy, you want a smoke? I'll provide the fixings if you do."

"I wouldn't mind one," the man said. "It's a filthy habit, but I took it up during the war."

"Blue or gray?"

"Blue," Deuce replied. "I served with the sheriff here and others in Laredo. Kurtz was one of them, and so is the Baptist preacher. Did you serve?"

Moses laughed. "Considering I was but thirteen when the war ended, I did not. Are there more of you Yanks here, then?"

"A few more," he said. "There's Jenkins over at the bank and the two carpenters that built the gallows out here. A lot of Johnny Rebs, though, like your brother there."

While Boone savored the smoke, Moses dug deeper. "I didn't know the blacksmith was a Yankee," he said, although he had.

"He was part of the Army of the Potomac like me, 93rd New York Infantry," Deuce said. "He wasn't worth the bread he ate, though. I had no use for the man."

In the middle of Moses' chest, a tendril of hope uncurled. "I'd heard he wasn't well-liked," he said.

The deputy finished his smoke and spat on the floor. "With good reason, he wasn't. My wife came from northern Virginia, and when the war came, she went back to her pa's place in Loudon County. In 1864, troops went through the Shenandoah Valley and burned a lot of farmers out, my wife's folks among them, and they were Quakers. I had been wounded and wasn't part of it, in an Army hospital, but Kurtz was. According to Lydia, he took carnal knowledge of her. He vowed he didn't, but she pointed him out to me when we came here and told me."

Moses' heart beat hard and fast, but he kept his tone casual. "No wonder you didn't care for the man. I didn't know you were married."

Since he'd been in town no more than a couple of days, he wouldn't, but he was fishing for more information. Deuce took the bait. "I ain't no more – she died of lung fever last winter."

"I'm sorry," Moses said, and though he didn't like the deputy, he meant it. "I hope you had some young 'uns, though."

Deuce shook his head and dug into a desk drawer for a half-empty bottle of whiskey. After a long swig, he said, "No, no little ones. After the way he used her, she couldn't have any children. I don't like to talk about it, but Lydia said he tore her up."

Moses looked at Boone, who nodded. "I'd best go before the sheriff returns, but thanks for the chance for a smoke."

The deputy took another drink and said, "That blacksmith deserved what he got. He didn't deserve to live. You'd best git."

"I'm gone."

Moses paused to exchange another word or two with Boone.

"He's been sippin' that liquor all day," Boone told him in a low voice. "Might have loosened his tongue some."

Moses grinned. "Might have, Boone."

With any luck, he might have found the blacksmith's killer. The deputy had motive, he thought, and opportunity. Now he would ask around, maybe find a witness or someone who knew, and then he'd do what he could to get a confession from Deuce.

He left the jail with a lighter step and a brighter outlook. He had a week – if God could create the heavens, earth, animals, and man in seven days, then surely, he could save his brother from hanging in the same amount of time.

# CHAPTER TWENTY-SIX

Early on Saturday morning, Rachel had made a trip to the mercantile to buy a knife for Ezekiel's birthday, as Boone had suggested. Then she returned home, and although she'd wept on and off for much of the day, Rachel baked bread to serve with the venison and noodles, then baked an apple cake as well. She would save the cake for tomorrow and had also bought some ham slices to fry for Zeke's sixteenth birthday meal.

Tomorrow, on Sunday, she'd take Boone ham along with fresh bread with butter as well some cake. She had baked to stay busy and keep her mind from the threat of Boone's hanging. From the window of their second-story rooms, she could see the gallows, built from fresh pine that was still yellow, so she avoided the view. As she worked, she prayed for a miracle, more worried now than when he'd been so ill after being shot. Rachel had been able to fight the infection and fever, but she was helpless against the sheriff's plans.

When they arrested Boone on the day after their wedding, she'd thought he would be back that day or within a few. But the days became weeks, then months, as she struggled to keep hope alive. Now that the sheriff announced his intention to hang Boone in a week, despair took root, and Rachel had trouble fighting against it. The single tear that had tracked down Boone's face hurt to remember, and so did his parting words after she'd referenced her promise not to leave him. He'd told her it might be better for her and the child if she did. *He might as well have slashed me with a blade,* she thought. *It couldn't have hurt more.*

He meant well, she knew, but she wouldn't leave him, not while he lived. If he did hang, Rachel would be there, although she knew very well how ugly and horrible hangings were. Hangings were still used as public execution, and she'd seen a few in the past. She recalled the details all too well, the struggle for breath, the way a hanged man's face could turn purple or black as he suffocated, the rank stench as they often soiled themselves at the moment of death, and the terrible dance on the gallows. Rachel couldn't bear to think about it now, or she'd go crazy. She also had a crazy fear that if she watched, it might mark the baby.

"I don't want to be a widow," she said aloud. "I don't. I can't be one."

"You won't have to be," Moses told her. He'd entered, and she hadn't noticed, caught up in her thoughts. Earlier, his expression had been as sober as a priest at a funeral, but now his eyes danced, and he wore a smile.

"Don't say it to cheer me," she replied. "I was there, same as you, and heard the sheriff. Unless something's changed, my Boone will hang."

"I believe I know who killed that blacksmith," Moses stated.

The words hung in the air between them with substance, and Rachel stared at him. She struggled to make sense of them, and when she did, she cried out.

"How? And who?"

Moses shrugged. "The deputy, Deuce," he told her. "And with a little liquor in him, he has loose lips. He more or less said he killed him, Rachel. Kurtz did wrong to his wife. I mean to find a witness or two, then get the man to confess. If he does, then they can't hang Boone."

She wanted to believe, needed to hope, but still, she said, "It won't stop that sheriff. He's got it in for Boone."

"Liam knows that much, but I gotta find him and tell him about Deuce. He already knows about that, Mad Mike, what you found out."

Rachel reached behind and untied her apron, then reached for her bonnet.

"Whoa, what are you doin'?" Moses asked.

"There's one person who might know something," she told him. "Mary at the saloon and I mean to go ask her."

"Boone wouldn't want you at the saloon, I reckon."

She narrowed her eyes and glared at him. "We spent a long time in an upstairs room there, Moses, and no, I don't suppose he would. I've been, though, a few times. Graciela in the kitchen's been teaching me to make some of the Mexican dishes Boone likes, the *frijoles,* tamales, and such."

"Kitchen's different," he mumbled.

"It's under the same roof, and I've no reputation left to ruin," she told him. "I'd go to hell and talk with the devil if it might keep Boone from hanging."

Her mind was made up. Although she liked Moses, she wasn't fond of his judgement, but he surprised her. "I'll go with you, then," he said after a few moments of silence. "I planned on going there anyhow, but she don't know me."

Rachel parted her lips to protest, but he shook his head. "Rachel, it's near evening. The saloon will be crowded, and you ain't walking in there alone. Boone would rip me but good if I let you go alone. In fact, we'd best go round the back and through the kitchen anyway. And we'd best hurry – Zeke and Liam will be coming for supper before long."

He made sense. "Then let's go."

She led him down the narrow alley behind the building and through the kitchen door of the Out of Luck. Graciela glanced up with a smile, then saw Moses and frowned.

"Mister Boone is out of jail?"

"It's not Boone but his brother," Rachel said, clipping her words short. "Get Mary. We need to talk to her."

Graciela protested, but Rachel refused to listen.

Mary exploded into the kitchen, as volatile as dynamite. Her face burned red, and her mouth was twisted with anger. "What the hell is going on?" she demanded. "It's busy out there, and I was told to go to the kitchen? Rachel Wilson, this better be worth my time."

Rachel didn't cower but stood her ground. Moses stepped out in front of her.

"It may be worth my brother's life," he told her. "You gonna listen?"

Some of the heat faded from her face. "I heard he was to hang within the week and I'm sorry to hear," she said. "I like Boone."

"He's not if I can prove who killed Kurtz," Moses said, arms folded across his chest. "And I believe I know who it was."

"Do tell," Mary said. He sketched out the story for her, and when he'd finished, she nodded. "That may well be. That deputy was here, getting drunker than a skunk that night. I saw him myself, and so did a lot of folks. Don't mean he killed the blacksmith, though."

"There might be someone who saw more," Rachel said. She moved toward the door, and Mary blocked her.

"You're not going out there in the saloon," she said. "Have you lost your mind?"

"I have not."

"Let me go ask," Moses said. "Maybe one of your gals or someone else saw."

"That might take half the night," Mary replied with a wicked grin. "They're working."

"I've got the time and the money if need be," Moses said. "Let me see Rachel home, and I'll be back."

"I don't want to go home," she told him.

"Rachel, it's gonna take time, and you've got to be there to give supper to the others. Tell them what I told you and what I'm doing," he answered. "If I'm to keep that noose away from Boone's neck, there's no time to waste, is there?"

She hated to admit it, but he was correct. "No," she said. "Stay – I can find my way back. Promise you'll come no matter how late to tell me what you learn – Liam and Ezekiel, too."

"I will – I'm bunking there, after all. I'll catch Ezekiel, and he can walk you home from here," Moses said with a sigh. "You're a hard-headed woman, Rachel."

For the first time all day, she smiled. "I am, and I'll wait for Ezekiel, then."

Dark fell before he traveled past the saloon from the livery, and the night turned cooler than the day. Rachel waited near the door on the porch where she'd first seen Boone with Moses at her side. He called out to his younger brother and told him the news.

"So, you're sure it's this deputy?" Ezekiel said as Rachel shivered in the frigid air.

"I am," Moses said. "Now I have to prove it or get him to confess. Both would be for the best. Would you take Rachel home? Liam will be along, and you can tell him what I found out."

"Aren't you coming?"

"Naw, I gotta do some asking around," Moses said. "I'll come there, but it may be late."

Despite being chilled and unable to feel her feet, Rachel smiled until Zeke studied her with an intense look. "You're likely to catch the ague," he said, with concern. "If you come down sick, Boone will lick me."

"I seldom take ill," Rachel told him and hoped it was true

in this case. "Once I get warmed up and eat, I'll be fine."

Ezekiel brought more wood and stirred up the fire in the stove. The venison and noodles were still warm, and the bread, placed on the back of the stove, was too. He carried up water as well while she let the heat take away the chill. By the time Liam arrived, she had set the table and had the food ready to serve. She kept back half of one of the loaves for Boone and a portion of apple cake. Rachel planned to save some of the meat for him as well.

They gathered at the table and ate the meal she prepared. Their mood was upbeat because, for the first time, there was genuine hope that Boone would be saved from hanging. Moses had not yet come, but Liam had seen him over at the saloon, so they were all aware of the revelation about the deputy, Deuce.

"If anybody can find a witness, it'll be Moses," Ezekiel said with confidence.

"I hope he can," Liam told them. "If not, we'll have to convince Deuce to confess, for I fear the sheriff won't accept anything less. I'll talk to Judge Masters on Monday since tomorrow is Sunday, though, and let him know what's in the works. To make sure it's all legal, I'll want him to exonerate Boone."

His use of big words reminded Rachel that Liam had once studied law, which eased some of her remaining fears. He would know and understand the legal system.

"What about the sheriff?" she asked. "If he hired that man to shoot Boone, can't he be jailed?"

"I hope so," Liam replied. "At the least, we can see he's removed from office. I don't know who will replace him, though, since Deuce is his only deputy."

"You could do it," Ezekiel suggested.

Liam laughed. "I could, but I won't. I'd have to be in Laredo all the time, and I'm missing my family and ranch now. Soon as this is over, I'm going home. There must be a former military man or someone who's worn a badge who can serve as sheriff."

Rachel thought of his ranch and knew if she were in his shoes, she'd be there. She had found the place peaceful and longed to return. Although Boone had often spoken of his plans to return to Kentucky, she would be content to live on the ranch, especially with the child on the way. For a few moments, she daydreamed about it, then wrenched her thoughts back to reality. She would go, as she'd promised, where Boone went without complaint or argument.

Moses did not appear during supper, so she set back food for him as well as for Boone. Liam departed for his hotel, and Ezekiel offered to assist her in cleaning up. Rachel almost yielded, but the chores kept her mind occupied, so she had him help, but she did most of the work. She was so tired by the time she'd finished that she planned to retire, but she knew, as weary as she felt, she probably wouldn't sleep. Her mind would race through the possibilities, both good and evil, keeping her awake. She probably wouldn't drift off to sleep until the early morning hours.

"Will you walk with me to church in the morning?" she asked Ezekiel.

"I will, Rachel," he told her.

"I'd like to go by the jail and see Boone first if we can." It would be early, but she had a desperate need to see her husband.

"I reckon we can," he said. "I'll plan to rise early."

Rachel had gone into her bedroom and was taking down her hair when Moses arrived. From the jubilant sound of his voice, she thought the news he brought must be good, so she returned to the main room to find him tussling and laughing with Ezekiel.

"Rachel, I did it," Moses cried. "I found a witness who knows Deuce shot the blacksmith."

The impact of that struck her like a thrown stone, and she

staggered. Her vision dimmed, and she thought she might swoon again. Rachel gripped the edge of the table, heart pounding and breath short.

"Then Boone won't hang?" she managed to say.

"No, ma'am, he won't," Moses hollered and slapped his younger brother on the back. "Found a witness who'll swear the sheriff paid Mad Mike to shoot Boone too, then hung him for it. He intended for him to kill him dead, but Boone didn't die."

Boone didn't die. Rachel hung onto those words and then repeated to herself, Boone won't die, Boone won't die, Boone won't die.

And please God and the Blessed Mother Mary, she prayed it would be true.

# CHAPTER TWENTY-SEVEN

Moses returned late, reeking of tobacco smoke, cheap perfume, and probably whiskey as well, but he couldn't keep from smiling despite a hammering headache that threatened to split his skull and deep weariness. His shoulders were taut, and his back hurt. He had accomplished his mission and had discovered a witness who could confirm that Deuce had killed Kurtz. It had taken long hours spent in the saloon, playing cards, talking until his throat ached from the effort, and the help of a soiled dove who said her name was Daisy. His first thought had been that she wasn't as fresh as one, not now, and the second was that he doubted very much that was her true name.

Until recently, he seldom smoked, but he had at the saloon, as much to pass the time as anything, and he'd had one drink. Whiskey wasn't a familiar taste for him, though his home state was as well-known for bourbon as it was for tobacco. Ma hadn't encouraged drinking, and Moses had never got into the habit. He realized he hadn't eaten since the previous night, so it was no wonder his belly growled and grumbled.

Although it seemed near impossible, he'd only arrived in Laredo less than a week ago after riding hard for the better part of two months. During the journey, he'd craved some rest when he arrived, but there had been little. He'd slept at Liam's ranch, but since hitting town, he'd slept when he could, consumed with the huge task of saving Boone from the noose.

For the moment, the rush of exhilaration at discovering the witnesses they needed kept him going. Moses realized he needed to eat and sleep, but for now, he didn't. Rachel poured him a cup of coffee, strong from staying hot on the stove, and brought him a plate of food. It was more than a little dry from the oven, but he ate it anyway and gulped two cups of coffee. Moses took the written page from his pocket and gave it to Rachel for safekeeping.

He wanted to go find Liam and share the news, but Rachel reminded him it was near midnight and he could wait until morning.

"You look tired," she told him. "Get some sleep, Moses."

That was his plan, although, despite his bodily ills and overwhelming fatigue, he couldn't sleep. Instead, his nerves were on high alert, and although he laid down, he couldn't unwind. Beside him, Ezekiel slept deep enough to snore, which annoyed Moses and kept him awake. In the end, unable to fall asleep, he rose and sat at the table. He rolled a cigarette and smoked it, then finished off the rest of the coffee.

The food he'd eaten lay uneasy in his belly, and when he thought he might vomit, Moses rose and started down the outside stairs. The idea of dunking his head in the horse trough on the street appealed as well because he had a notion it might ease his headache. The cold water in the night air made him gasp, but it didn't do anything for the pain in his head. He all but crawled back up the steps but never made it to bed. Instead, he sat down at the table and laid down his head.

The next he knew, he roused as sunlight illuminated the room. He winced against the glare.

"Moses?" Ezekiel said. He sounded both exasperated and concerned.

"Yeah?"

"You sick?"

Moses sat up and rubbed his eyes. "I don't reckon," he said. "Just worn out."

"You never went to bed."

"I fell asleep here." He hadn't lost the headache, but it had diminished, and he didn't feel quite as wretched as he had.

"We were worried," Rachel said, biting her bottom lip. "If you're hungry, I just made flapjacks. I'm taking some to Boone while they're still hot, along with some bread and butter, some cake I baked for Ezekiel's birthday, and the last of the venison."

He caught the word 'birthday' and remembered.

"Kid, it's not that I forgot, but I didn't get anything to remember the day…" he started to say.

Zeke grinned. "You gave me the best birthday present ever, finding those witnesses, and Rachel give me a knife from Boone," he said. "I even had a silver dollar to give her back for it, you know, like Ma always said."

"Happy birthday, Ezekiel. So, you're off to the jail?"

Rachel nodded, "We're going to see Boone, then church. Then I'll be home to cook rabbit stew for supper. Do you want to come with us?"

Moses did, but he didn't. "I'm gonna eat, then clean up first. I reek like the saloon after last night."

"I figured you'd want to tell Boone what you found out," Ezekiel said, with a slight frown.

"I will, but I don't want the sheriff to catch wind of it," Moses told him. "He might get angry and hang Boone before we can get the judge up to speed. I gotta talk to Liam, and tomorrow, he can get Judge Masters. Rachel, can you put up that paper from Daisy?"

She nodded. "I'll put it away, hide it with our money. That's about the murder – you said you had a witness that the sheriff hired that man to shoot Boone, then hung him to hide it, too?"

"I do. It's one of the hands from the Galloping Paint Pony Ranch," he told them. "He was drinking at the next table, overheard the whole thing, and saw the sheriff pay that Mike to try to kill Boone. Name's Caleb, but he can't read or write, so he'll have to tell his tale in person."

Rachel put a plate of flapjacks before him, patted his shoulder, and headed out the door with Ezekiel. She wore her best dress, he noticed, the one she was married in and her bonnet. Moses ate the food, then he washed up as best he could and changed to a fresh shirt. He walked down to the jail, squinting against the sun, which revived his headache. He resisted the urge to dunk his head in another horse trough and entered to find Boone finishing the last of Rachel's bread. He glanced up.

"Son, you look like you been rode hard and put up wet," Boone said with a mixture of amusement and concern. "Are you poorly?"

"I've been better," Moses said. "But I'll do – I'm played out and got a misery in my head. Stayed too late at the saloon last night, I reckon."

The wrinkle in Boone's forehead evened out. "Do tell," he replied with a faint grin. "Did you win at cards?"

Moses waggled his hand up and down. "Won some, lost some, but I did get the jackpot I was hoping for."

From the light in his brother's eyes, he could see Boone understood.

"That's likely to come in handy," he said with a sideways glance toward the sheriff.

Johnson grunted. "For him, maybe, not for you," he said. "You already had your visitors for the day – what's he doin' in here anyhow?"

Now that he'd passed along the message, Moses would go. "Leavin'," he said, his battered hat in his hands. "I'll see you tomorrow, Boone, probably be Liam and me. Reckon maybe Rachel ought to stay at home – she's got cooking to do, looking out for some company."

"Sure," Boone answered. "Can I get a smoke from you before you go?"

Moses rolled a cigarette and handed it through the bars, then lit a match on his heel. The aroma reminded him too much of the Out of Luck, and he thought he probably wouldn't spend another evening in the saloon for a long while. He craved the wind in his face and the smell of the outdoors. If he had the time, he'd take a long walk along the Rio Grande, but instead, he marched off to find Liam to share the news.

He found the rancher lingering over a late breakfast at the hotel. It took some urging, but Moses insisted he couldn't share the latest unless they had privacy, so they ended up along the river bank after all. They walked beside the water as Moses sketched out what he'd learned and what evidence he had. It pleased Liam. His eyes sparkled, and he slapped Moses on the back.

"I'll see the judge first thing in the morning," he cried. "Then we'll round up this Caleb character and the statement from Daisy. It should be more than enough to spring Boone and to get charges filed against both the deputy and the sheriff. We need to send for a lawman, though, to take over or find one."

"I might have a lead on that, too," Moses told him. "I met a man named Amos Murdock while I was in the saloon for so long. He graduated, like General Lee, from West Point back before the war and was an officer before he resigned his commission to wear gray. He talked about being a sheriff of a little town up Virginia way, and he seemed solid."

"I'll see if I can track him down today," Liam said. "I'll be glad to see Boone freed and an end to this mess. I want to go home. I've missed most of the calving season as it is. Then, it'll be branding season. Summer will be here before I know it, and I'll need to be trailing cattle. My wife's most likely forgotten what I look like, and I expect young Grace doesn't remember she has a Da. I wish Boone would take on that top-hand job instead of heading off to Kentucky."

So did Moses. "He might," he told the other man. "Now that Rachel's in the family way, he might change his mind."

"I'd be happy if he did," Liam replied. "As for you and young Ezekiel, I'd be proud to take you on as hands as well if you were interested."

Moses thought of the long trek he'd made to get to Laredo. He recalled how the tobacco crop had been lost to grasshoppers and how times had been more than a little lean. Jacob and Garrett had begun working more with the horses after that. Once Moses announced he was heading to Texas, they took over the horse work. If they all went back, he feared there wouldn't be enough work to go around. Guilt smote him as he realized he'd yet to tell either of his brothers about the crop. The few days since he arrived seemed more like a month, and he'd been fighting to free Boone hammer and tong. He liked this country, though. and wouldn't mind remaining.

"I may well be," he told Liam. "I'll let you know once all this business is done."

"If you do and I've already gone, just come to the Double B," Liam said. "There'll always be a place for any of you three brothers on my ranch."

"I appreciate that, and I'll see," Moses replied.

"Fair enough."

They parted ways so Liam could see if he might find the lawman and see if he'd have an interest in becoming sheriff. Though Liam didn't live in Laredo, he took the business of the community to heart. Moses headed back so he could grab forty winks. He'd need the rest to face the events Liam had planned for tomorrow.

Rachel had returned from church, and Ezekiel had gone hunting in his absence. She offered food, but he turned it down, promising he'd wake in time to eat at supper.

"I'm gonna see if I can sleep," he told her. "I'm near about dead on my feet, and I need my wits for tomorrow."

"Do you truly think that Boone will walk out of that jail?"

"I do, Rachel."

"I want to hope," she said. "But I'm almost afraid to, but I'll pray."

"Prayer never hurt and will likely help," he said, wondering if he ought to ask her to pray his headache would go away, but he didn't.

She put the back of her hand against his forehead.

"I'm not fevered," he stated. "Boone and everyone else told me how bad I look, but I'm just tired."

"Go rest," she told him.

Moses headed into the smaller bedroom and the bed he shared with Ezekiel. He sat down, pulled off his boots, and set them aside. Then he stretched out, still fully dressed, and pulled a blanket up to cover his body. He never could sleep cold. His mind spun with thoughts of Boone, of how tomorrow would play out, and scenes from the saloon. He'd kissed more than a few of the gals but nothing more, although Daisy and another one had offered. Moses also reflected about Kentucky, thinking of his mother and hoping they could send her good news soon. He sighed to recall the tobacco crop, stripped bare by the insects, and hoped that the family fared well. Tobacco was their cash crop, and the loss of it would sting, although the farm – and the horses – should provide their basic needs.

His headache had receded in the clear, cool air by the river, but it had returned, and he feared he might not be able to sleep after all. At some point, he thought Rachel came into the room and straightened the bed covers over him. Later, he woke once to the sound of Ezekiel's voice, but he didn't rouse, and when he did wake for good, it was morning. He'd slept through supper and the night.

The bed was rumpled where Ezekiel had slept and had already gone. The aroma of coffee wafted through the rooms, along with bacon. His headache gone, Moses sat up, scrubbed his face with both hands, and put his boots on. There was enough water in the pitcher. He washed both hands and face, then joined the others for breakfast.

Today, everything would change, he thought – and with any luck at all for the better.

# CHAPTER TWENTY-EIGHT

Boone slept little, keyed up with anticipation that he might walk free. From what Moses said – or didn't say but couched in vague terms – he thought his brother had found a witness or evidence that would clear his name. After almost three months locked behind bars, he had trouble imagining walking into the street, but he wanted it. More than that, he ached to hold his wife close and to pick up the life they had barely begun when he'd been taken into custody. Sometimes, it seemed unreal, like a terrible nightmare, and in other moments, he lived the harsh reality of jail life.

From what Moses told him, Rachel wouldn't be coming to visit. She'd be at home, cooking, hoping he'd be there to eat. That meant no food or coffee, and that was fine, he mused, unless he didn't get released. If that happened, he would be hungry for at least a day, but after all he'd endured, Boone figured he could manage his belly. He wasn't at all sure he would be able to handle his emotions.

From a prone position, arms tucked under his head, on the bunk, he watched the sheriff and deputy. Neither seemed to have any inkling a change was coming, so Boone waited. Time dragged more than usual, and jail time was slow enough, but mid-morning, Liam entered, followed by the judge who'd married him to Rachel, his two brothers, a man named Amos

Murdock, and a hand he recognized from playing faro. Boone sat up, then stood, more than a little nervous.

"What's all this?" Sheriff Johnson said, coming to his feet. His face flushed brick red. "The prisoner can't have all these visitors. What's the meaning of this, Rafferty?"

Judge Ike Masters replied. "It's legal business, sheriff. I've got evidence that this man, Boone Wilson, is innocent of all charges and should be released immediately."

"That's nonsense! He's guilty as charged."

"Do you have evidence?" The judge's voice was smooth and even.

"I don't need any – everyone in town knows he tussled with that blacksmith who turned up dead."

"That's not enough," Masters said. "I have evidence from two eyewitnesses. Donald Baines, known as Deuce, you're under arrest and will be tried for the murder of Harold Kurtz. Sheriff, let Boone out of that cell now. He's free to go."

"I won't do that," Johnson shouted. "I don't believe you."

Liam spoke up. "Believe him, sheriff, and there's more. Murdock, get the keys."

Amos Murdock stepped forward, a stocky man with a large moustache. "It's my pleasure."

"He has no authority," Johnson said.

Judge Masters stared at the man. "He does or will in about five minutes. I'm swearing him in as the new sheriff as an emergency act. And I'm arresting you for attempted murder."

Johnson put up his fists as if he meant to fight. Before he could lash out, Murdock slapped him into handcuffs and then retrieved the cell keys.

"Amos Murdock, by the power invested in me by the state of Texas and with the governor's consent, I hereby swear you in as sheriff of the city of Laredo, Webb County, Texas. Do you swear to uphold the law?"

Right arm raised high, Murdock said, "I do, the law for the state, the country, and the Almighty, so help me God."

"As your first official duty, would you release Mr. Wilson?"

"Glad to," he said and unlocked the cell.

Boone exited the small space for the first time in three months. He stepped over to his brothers and embraced both.

Murdock then led the former sheriff into the cell and turned to Deuce.

"Do I need to use the handcuffs?"

Deuce shook his head. "I'll go without a fight. I'm guilty as charged, but it's not what it seems. Wasn't cold-blooded murder. That man did my wife wrong during the war."

"You'll have a fair trial," the judge said. "That's more than Johnson here gave Boone. You have my word on it."

The former deputy joined the former sheriff in the cell, and Murdock locked them both behind bars. Boone watched, heart pounding, hands shaking a bit. It had happened with such speed he had trouble wrapping his mind around it.

"Boone, go home," Liam told him. "I'm about to do the same. It's early enough I can make it to the ranch before supper time. If you need anything, give me a holler, and don't forget, that offer to be my top hand is still on the table."

*Home.* To Boone, that meant Rachel, not Kentucky. He shook Liam's proffered hand and turned to his brothers. "I'm free?"

"Yeah, you are," Moses said. "Let's get out of this place."

Flanked with Moses on his right and Ezekiel on his left, Boone walked out onto the street. It was a fine day, and the sunshine all but blinded him. After months inside, it was almost too much, and he ducked his head against the brilliance. When he'd gone to jail, it had been bleak winter and cold. Now, a March wind swept between the buildings on the street, and there was a hint of spring in the air. He inhaled to enjoy it, then almost tripped over his feet as he reached the muddy street. His legs were rubbery from lack of use, and Moses grasped his arm to stave his fall.

"Take it easy, Boone," he told him. "Wouldn't be any good at all if you got out of jail to be trampled by horses or run over by a wagon."

Boone almost laughed, but he didn't. He caught sight of the gallows, complete, although more than a little shoddy, where he would have hung by his neck until dead in a few more days. The realization of how close he'd come to the noose evoked a shudder, and he trembled.

"You alright?" Ezekiel asked him with a frown.

"Yeah, it's just a big change, being out in the world and knowing I'll live," Boone said. A variety of smells filled his nose, horse flesh, baking bread, beer, and whiskey from the nearby saloon, someone's slops emptied, and more. He sniffed and realized he smelled, too. "I'd like a chance to shave and maybe bathe before Rachel sees me, though."

Moses laughed. "I'll spot you at the barber if you want – don't know about the bath unless Mary over at the saloon will let you take a bath. She might – the woman likes you, Boone."

"I've no notion why, but she does," he said. He also wanted to ride Sprat fast and furious along the river to blow away the cobwebs that cluttered his brain. It made sense to do that first, so he told his brothers. The next thing he knew, he'd saddled Sprat and was off, riding hellbent along the Rio Grande with the sun on his back and the wind in his face. He couldn't resist parting his lips for a Rebel Yell as he marveled in God's outdoors. When he'd finished, he surrendered his mount to Ezekiel and headed for the barbershop. Since it turned out that the barber had limited bath facilities, he had a good wash, his hair trimmed, and a shave. When he'd finished, he dressed, eager now to see his wife.

His brothers withdrew to provide privacy for the reunion,

but as Boone mounted the steps to the rooms he shared with his wife, he almost wished they were at his side. An odd shyness crept over him as he climbed. He loved Rachel beyond any doubt, but their courtship had been anything but ordinary. They'd met when he was sure he would die very soon, but instead, she'd nursed him back to life. They fell in love over his sickbed, and once he healed, they wed, but on the day after their wedding, he had been arrested for a crime he didn't commit and had sat in jail.

Somehow, the world seemed larger now, and the space he'd craved while locked up now daunted him. He wanted to make himself small, he thought, almost hide away so he wouldn't be seen.

Boone realized he'd spent as much time away, if not more, from her in jail than he had known her before the wedding, and that made him a little shy. Over the past three months, he'd seen her no more than a few minutes each day except once, the day he learned he would be a father.

Wondering what he might say and how she would react filled his mind, and he almost turned around to bolt, to return later once he'd figured those things out. But Boone steeled himself and opened the door to walk into the main room.

Rachel stood in the kitchen, her back to him, as she stirred something on the stove. Aromas wafted toward him, bread baking, something cooking, and the sweet scent of a cake. Her hair was braided, then pinned into a bun at the back of her head, and Boone paused, struck at the sight of her.

"Rachel."

When he spoke her name, she didn't turn around as he expected. "Moses, is Boone still in jail?" she asked, in a voice as brittle as old bones.

"I'm not," he said. "It's me, honey."

This time, she whirled around and dropped the spoon in her hand. She stared at him with wide eyes, face gone pale. Time seemed to stop, and he wondered for a long, terrible moment if she wanted nothing more to do with him. Boone couldn't blame her if she had, but his heart would shatter if that proved to be so. He scrutinized her, noting that her face was thinner, gaunter than he recalled, but beneath the apron she wore, her midsection was a bit thicker. If he wasn't aware of her pregnancy, he doubted he would notice, but he did.

"Boone," she said, her voice low, somewhere between a moan and a whisper. "Oh, Boone."

He took a step toward her as she flew across the room, then she was in his arms. Boone held her close against his chest, his arms locked, holding her in place. Rachel rested her head against his chest. She smelled of faint lavender and cooking, a scent he savored. The reality of having her in his arms brought tears to his eyes. He'd almost given up on the notion he'd ever be free or with his wife again. She wept a little, face buried in his shirt, and he tightened his embrace. Right now, he never wanted to let her go, and he could stand here forever.

After what seemed like a long time, she raised her face to him.

"Is it over? Are you free?"

Throat clogged with emotion, he nodded. "It is, and I am, honey."

Rachel lifted one hand to caress his cheek. "Are you well?"

Boone nodded. "I'm fine, Rachel, better now than I've been in a long time. Are you alright?"

He released his grip and freed his left hand to lay across her belly. He could feel the slight curve there and knew it for his child.

"I am," she told him with a smile, the first since he'd walked through the door. "I still get sick some mornings, but otherwise, I feel good."

He kissed her, sweet and lingering, the taste of her pleasant to his mouth. She brushed her fingers across his face. "You've shaved."

"And bathed," he said. "I wanted to come home to you without the stink of the jail on me."

Rachel laughed. "As long as you're here, I wouldn't mind, but I'm glad. Are you hungry?"

"My belly's as empty as a church on Monday," he told her. "I'm near starved."

"You're skinny," she said. "There's coffee made. Come sit and have a cup while I fix you something to eat."

"What are you cookin'?"

"Turkey and dumplings," she replied. "Ezekiel got a turkey rather than a chicken, fried squirrel, ham, beans – frijoles the way you like, and green beans cooked with a ham bone. I'm going to fry potatoes later and bake another cake. There's some left of what I baked for Zeke's birthday, and I plan to make bread or biscuits. I have sausage, too. I can make biscuits and gravy if you'd like."

His mouth watered at the list of food. "I would," he said. "I'll drink coffee and have a piece of that cake while you're cooking if you don't mind."

Her smile became a grin. "I don't, Boone."

Before he released her all the way, he held her close. "Woman, I love you."

"I love you, Boone, so very much," she replied.

He kissed her again, another long, sweet kiss, then took a seat at the table. Rachel brought him coffee and cake. He sipped the coffee, savoring it, and ate the sweet as he watched her work. Boone admired the way she moved with such deft precision and grace.

As she cooked, he talked to her, telling her how he'd been released, and she listened.

"I'm glad your brother Moses came," she said as she put a

plate of biscuits and gravy before him. "He's been a help, Ezekiel, too, of course."

"It's good to have them here, both of the yahoos," he replied. "Need to send a letter off to Ma, though, to let her know I wasn't hanged after all. Come eat with me, come sit down."

She protested, and then she did. "I'll get heavy," she told him.

"You're eating for two," he replied. "You won't."

Eating at a table again, with his wife for company, brought a deep delight. Boone enjoyed the food, but he liked the company more. Doing such a simple, normal thing as sharing a meal seemed like a miracle after his months in jail. When he'd finished, he yawned, and she noticed.

"You're tired," she said. "You should go sleep awhile. The rest of the food won't be ready for hours yet, not till supper time."

"I ain't slept good for three months," he said. "I'll rest a spell, but only if you lay down with me."

Boone ached to make love to her, but he worried about harming the child, although he thought it was too early to matter. He was weary, though, and he figured they had time for lovemaking later. Sleep called him, and when she nodded, he took her by the hand, and they retired in broad daylight.

He removed his boots and tossed them to the corners of the room, then lay down beside her. Boone spooned against her, and when she sighed, he knew she was contented, too.

He was home, a place he had feared he'd never be again, and it was all he'd dreamed about and more.

# CHAPTER TWENTY-NINE

He seemed bigger but thin, she thought, almost larger than life. Rachel woke long before Boone and watched him sleep, his face slack in repose. She cuddled against him, glad for his proximity, still wanting to pinch herself to prove she wasn't dreaming. Boone was home and free. The last few months had been terrible, worse in many ways than when he was so ill after being shot. Then, she'd been able to work toward a goal, but while he was locked up, Rachel could do nothing but wait.

Although she longed to stay beside him, she had cooking to do, so she untangled without waking him, smoothed down her dress, put her apron back on, and found her shoes. She walked into the kitchen and washed the dishes they'd used earlier, ones that had been soaking since their late breakfast.

She had two loaves of light bread rising, the turkey roasting after being parboiled first, and was sifting flour for dumplings when Moses and Ezekiel walked through the door.

"Isn't Boone here?" Zeke asked with a dismayed expression.

"He is," Rachel replied. "He's sleeping."

Moses yawned. "I could sleep for three days, I reckon."

"Grab a nap, then," she suggested. He didn't look as haggard as he had, and she figured Boone's release had eased most of his worries.

"I might," he said. "I don't want to sleep through dinner."

"I'll make sure you wake," Zeke said. "Got anything I can eat now, Rachel? I'm hungry."

"I do," she told him and fixed a plate. "Moses, do you want to eat a little now, too?"

He shook his head. "I'd rather catch some shut-eye while I can."

By six, dark had fallen, and the feast she'd spent the day preparing was ready. There was the promised turkey and dumplings with some of the bird sliced placed on a platter, a dozen fried squirrels, some fried fish from the river, fried potatoes, light bread, frijoles, green beans with ham, some fried ham slices, biscuits, and a dried apple cake. Rachel roused Boone with a kiss. He rolled over, bleary-eyed, then grinned at her.

"Thought for a minute I'd dreamed being out of jail," he said. "But it's real enough, I reckon."

She kissed him again. "It is. Supper's ready if you want to come eat a bite."

At the sight of the laden table, he paused. "Woman, I'd almost swear it was Christmas."

"We missed Christmas," she told him. "It can be Christmas if we want it to be and a celebration that you're here."

"Then we will," he said. "I haven't had much of a holiday in years. Oh, Liam does it up brown at the ranch but it wasn't like having family. Well, you know – didn't you go there at Christmas?"

Rachel nodded, recalling the pleasant ranch, Liam's wife, Maggie, and the little cabin that they could call home if Boone accepted the job Liam kept offering. "I did, and I liked it very much."

Boone narrowed his gaze as he looked at her, and she wondered why. "Let's eat. I'm hungry again."

They gathered around the table with his two brothers,

asked a blessing over the meal, and ate until they were all full. Rachel received compliments on the food she'd cooked, but her eyes remained on Boone. Maybe her cooking was as delicious as they said, but she didn't care. Her husband was back, and that meant more than anything else but the child she carried. Almost every time she chanced a glance at Boone, she caught him looking back at her, although he talked and laughed with his brothers. After the meal ended, Moses offered to clean up, and after a slight hesitation, Rachel nodded.

"Thank you," she told him. Weariness clung to her like a heavy blanket. After today, she figured she wouldn't cook so much in one day, not until after the baby came. "Moses, you're a gentleman."

All three Wilson brothers hooted, and Moses blushed. "Not me," he said. "Ma just raised us right."

With the table cleared, Boone lit a smoke, and Rachel smiled to see how much he enjoyed it. "I figured on writing Ma a letter," he said. "Maybe send a wire, but that would mean someone's gotta go over to San Antonio."

"I can go, Boone," Zeke said.

"All right. Guess we'll get the letter mailed soon, or else Moses can take it when he goes back to Kentucky."

Rachel sighed. She'd miss Moses if he returned although unless Boone had changed his mind, they would follow in the future. It wouldn't be in the spring, not with her condition unless Boone insisted. They couldn't travel easily with a newborn, either, and if the baby was born in the fall as she expected, it might be a year from spring before they could go.

"Uh, Boone, about that," Moses said, returning to the table as he wiped his hands dry on a cloth.

"Yeah?"

"I don't know that I'm going back, but we need to talk, brother."

Rachel stilled, aware that whatever would be said must be momentous.

Boone stared at his brother, and she couldn't tell if he was angry or curious. "What is it, Moses? Is there ill news from home?"

Moses sat down backward in a chair and faced his brother. "I wouldn't say it's bad, Boone. Everyone's well or was when I lit out, but times are hard. I don't know how to say this, so I'll just tell you – grasshoppers came last fall, a plague of them, and they ate up all the tobacco standing in the field. We didn't get a crop, not at all. Both Jacob and Garett started working with the horses, nothing else, and took it over when I left."

"How bad is it?" Boone asked in a quiet voice. Rachel scooted closer and took his hand in hers to offer comfort.

"Nobody's starving," Moses told him. "We still got the other crops in, mostly. Garrett don't mind farming – I think he likes it even more than the Morgans. It's just that there's not as much there to support another mouth or work for my hands if I return. Fact is, I like Texas right well. Maybe not Laredo so much, but this country. I spent a night at the Double B when I first got here after my horse keeled over dead, and I liked it. Liam offered to take me or Ezekiel on as hands should we want to stay, and Boone, I do."

Watching Boone's face, he gave no reaction, but his hand tightened around hers.

"I'll be," he said after a long pause. "I never thought but that you'd be heading home soon as my business was done, one way or another. What would Ma think if you don't return?"

All this was a revelation to Rachel, and she waited to hear the answer.

Moses dug out his tobacco and papers, then rolled a smoke. He fired it with a match Boone handed him, then blew out smoke. "We talked about it some before I left," he told them.

"We didn't know what I'd find when I arrived. For all I knew – and feared all the way – you might have been already hanged and planted. If that had been the case, I figured on bringing the kid back home. I didn't know, though, he'd grown up since I'd seen him, and I wasn't sure what your wife might want to do. Ma did get the letter you'd married. I hoped to find you living and did. I didn't think much after that about home, just did all I could to get you out of that jail and see you didn't swing. But, Ma, she said it might be different now, and she talked about how losing the 'baccy changed things."

Boone's voice was a quiet drawl. "So, you're telling me there ain't much to go home to and that it might be best if I don't?"

He sounded distraught, and Rachel reached up to touch his face with her free hand. He cupped his over it and turned his head to plant a brief kiss on her mouth.

"I ain't sayin' that at all, Boone. You know well you'd be welcome if you go home. You been missed all the time you been gone, first in the war and then being a cowboy. But if you don't, Ma's a strong woman. She's got Garrett at home and Jacob near. Hells bells, I'd miss the lot of them too if I do stay, but sometimes you gotta do what you gotta do."

"That's true. Ezekiel, what about you? Are you wanting to stay in Texas?"

The young man ducked his head and then nodded. "I'd rather, Boone, but I'll go with you if you go, when you go. I'd rather not be parted, and that's a fact."

"What about Peggy?"

Ezekiel's face turned scarlet. "That wasn't nothing but flirting," he said. "Besides, she's moved up from dancing to all of it."

Rachel hadn't known, and from his face, neither had Boone.

"I'm sorry, kid," he said. "Rachel, I reckon we need to talk a minute."

She nodded, and her heartbeat increased. Her head spun a little, too.

"We can clear out for a spell," Moses told them. "Zeke and I can go to the livery or the saloon or somewhere."

Boone nodded, and they went in a rush of clattering boots and quick remarks.

Once they'd gone, Boone turned to her, his gray eyes dark with emotion.

"Rachel?"

One word, and she knew what he asked. "I meant what I said the day we wed," she told him. "Ruth's words are mine, too. I will go where you go and lodge where you lodge, Boone. If I'm with you, I'm not particular as to the place."

"I meant to head out for Kentucky come spring," he said. "And it's almost that now. I figured we'd go back and take up a life there in the old house with my mother. I thought about it often when I lay with fever and when I reckoned maybe I'd die."

"If that's where you want to be," Rachel said. Her throat was tight with unshed tears. If he hurt, so did she.

"It is, and it isn't," he said, confusing her. "I ain't been there for five long years, more than that if you count the war. I went back afterward but didn't stay. It wasn't the same, and neither was I. That war changed me, Rachel, and I didn't fit the place anymore. When I thought I'd die for sure, I thought about home, and I yearned for it. Then you came into my life, and I want you more than Kentucky. It was my place, not yours, and I know that."

"I came from the same country, not so far away," she whispered.

"I know, but as soon as I knew you were with child, I figured we couldn't go this spring. It's too long and hard a trip. I'd worried any way how you could make it, but in your shape, there's no way. I won't risk you or the baby. I've studied on it a lot. We could still go after the baby comes, but probably not till spring again. It would be hard on a young 'un like that too, and I can't say, but you might be in the family way again."

His voice was low and rough with emotion. Rachel still held his hand, and his fingers wrapped tight around hers. "Boone, if Kentucky's where your heart is, I'll go with you."

"Woman, you're my heart," he told her. "You quoted the Book of Ruth to me from the Bible, and there's a verse I've had on my heart too – it's Matthew 6:21, and it says, "Where your treasure is, there's where your heart will be also." I want to be where you are, where you're happy, Rachel."

"I'm not sure what you're trying to tell me, Boone," she said, her voice cracked and breaking.

"I wouldn't mind staying in Texas," he said. She released the breath she'd been holding. "I'd like to be Liam's top hand as long as you're my wife, and you're good with that. All the more so if my brothers stay. I got two more at home, and though I love them dearly, what we've gone through together here has bonded me with Moses and Ezekiel. I don't want to stay in Laredo, but if you do or you'd rather go to Kentucky or off where you got kin, I'll go. That's what I'm saying. Tell me, honey, if you want to stay in Texas or not."

Her tears came fast and hard like a summer thunderstorm. She couldn't contain the sobs and she struggled to stand up to say what she must. When she pushed her chair back, Boone leapt to his feet.

"Hold me, Boone," she cried. "Hold me close."

He wrapped his arms around her and cuddled her against his chest. She struggled to calm and to put together the words.

"I love you," she began when her sobs had quieted. "I love you today, and I'll love you tomorrow, but Boone, if you ever loved me, love me now."

"I do love you now — just tell me where that's likely to be, all this lovin'," he said, his voice almost harsh.

"I want to live on the ranch," she told him. "Ever since I spent Christmas there, I've hoped we could live in that little dog trot cabin and raise our baby. I liked it there. It was peaceful, and come summer, it's likely pretty. It's not so far away, so the trip wouldn't be too awful, though I'd have to ride in a wagon now. But I only want it if you do, Boone."

"I do, honey. That's the life I'd like now. We'll have to write to Ma, but I think she'll send her blessing, and maybe someday we can go visit. I would like you to meet her."

"Then we'll go to the ranch?" She couldn't believe her secret dream, the hope she'd shared with no one, would be reality.

"Rachel, we'll go as soon as we can pack, and the weather's good," Boone said. "And then we'll get started living this life together."

His words were sweet in her ears. It was all she wanted and what she needed, now and always.

# CHAPTER THIRTY

Three weeks and a day after he was freed from jail, Boone hitched up the sturdy pair of draft horses to the covered wagon that Liam had provided and drove it over to the place they'd been calling home. His brothers were ready to load the goods. Rachel had spent hours packing up their possessions with his help, along with both Ezekiel and Moses.

A light March wind teased between the buildings in Laredo and rippled the waters of the Rio Grande. The sun shone, and the day was warm, both things that made Boone glad. The trip out to the ranch would take longer with the wagon, but he wouldn't allow Rachel to ride, so they would go slow.

It wasn't far past dawn as they loaded the wagon, and he figured the journey would take five or six hours, maybe more. They would reach the Double B by evening at the latest. When Ezekiel returned with the wagon, he brought greetings from Liam, who apparently was delighted that they would be in his employ.

The weeks had passed in a swift blur, but it had been a time of healing for Boone. He basked in his wife's love and the affection of his brothers. He had been able to sleep well, enjoy meals Rachel prepared and savor the world in a way he never had before, not even after the war.

Today, he enjoyed the warmth of the sun falling on his

shoulders, and the breeze carried the smell of spring. Boone relished both as he reflected how delighted he was to leave Laredo. Until he'd been shot, it had been nothing more than a place he came once in a blue moon to play cards. He'd never expected it to become a place where he lived – or where he almost died, twice of two different causes.

"You're the only good thing that I found in Laredo," he said to Rachel, who waited with her shawl tucked about her shoulders at the foot of the steps.

She smiled. "Your brothers found you here, too," she reminded.

"That's true," he said. He tilted her face up for a kiss beneath her bonnet. "But I'm not sad to leave the place behind, are you?"

Rachel shook her head. "No, not at all. I came here figuring I would stay, but I'm happy to be going to the ranch with you."

"Are you ready?" he asked, indicating the wagon seat. At her nod, he put his arms around her still slender waist and lifted her in place. Boone held her until she had settled into place. "Are you good?"

He wanted her safe and treated her as if she were made from fine, thin porcelain. He had before she carried their child, but now, Boone's focus was on Rachel's safety.

"I'm fine, Boone."

He climbed up beside her and picked up the reins. Zeke and Moses mounted, Moses riding Sprat. Boone clicked his teeth at the draft horses and hollered, "Gee haw!"

The horses lurched forward, and so did the wagon. "Hang on tight," he told Rachel. "If you need to stop, say the word, and we will, all right?"

"I will," she said and put a hand on his arm. "I promise, Boone."

The road that led out of Laredo and wound toward San

Antonio was more of a trace, narrow and rutted. Boone kept their pace to a slow walk, mindful of his wife. The open country on either side of the road had greened with early spring growth. Birds flew above the vegetation, and he could hear their bright songs in the morning air. A few bluebonnets were blooming, and Boone listened as Rachel prattled about the sights.

"Boone, you're slower than an old hound dog on the hottest day of summer," Zeke said, riding back to offer his opinion. "We ain't never gonna get there at this rate."

"We'll be there by supper time, probably before," Boone told the kid. "This wagon ain't built for fast travel, and neither is my wife."

"I'm gonna ride ahead, then," Ezekiel replied. "Maybe I'll shoot some game or something."

"Once we're there, Liam will provide the grub," Boone told him. "Still, it won't hurt to add something to the pot now and again. He's heavy on the beef."

Speaking of food reminded him how hungry he was. With everything packed and loaded, breakfast had been some cold biscuits washed down with hot coffee he'd begged from Graciela at the saloon. Rachel had packed some fried ham and bread for a noon meal along the way, and when they arrived at the ranch, Boone didn't expect Rachel to cook. Liam would likely invite them to supper, which he anticipated with pleasure. Whether they ate at the main house or at the bunkhouse with the hands, Liam put on a fine spread.

From a distance, he heard Zeke yell with urgency and wondered why.

"Something's wrong," Rachel said, her brow furrowed with a worry line.

"I reckon not," Boone replied and hoped he was right.

"Do you think it might be Comanches?"

She sounded more than a little afraid, and he reassured

her. "No, honey, I don't. There aren't many left these days, and those that are wouldn't be around here. We'll hear whatever it is when he rides back this way."

A good half hour or so later, Ezekiel returned at a gallop, with Moses riding behind him. Rachel had just shared a need to make water, and Boone had stopped the wagon. He had jumped down and come to help her when his brother rode up.

"Why are you stopped?"

"Rachel has a need," Boone replied. "What was all that ruckus a while ago?"

"Rattlesnakes in the bluebells," Ezekiel said. "Lots of them, Boone. I near got nailed when I stopped to do a bit of hunting. Best keep Rachel close."

Boone rested one hand on the butt of his Griswold, worn in a holster on his hip, as he scanned the fields of flowers and scrub. He didn't like snakes and had killed many on the trail. He'd seen a few men die from snakebite, and he'd saved Liam's life once after a large rattlesnake bit him. "I will, kid. Are you wearing your gun?"

Ezekiel nodded, and so did Moses.

"Don't hesitate to shoot if you need to," he told them. "Getting bit is a nasty business and often fatal. I'd rather not bury any of you or tend you if you get fevered."

Rachel peered down at him. "If there's snakes, I can wait, Boone."

"You ought not," he answered. "Let me get you down, and I'll keep you right here by the wagon. It's fine unless you go out into the field."

"Are you sure?"

"You can trust me with your life, honey."

She nodded, and he lifted her down to the ground. Then he led her behind the wagon as his brothers moved forward fifteen or twenty feet. Boone surveyed the area and saw no snakes. "Go ahead. I'll turn my back, and you can make water."

He listened and waited, then when she'd finished, he scooped her up into his arms.

"Boone!" she cried, but he could tell from her tone she liked it fine.

"What?"

"Put me down. I want to walk a little and stretch my legs."

He shook his head. "You're gonna have to walk right here, honey."

"I will. Don't worry – I'm scared to death of snakes, so I won't be getting in the field at all, not even to look at the bluebells."

Boone laughed. "I wasn't gonna let you."

He walked with her, one hand resting on her waist. Although he doubted any snakes would be in the road or near the wagon, he wasn't taking any chances.

"Are there a lot of snakes on the ranch?" she asked.

"No," he said and lied. There weren't a lot, but there were some. He recalled when Dexter Yates had killed a six-footer near the corrals, but now wasn't the time to share that with his wife.

"They won't get in the cabin, will they?"

"It ain't likely," he said. If she asked Maggie, she'd hear a different story, though. Snakes, especially rattlers, inside were uncommon, but it did happen. "That cabin sits up off the ground, honey, so they can't get in."

"I hope not," she said with a shudder. "I've helped nurse people who were bitten, and I've seen Granny kill a few with a hoe."

"Can you shoot?" he asked.

Rachel shook her head. "My brothers taught me how, but it was a long time ago."

"I'll teach you, first chance I get," he said. "Then maybe you won't fret so much about snakes."

She'd never been nervous since he'd known her, Boone mused, or afraid. She'd worried, sure, mostly about his health, but this fearful side was new. It came from being in the family way, he figured, and he remained patient with her.

"Oh, Boone, I don't know," she said.

He muffled a sigh. "We don't need to think about it this minute, honey. Let's get back on the road. We've got a long way to go, and we'll be stopping to eat a quick bite before you know it."

"You're right."

Once he had her boosted back on the seat, the reins in his hand, and the wagon in motion, Boone began to sing. He figured it would distract her from the snakes, and she'd liked it when he had sung to her once before.

"It's of a bold, young highwayman. This story we will tell," he began, and his brothers, who had returned to stick close to the wagon, joined in. "His name was Willie Brennan, and in Ireland, he did dwell."

Rachel scooted close to him, one hand resting on his leg, and listened with a calm expression as they sang many of their Ma's old tunes, from Brennan On The Moor and other ballads carried across the water to popular songs by Stephen Foster. They sang, Rachel sometimes joining in, especially on the few hymns they belted out. By the time the sun stood straight overhead in the sky, Boone was more than ready for a bite to eat.

He found a small creek nestled in a cluster of young trees and drove down to it. In the shade, he figured there would be few snakes, and the water would provide a drink for the thirsty horses. Rachel dug out the fried ham, bread, and the cheese he'd bought at the mercantile for sandwiches.

In the afternoon, it became hot, and to the west, thick clouds gathered. There would be rain by nightfall, Boone thought. If he remembered right, they had another hour or so to go to reach the

Double B. If it hadn't been for Rachel, he would have increased speed, but he didn't, so they plodded along. Ezekiel rode far ahead and returned, grinning with a wild hog he'd shot. He slung the gutted animal on the back of the wagon upside down.

"We'll have fresh pork tomorrow," he cried.

"And then we'll salt down the rest to have on hand," Boone said, thinking of the work that would lay ahead. He liked the idea, though, of some salt pork on the menu to break up the frequent beef.

By the time they reached the edge of the Bonnie Blue, the sun had dropped halfway down the sky. The glorious orange glow was framed by the heavy gray clouds that would bring rain. Rachel dozed beside him, and he roused her with a gentle hand.

"Honey, we're on the ranch. We'll be at the main house soon."

She smiled, and he thought his heart would burst straight out of his chest with love.

Moses sidled his horse beside the wagon. "Boone, you want me to ride ahead and tell Liam we're coming?"

"Yeah, I do, you and Zeke both. I'm hoping to get there ahead of the rain."

The air hung heavy and humid. When Boone glanced back, he saw lighting illuminating the dark clouds. The setting sun was no longer visible. He'd lived in Texas long enough to recognize a thunderstorm in the making, and he did step up the horses' pace a little.

He pulled up to the main house, leaped down from the seat, and set the brake. Liam burst outside to greet him.

"Boone Wilson, I thought you'd never get here," he hollered. He slapped Boone on the back and greeted Rachel, still seated in the wagon. "Welcome to the ranch. I do believe it's fixing to rain so if you'll help your Missus down, you can park this wagon in the big barn. Maggie's got a room ready for you tonight, and I figured that the boys could sleep at the bunkhouse. Supper's near about ready, if you're hungry."

"I'm starved enough to eat a saddle blanket," Boone replied. "I'm glad to be here, Liam, and I thank you for the job."

"It's good for you, good for me," he said. "I'm over the moon you finally agreed to be my top hand. We'll start branding soon – likely as soon as the rain quits."

Thunder grumbled in the distance, and more lighting flared. A sharp wind brought a rush of cooler air, and he knew the storm was almost there. Boone lifted Rachel down and held her close for a moment. They had made it to the ranch in one piece and without incident. "We're here, honey. Get on in the house – Maggie's waiting, and I'll get this wagon put up."

She put her arms around him for a moment, and he kissed her, sweet and swift.

The rain hit before he returned, dashing through the downpour with his brothers beside him. Ezekiel had dealt with the hog, hanging it from a tree till morning. The rain wouldn't affect it in the least and it would be fine as long as no critters got to it, unlikely with the weather. Moses had helped unhitch the dray horses for the night and park the wagon. All three were wet when they entered Maggie's warm kitchen, where Rachel sat at the table with a cup of coffee and a half-eaten plate.

"I told her not to wait, Boone," Magdalena said. "Soon as you dry off a bit, there's plenty of grub. Come fill a plate and sit down. Everyone else already ate."

He did his best to wipe off most of the rain with a towel, but a change of clothes would have to wait. Boone loaded his plate with tender beefsteak, fried potatoes, beans, and a pair of biscuits. He ate it all and had another biscuit. Ezekiel managed to wolf down two steaks and half a bushel of potatoes. Moses ate his fill, and then the pair dashed back into the rain to the bunkhouse.

"Let me help you clean up," Rachel said, but Maggie

shook her head.

"You've traveled all day, and I hear you're in the family way. You head upstairs to get some sleep. It's the same room where you stayed at Christmas."

By the time they climbed the steps, Boone was more than ready to lay his weary body down. Rachel removed her shoes but slid under the covers in her dress, an old calico. Boone stripped off his damp garments and hung them on the room's single chair to dry. Then he joined her, cradling her against him. Rain pounded down hard on the tin roof above them, and he liked the sound.

"We made it," he whispered to her. "We're here."

Her contented sigh filled him with joy. "I'm glad, Boone. I'm so tired."

"Sleep, honey. You just go to sleep and don't fret about a thing."

"G'night," she mumbled. "I love you, Boone."

Before he could tell her that he loved her too, she slept, and then so did he.

# CHAPTER THIRTY-ONE

Rachel woke, and for a moment, she was disoriented. Boone lay beside her, one arm still holding her tight. She inhaled his familiar smell, a bit wet and a lot horsey this morning, and relaxed. They were at the ranch, she remembered. Her back ached a bit, and when she untangled from Boone, she found her limbs more than a little stiff after the long wagon ride. It was cool in the bedroom and still raining outside. The sound of it made her need to pee, and so she rose to use the chamber pot in one corner. Her nose twitched as she inhaled the delightful aromas of coffee and bacon. It smelled wonderful, although her turbulent stomach threatened to revolt.

Boone stirred. "Honey?"

"I'm right here," she said and sat down on the edge of the bed. He wore a worried frown, and before he could ask, she added, "I'm fine, a bit stove up but good."

"Are you fixin' to puke?"

She laid one hand over her stomach. "I hope not."

"If you dig in my pockets, there's a peppermint leaf or two."

Rachel found one and chewed it. She'd found that it eased the nausea, but she hadn't realized he'd brought some in his pockets. It helped, so she put her shoes and stockings on. Boone, bare-chested, shivered a bit and reached for his clothing.

"They're not quite dry," she said. "I wish you had dry things to put on. I don't want you to catch a chill."

"I won't," he promised. "I'll sit by the fire when we get downstairs."

They breakfasted on bacon, which Liam called overland trout, which was apparently a cowboy joke, fresh eggs, and biscuits. Rachel slathered one with both butter and honey, then devoured it. After they'd eaten, she noticed that neither of her brothers-in-law had appeared. "Where's Ezekiel and Moses?" she asked Boone.

"Bunkhouse," he said. "They likely ate there with the weather. Deke and Mac are there, too."

Liam finished off his third cup of coffee. "By now, they're likely out gathering cattle," he said. "Gotta start spring round-up, Boone, and soon."

"In the *rain?*" Rachel asked.

Both Liam and Boone laughed. Even Maggie giggled a little bit.

"If we waited on the weather, we'd never get anything done," Liam said. "You're new to ranch life, Rachel, but you'll learn. Maggie did."

Rachel bit down on a sharp answer. They owed Boone's freedom in good part to Liam, as well as his new livelihood. "Do you have to go out, too, Boone?"

He shook his head. "Liam said I can get the cabin ready, so when it quits raining, we can get our things moved in. I've got that pig to cut up and salt down, too."

Her pique faded. "I want to help."

"Maybe if the rain eases," Boone told her. "I don't want you wet, woman."

"I won't melt – I'm not made of sugar."

Although they weren't alone, Boone leaned over and kissed her. "To me, you are."

"You can help me today," Maggie said. "I'm cooking beef and noodles."

"Do you cook for the hands, too?"

"They have Cookie," the other woman told her. "He does most of the meals for the bunkhouse. I sometimes cook for them, but usually not."

"I won't let her," Liam stated. "She's got enough to do as it is, and she can use the extra help, Rachel."

Maggie began stacking the empty plates, and Rachel followed her lead. Boone lingered over one more cup of coffee, then had a smoke. So did Liam. When they prepared to head outside, Rachel caught Boone's arm.

"You'll get wet again."

"Naw, this time, I'll put on a slicker," he said. "We'll be in for dinner around noon, honey."

Although dinner, served midday, was often the larger meal of the day, Maggie explained that on the ranch, they switched it, providing the heartier fare in the evening when the men had finished work. She had beans cooking for noon, and soon, Rachel helped make and roll out noodles to dry, then cut up beef to brown and simmer. Then, at Maggie's request, she made several loaves of bread. "They would like a switch from biscuits, I have no doubt," Maggie told her.

Boone brought them fresh pork from the pig Ezekiel had killed on the journey and salted the rest. The two women made the pork into sausage, seasoning it with black pepper, salt, sage, and onion. When they served it at breakfast, it proved to be a hit, different than the usual fare.

Adjusting to a working husband was more difficult than Rachel expected. Their courtship, such as it was, had been spent under extraordinary conditions in a single room, and then their marriage began with the groom jailed. Since then, they had prepared to come to the ranch, so she hadn't imagined her life while Boone worked. For the first time, although they spent the night together, he was up and gone for much of the day. At present, he wasn't far afield, just across the way in the cabin they would soon call home. Rachel missed him, and she missed Ezekiel and Moses, too.

It rained steady for the first few days after they arrived, and Boone's brothers were out rounding up cattle to the far edges of the ranch. Late on Friday, the rains ended, leaving a muddy expanse around the main house. The sun shone, and after the long day's work, both Moses and Zeke came up to the main house. They feasted on chicken fried steaks with mountains of mashed potatoes and cream gravy, then played Faro for nothing but fun with Boone and Liam until late.

On Saturday, Boone's brothers, along with his pards, Deacon and Mac, unloaded the wagon's cargo into half of the dogtrot cabin. For the first time, Rachel, who had admired it on her earlier visit, walked through the two rooms that they would call home. She entered from the covered dog trot between the cabins into the main room, finding it spacious. A large fieldstone fireplace covered much of one wall. A food hutch sat in an adjacent corner, and there were shelves to the right. Boone had already unloaded the table and chairs that Ezekiel had bought back in Laredo, and her rocker, another gift from Zeke, sat near the fire.

Behind it lay a smaller bedroom where the Wilson brothers had already set up the bed Boone bought before they left town. Her trunk rested in one corner and the washstand in another. A small chest rested against one wall, and there was a straight wooden chair as well.

Two windows, with glass, looked out across the porch to the main ranch house and the rest of the place. There was a door leading from the breezeway into each room, and as Boone had promised, the house sat off the ground with a space beneath.

Seven wide steps led up to the porch. Piles of their household goods sat around, some on the floor, some on the table.

"What do you think?" Boone asked, standing beside her.

"I like it," Rachel told him. The rooms above the saddler's shop back in town had been sufficient but plain. The cabin boasted a homey appeal, and she knew that they would be very comfortable in this space. For the first time, she realized it would be home to her and Boone, the first one.

"Don't frazzle yourself putting things away," he told her. "You tell us where to put things, and we'll put them there."

By the end of the long day, her cast iron pots and pans were hung on the wall, her utensils, dishes, and such had been stacked on the open shelves, and the food they'd brought was stored in the food hutch. Her trunk had been unpacked for the first time in years, and she'd arranged her brush, comb, and mirror on top of the chest in the bedroom. Their clothes hung from pegs on the wall in the bedroom or were tucked into the chest. Rachel had made up the bed with fresh bedding and topped it with a quilt, also from her trunk. Boone's gear was stacked in the small closet, and his Springfield rifle had been hung on the wall near the door.

The calico curtains she made in Laredo graced the front windows, and she thought, if she had time and energy, she would make a round rag rug for the floor in that room. A few of her prized possessions, a pair of candlesticks, a carved horse, and a vase rested on the mantle. When he saw the vase, Boone went out and picked spring flowers to fill it. Last, Rachel hung a calendar that Liam had given her and said, "It's the first day of April, Boone!"

"Springtime is here," he replied. "We start branding on Monday, and Easter is a week from Sunday."

It seemed impossible, but she knew it was so. Rachel grabbed a crockery bowl to mix biscuits for supper and a skillet to fry some salt pork, but Boone stopped her.

"We'll go eat at Liam's," he said. "Meals are part of the wages, Rachel, though I'd like it well if you cook here sometimes. But it's been a day, and I know you're tired. Besides, my brothers have already headed to the bunkhouse. So are Mac and Deke."

He made sense, and she knew it. "I'll cook tomorrow, though," she told him. "And then Ezekiel and Moses can come eat with us."

"Liam will also provide food to us," Boone said.

"I know, but I thought I'd cook those three prairie chickens that Ezekiel shot this morning."

They dined with the Raffertys and enjoyed the simple meal of beef stew with potatoes and carrots. Afterward, they came home together for the first time with a fire in the hearth and a sense of home. When Rachel would have retired, Boone pulled her into his arms. He kissed her slow and sweet, then began to dance with her.

"There's no music," she said, and he laughed.

Boone began to sing the hauntingly lovely tune that had been Stephen Foster's last, the romantic *Beautiful Dreamer*. As he sang and whirled her about the room with grace in a waltz, Rachel held tight to her husband. She enjoyed the dance and the contentment that accompanied it. They were finally home, and no threat of death hung over Boone. The love song delighted her, and afterward, Boone loved her with tender hands and slow, gentle caresses.

On Sunday, missing the chance to attend church, Rachel busied her hands with dinner. She roasted the chickens and seasoned them with onions and sage with a bit of salt. Near the last, she drizzled a bit of honey over them to sweeten the skin and make it crisp. She riced some potatoes for a side dish and made gravy. She used the last of the dried apples to make a pie, and they feasted on the first meal in their new home.

***

By late August, Rachel was clumsy, her belly large and her energy short. She stayed home most of the time, sewing small clothes for the coming child and waiting. Liam and most of the hands were gone on a trail drive to Abilene, but Boone, as top hand, remained on the ranch. Although many days he was gone from dawn till dusk, working cattle, riding the ranch boundaries, or other tasks, he came home each night. Sometimes, she still cooked a meal, but most nights, he walked her over to eat at Maggie's table, handling her with extreme care as if she were fashioned from fragile glass.

Once or twice a month, he rode into Laredo for supplies and to bring back any mail. On the last Saturday in August, Boone returned with two letters and a package from his mother in Kentucky.

"We've got mail," he announced as he burst through the door. Rachel sat in her rocking chair, all but dozing over needlework. "Ma's written us."

"She must have received the letters, then," Rachel said. She stood, put a hand to her lower back, which ached, and waddled to the table. Although they'd sent a wire before leaving Laredo, they waited to write until they were settled on the Bonnie Blue. Otherwise, any answers might have been lost somewhere. "I'm glad."

Boone sat down, rolled a smoke, and lit it. "I am, too, honey. I just hope she's not angry. None of us came home after all."

He ripped open the first envelope and read it aloud to Rachel.

*"Dear Boone, Ezekiel, and Moses, I received your telegram and then your letters, then rejoiced that you all are alive and well. I looked for you to return to Kentucky, but I understand why you have not. By the time you receive them, it may be near the time your child, Boone, will be born. Write and tell me of the birth and the name, if you will.*

*We are well here but still have some hard times due to last year's crop failure. I pray for each of you daily and pray that we will meet again, if not in this life, in the next. Your loving mother, Jemima Wilson."*

Rachel saw the tears in Boone's eyes as he read and reached out to grasp his hand in hers. He shot her a sideways grin, then opened the second letter.

"Boone, this is a baby shawl I made for you before you were born. I wanted you to have it for your child. Maybe it will be born on your birthday. Love, your Ma Jemima Wilson."

He handed her the shawl, a bit faded and worn but still serviceable. It was fashioned from soft flannel with hand stitching around the edges, a priceless heirloom and gift. Tears leaked down her cheeks, but Rachel smiled as she held it in her hands.

"When's your birthday?" she asked.

"September 26," he replied. "That's why I'm called Boone – 'twas the day Daniel Boone died in 1820 or so, and Ma wanted to remember. He's some kin to her, or so she always said. When were you born, honey?"

"The 20th of October," Rachel told him.

"It must have been a Monday."

"I believe it was, but why?"

Boone quoted an old poem. "Monday's child is fair of face, and you are."

Then he leaned across the table and kissed her.

Within, the child kicked, and Rachel took that as a good omen that he or she knew their daddy and the love he had for his family.

# CHAPTER THIRTY-TWO

The longer Rachel was pregnant, the more Boone worried. Every time he had to go out on the ranch to work, he feared she might fall into labor in his absence. Although she looked very well, no different except for the huge mound of her belly, he was afraid she might have a hard time in childbirth. Every sad story he'd ever heard about a woman who died giving birth haunted him, although he said nothing of it to his wife.

He might have confided in his brothers or in Liam, maybe asked them to allay his fears, but they were all out on the trail and likely wouldn't return until after the baby came. Boone didn't know Maggie well enough to talk to her about it, and he wished for his mother's wisdom. She would have the right words to calm his concerns, he knew.

The nausea that dogged Rachel in the first few months had gone. The first time she felt life, he had rejoiced. When the kid kicked, and she put his hand on her belly so he could feel it, Boone thought he'd bust his buttons with pride. He thought it might be a boy, although he'd be happy with a girl. Boone just wanted his wife to survive and the child, too.

September remained hot and dry, good for the haying but hard on Rachel. By mid-month, Boone spent many hours with the hay crews, ensuring that the hay that would see the herd through winter was cut, dried, and put up. He rode the fence lines with the new-fangled barbed wire Liam had brought last fall. On the 15th, he left the crews at work midday and rode back to the cabin with speed. Rachel had slowed over the past few days and had said little.

He found her rocking before a low fire, all doors to the outside open in the heat. Boone knelt before her and put his hands on her belly.

"How's my pretty wife?" he asked.

Her smile seemed forced. "I'm ready to have this baby," she said. "My back hurts, and I feel bigger than a buffalo."

The kid kicked hard against his hand, hard enough that her dress moved with the force of it. He'd seen it happen before, but it still shocked him. "Does that hurt?"

This time, though faint, the smile was genuine. "No, Boone. You're home early."

"I wanted to see you," he said. "You've been awful quiet, honey. Do you feel bad?"

Rachel shook her head. "I just don't feel good, Boone. My back hurts, and my belly's griping me today."

She leaned forward in the chair to rub the small of her back, and he stood up. Boone turned to pour a cup of the coffee from the pot, which was always over the fire, and found it empty.

"Have you ate today?"

"No, I didn't want anything. If you're hungry, I can fix you something."

"I'll go bother Maggie when I want some food," he said. "You just sit right there, honey. Would you be better to lie down for a spell?"

Rachel sighed. "I doubt it, but I can try. Help me up."

Boone grasped her hands and pulled her upright. As he did, a strange expression flitted across her face, and he heard a soft, wet noise.

"My water broke," she told him. "Oh, Boone, that means

I'm going to have this baby."

Fear clenched him hard and tight until his belly hurt, too. He needed to find a midwife, he thought, then realized the only women on the ranch were Rachel and Maggie. Boone drew a sharp breath and held it. He knew all too well that there were no neighbors close to the large ranch. There wouldn't be a midwife any closer than San Antonio or Laredo. He didn't have time to ride out to either place. A doctor, then, he thought, then knew the same applied. His pal, Deke, used to help tend those who took sick or got hurt on the trail, but he was out on the cattle drive now, along with his brothers and Liam, the sole other person who might know a bit about bringing a baby. Panic threatened to swamp Boone, and he tried to hide his fear from Rachel. "I'll go fetch Maggie, then," he told her.

Rachel stared at him. She'd gone paler than he'd ever seen, and her forehead was creased with a worry line. "Maggie can help, Boone, but she can't bring the baby, and she would have to have little Grace along."

The question shot from his mouth. "Then who's going to bring it?"

"You are," she said. His guts twisted into snakes that bit with pain. "I thought you realized it, Boone. You've delivered calves and foals, haven't you?"

He had many times. "It's not the same, honey. Who helped Maggie when Grace came?"

She shook her head. "Liam did."

Rachel gasped and gritted her teeth as her face changed. Boone recognized the look of pain. "What's wrong? Are you hurting?"

"I'm in labor. I think I've been having pains since early this morning, Boone. I thought it was just my belly bothering me, but now, I don't think so."

If he hadn't come in early, she'd been alone. A cold sweat

drenched him. "I'm going to get Maggie. I'll be right back, honey. Is there anything I can do first?"

"No. I need to get out of this dress, but I can manage. Just hurry, Boone, please."

He hurried from the cabin, jumped from the porch to the ground, and ran to the main house. Twice, he almost stumbled, but Boone didn't slow. He reached Liam's home and dashed to the back door, expecting to find Maggie in the kitchen. When he burst into the room, breathing hard, she looked up from stirring a mixing bowl.

"Is it Rachel's time?" she asked, with a calm he envied.

"Yeah," he gasped. "Her waters busted, and she's having pains. Can you come?"

Maggie paused, wiped her hands, and called for her daughter. "I'll be there, Boone."

"Have you ever brought a child into the world?" he asked.

"I have not," she replied. "I'll help you, Boone, all I can."

Stubborn and scared, he wanted to make the impossible possible. "There's no one on the ranch who can bring a baby?"

"Just you."

He had to return to Rachel, so he swallowed hard and nodded. Boone hurried back to the cabin as fast as he'd come, bursting in to find Rachel changed into a nightgown and sitting on the edge of the bed. Although the day was hot, she shivered as if it were winter, and he realized she was afraid.

"Don't fret, honey," Boone told her. "Maggie's on her way, and I'm ready to meet our baby.

"Any more pains?" he asked, and she nodded. Before Maggie and her young daughter arrived, Rachel suffered another contraction, this one stronger and longer than the first one he'd seen. She grasped his hand, panting, and squeezed so hard it hurt. If she'd had the strength of a man, Boone figured she'd broken a bone or two, but he never complained.

Since his sole experience with birth was calving, Boone figured it would be over by supper or early evening. Although he was the oldest, he didn't remember much about the birth of his siblings because Ma always sent him to a neighbor or one of the aunts. He'd come home to find a new baby and never thought much about how it arrived. Calves tended to come fast. He'd delivered one in an hour and a few that stretched out over six hours. Human babies couldn't be much different.

But supper time came and passed without a child. Rachel's pains grew closer together, and he could see how uncomfortable she'd become. It was hot in the cabin, even with the fire banked, and Maggie bathed Rachel's forehead with a wet rag. Boone sat with her, often holding her hand, sometimes pacing around the room.

"Talk to me, Boone," she told him, so he did. He told her stories about growing up in Kentucky, good times picking blackberries with the family or crab apples so Ma could make jelly.

"One time when I was about twelve, me and Jacob, he's next oldest, ate as many crab apples as we picked," he told her. "They ain't that great to eat, but we were hungry, so we kept nibbling at them. Ma never noticed, minding the little kids, till we went home for supper. She'd baked sweet 'taters in the fireplace and made rabbit stew, but neither of us wanted to eat."

"Oh, Boone," Rachel said with a faint laugh. "You ate too many, didn't you?"

"We did, and we were sicker than dogs," he replied. "Makes my guts gripe just remembering it. Never cared much for crab apples after that, though the jelly's good."

He put a hand to his belly, which did hurt but not from crab apples. For one, he was hungry, but he didn't think he could eat, and he was worried about Rachel. He told more tales, and then she suffered the hardest pain yet. She didn't scream, but her groan wrenched his heart.

When it had passed, she said, "Would you sing to me?"

"Yeah, honey."

As Boone began to sing, he realized it was dark. Maggie rose, lit a kerosene lamp, and carried it into the bedroom. Then she lit another one in the main room, high on the mantlepiece out of reach of her child. She made a pallet for the little girl and rocked her until she went to sleep as Boone sang.

He continued until he was hoarse because it comforted Rachel, but as the night continued, her pains increased until nothing helped. Maggie helped Rachel to sit with her back against the headboard and urged her to open her legs wide. Boone scrubbed his hands with lye soap for the twentieth time and rolled up his sleeves. He'd always heard that women screamed in childbirth, but Rachel didn't, although she moaned and bit her lip so hard that it bled. Her breathing increased until she was panting, and he was terrified, remembering all the terrible tales of mothers and babies lost at birth when he saw the head emerge.

His breath caught and held. Boone could hear Rachel's cries and Maggie's patient voice, sometimes slipping into German, urging her to push, but it seemed distant as he focused on the child. After what seemed like an eternity, the child slipped from Rachel's body, and he caught it. The baby was covered in a white, waxy substance and blood. It made no sound, and without thinking, through instinct, he tapped the kid's feet with his fingers. A loud cry erupted from the baby's mouth.

"Is it a boy or a girl?" Rachel asked, panting, still pushing.

Boone hadn't looked, but he did now. "It's a little gal," he told her as his lips turned up in a grin. "A pretty girl."

When her face contorted with another pain, he gulped, wondering if that meant there was another child or if it signaled a problem. Maggie's expression remained unruffled.

Within a few minutes, a blood red mass slid out of Rachel

with the umbilical cord attached, the other end to the child. He panicked, then realized it must be the afterbirth. If he recalled his folklore, he'd have to take it out and bury it in a little bit.

Maggie handed him a knife she'd splashed with whiskey. "You have to cut the cord, Boone."

His hands trembled as he did so, and then he handed the squalling infant to Rachel, who cradled her close. Boone kissed his wife's forehead, then watched as she kissed the tiny baby on the forehead, then surrendered her to Maggie, who washed her with gentle hands and then wrapped her tight in a blanket.

He expected her to hand the child back to Rachel, but Maggie put the bundle into his arms. Boone wrapped his arms around the precious child, almost afraid to hold her. She was smaller than he expected and somehow fragile. He figured he'd be fond of the baby, but the rush of love and the need to protect this tiny creature swamped him. He felt tears burn in his eyes, then escape down his cheeks as he cradled his daughter.

They talked about names and had chosen the name Robert William for his late father and for Liam. Rachel had been certain she carried a boy, but they'd decided to call a girl for his Ma, Jemima, with the middle name Ann for Rachel's granny.

"Howdy, Miss Jemima Ann," Boone said to his little girl.

She opened her eyes and looked up at him, then squalled.

"Boone, let me have her."

He put the child in Rachel's arms, then took off his boots so he could crawl beside his wife on the bed. Boone lay beside her, watching as she gave the baby her breast.

"Is she gettin' anything?" he asked.

Maggie and Rachel both laughed. "Not yet. The milk hasn't come in yet, but she'll be fine," Rachel said.

"Do I need to go milk the cow and bring some?" Boone asked.

"No, she's fine," Rachel assured him. "You can put her in

the cradle when she's finished."

The cradle, handcrafted by Moses, rested beside the bed. Rachel had prepared it with soft covers and a quilt. Boone placed his daughter in it and watched as she slept, then turned to Rachel.

"Are you well? Do you hurt? Can I get you anything?"

Her smile was as brilliant as the morning sun. "I'm fine, just weary and a little sore. I doubt I'll be jumping out of bed for a day or two, but I'm a bit hungry."

"It'll be a week before you're up," Maggie said with authority. "I'll go fix you something to eat, Rachel. You, too, Boone, if you'll carry Grace home for me."

Until he stepped outside with Liam's daughter in his arms, Boone hadn't realized it was near dawn. The eastern sky was streaked with rich pink and gold, highlighted by a soft blue. He didn't linger at Liam's, almost desperate to return to his wife and daughter. As he walked across the yard, he heard multiple hoofbeats in the distance and waited. A band of cowboys, led by Liam, galloped up, the men whooping and shouting with joy to be back.

"You're up early, Boone," Liam commented as he tied up his mount and swung to the ground. "Is anything amiss?"

Boone felt his grin stretch the muscles of his face wide. "I'm a pa," he said. "Rachel had the child, a beautiful little gal, Jemima. They're both well."

His brothers rode up in tandem and heard the news. Both dismounted, hollering and pounding Boone on the back. They were dirty, they smelled, and he'd never been so glad to see either one of them.

By noon, they'd all eaten the rich chicken and dumplings Maggie prepared, delicious, but Boone thought they were not as good as Rachel's though he kept that thought to himself. His brothers had made a brief visit to see their niece, followed by Deacon and Mac. Liam came, toting the food and to wish them well. He gifted Boone with a gold double eagle, a $20 coin, for the baby, and then everyone departed to let the small family rest.

Rachel rocked the cradle with one hand, although she looked drowsy. Boone brought the rocker to the bedroom and sat it. He could sleep, he realized, without much trouble, but he would rather watch over his women. When both the baby and Rachel slept, he knelt before the rocker, his face buried in both hands. Boone Wilson wept with joy as he thanked the good Lord for the safe arrival of the baby, for Rachel, for Jemima, for his brothers, for the ranch, and for good friends. He still longed for his ma and his family in Kentucky and always would, but this was home, this cabin, this ranch, this Texas. Maybe someday they'd go visit, and he'd like that very much.

Tomorrow, he'd write his mother about the baby, but now, he needed to be here, in this space with Rachel and his daughter.

It'd been almost a year ago since he'd been shot for no good reason, as he played faro in Laredo. He'd been certain he would die and that it had been the worst thing that had happened to him. Then, Rachel came to him, and everything changed. He survived, and now he'd never been happier.

The words Rachel spoke on their wedding day returned to him, and he repeated the last aloud, "thy people will be my people and thy God, my God." It was a vow he made, and he wiped away his tears, smiling now.

This was his life, and beyond that, this would be his legacy.

Lee Ann Sontheimer Murphy is a former newspaper editor and reporter who makes her home in the Ozarks. As a widow with three grown children, her focus is on writing romance novels that range from sweet to heat, from contemporary to historical. She has written more than twenty-five novels and novellas, along with a variety of non-fiction and freelance works. A native of St. Joseph, Missouri, where the Pony Express began and outlaw Jesse James met his end, she is a graduate of Crowder College and Missouri Southern State University. She lives in what passes for the suburbs in far southwestern Missouri, a little north of Arkansas and just east of Oklahoma.